THE
MEDICINE
SHOW

MARSHALL SEDDON

NFB
Buffalo, New York

NFB Publishing
119 Dorchester Road
Buffalo, New York 14213
For more information visit Nfbpublishing.com

for my family

1

Horses, like humans, have a limited capacity for effort; they can't go any faster than they are able, but they can go slower. That's why the driver snapped the carriage whip every so often, not hitting the horse but reminding him to keep up the pace which, due to circumstances beyond the driver's or horse's control, was a slow, desultory plodding. The horse in question was a Percheron, a large draft horse originally bred to carry an armored knight into battle. This one was a gray, standing sixteen and a half hands high, big boned and well-muscled. But it had been towing the big wagon down a rutted, muddy road all night, and its energy and resolve was flagging. And so, the driver snapped the whip every now and then.

The wagon was a vardo, an enclosed carriage set on four wheels. About ten feet long, it flared up from the base and had an arched, curved top. Often used as a living space, it had a stove, a tin chimney and plenty of room inside for eating, sleeping and storage. Among his many talents, the driver was a skilled carpenter and had converted the wagon to suit his purpose. It was the type of conveyance favored by Gypsies and medicine shows. The driver was no Gypsy.

Two riders rode behind the wagon, and they were miserable. They were brothers in their late teens, Joshua, and Jason and they were wrapped in blankets against the cold, rainy night. Each had a scarf pulled tightly over his mouth. Their hats were pulled down over their foreheads and they drifted in and out of sleep, their horses following the wagon blindly. They had been traveling all night and had traveled all day the day before. Yet on they went, not even stopping for a short rest and a warming cup of coffee by a fire. The Doctor insisted.

Dawn was just breaking as the wagon and two riders entered a small town and traveled down the main street to the town square. Other vendors were already there and were setting up their stands, but there was an open area on the far side of the fountain that would suit. The Doctor drove his wagon over to it and began unlimbering his horse. Joshua and Jason dismounted and unsaddled their horses. Not a word was spoken; they had all done this many times. The brothers took the three horses to a nearby livery stable and paid the stablemaster for the week with the coins the Doctor had given them. By the time they returned the Doctor had a fire started in a small iron stove inside the wagon. A large metal coffee pot sat atop it, emitting the welcome aroma of boiling coffee. When it was ready, the Doctor poured three cups and they sat around the fire, warding off the cold that had settled in their bones. They sipped coffee and munched on biscuits. The sun was beginning to warm the day nicely and soon their flagging energy returned. They began setting up the exhibition, stacking crates of bottles on two tables on either side of a small stage on which the Doctor would stand. The Doctor changed into his suit; a cream-colored three piece with brown leather facings. He wore a silk cravat at his throat, highly polished black boots and a brown felt top hat.

Joshua and Jason dressed in identical Zouave outfits: soft black boots, red ballooning pantaloons, white shirts, and tight green jackets. On their heads, each wore a red fez. Joshua got his fiddle out of a battered black case and meticulously tuned it while Jason began practicing his juggling routine. It was called a medicine show and they were good at it; they'd been plying their crafts for years in towns across the state. After a while a crowd began to gather. Joshua played a lively tune as Jason juggled a variety of balls, wooden pins and his specialty, long sharp knives that glistened in the morning sun as he spun them. The Doctor began barking to the crowd in a sonorous baritone.

"Ladies and gentlemen," he boomed. "Let me introduce you to a life-changing potion I call: "Doctor Mulroney's Exemplary Elixir." He held a light blue rectangular glass bottle with the name and a coiled rattlesnake embossed on it. He held it high for everyone to see, panning the gathering crowd with it. "It's a patented potion guaranteed to cure, soothe, vitalize, stimulate, innervate, and motivate. It cures sore throats, headaches, dyspepsia, and humors of the bowels. Applied topically, it eases aches, pains, poison ivy and insect bites. It will reduce hemorrhoids and itchiness of the anus. Rub it into your scalp and it will not only stimulate hair growth; its emollients will turn dry hair into a luxuriant mane."

"What's in it?" A slurry voice from the crowd asked. The Doctor was ready for the question; he'd paid the man good money to ask it. "I'm glad you asked that question, my good man," the Doctor said. "It's a patented formula, the exact configuration of ingredients and amounts are on file in the Library of Congress, but I can tell you this, there is, among many other things, oil of licorice, willow bark, essence of peppermint, eucalyptus, ginseng, ginger root, and turmeric. There is a liberal quantity of rendered poppy seed. But... (this said with a dramatic flair) this is the coup de grace! The holy grail of ingredients! I get it from this friendly little creature." His two assistants, Joshua, and Jason, right on cue, brought forward a large container covered with a purple velvet cloth. The Doctor swept the cloth away with a snap, revealing a glass terrarium in which a large eastern diamondback rattlesnake lay coiled, its tongue flicking dangerously. Behind his back, the Doctor shook a large rattle. The crowd gasped in unison, recoiling at the sight of the large serpent. The two brothers carried the container forward as the crowd backed away.

"This is Alexander the Great," the Doctor intoned. "He provides me with the finest, purest snake venom east of the Mississippi." The brothers set the terrarium down on a table in front of the Doctor and stepped away. "Let's see you milk him," the man with the slurry voice demanded.

"Why certainly," the doctor said. He pulled out a large glass jar with a rubber top fastened tightly with sinew. "I just need to have someone hold the jar." He gestured toward the man, shaking the jar invitingly. The man shook his head and backed away, drawing some contemptuous laughter from the crowd.

"Anyone?" the Doctor said. There were no takers. He looked toward his assistants, who backed further away, shaking their heads. The Doctor shook the rattle again. The snake adjusted its coils slightly, still flicking his tongue.

"As you can see," the Doctor continued in his booming baritone. "Gathering snake venom is not for the faint of heart." He pulled his sleeve up slightly, revealing a pair of puncture-wound scars. "I got these early in my experimentations…" He paused and spread his hands wide, taking on a bemused tone, "Before I realized that I needed a lab assistant for safety."

The crowd tittered, the people looking from the Doctor to the snake and then back again.

"But I was convinced that an amount of snake venom was imperative for the efficacy of my product…and I was right!" He lifted his hands and his gaze to the sky in dramatic fashion.

"There are many brands of cure-alls, all of them claiming to do what mine does. But the difference is that the men who purvey their products are mere salesmen. Hirelings, if you will. They have no more knowledge of their product than the man in the moon! I, on the other hand, am a board-certified medical doctor and patented inventor. I stand behind my product because I developed it. I patented it; and I take it!"

The Doctor paused again and looked meaningfully around the crowd, nodding his head as he did so. "Now, who is ready to purchase a bottle of my life-changing elixir?"

"I'll take two," the man with the slurry voice announced. Good! The Doctor thought. At least the man hadn't drank up all the money he had paid him. As the man stepped up a line began to form behind him. Joshua took money and made change as Jason handed out the purchases.

"I'll be here for a few more days and, once people have tried it," the Doctor announced. "I expect there'll be many satisfied return customers!"

He continued his pitch throughout the day, with Joshua playing fiddle and Jason juggling for the new crowds that gathered. The biggest surprise of the day though, was the purchase of a bottle by a tall, well-dressed lady of incomparable beauty. She watched the show from the periphery and, when the last person in line had made his purchase, she stepped forward and, taking off her bonnet, asked quietly, "I've recently recovered from an undiagnosed illness, but I'm afraid my once beautiful locks have not. Will your tonic help?"

The Doctor motioned her closer. She stepped up to him and bent her head forward. "May I?" the Doctor said, his hands poised above her scalp. She nodded yes and he gently ran his fingers through her short hair.

"Hmm," he said. "It looks as though your illness has ravished your scalp, impeding the natural oils in their delivery of nutrients to your follicles. He stood up and picked up one of the bottles. "Take this and apply it to your scalp tonight. Don't wash it out 'till morning. Come back tomorrow and I'll examine you again. I think you'll be surprised and gladdened by the results."

The woman took the bottle and reached for her purse. The Doctor held his hands up in a gesture of refusal. "There's no charge. My payment will be your cure."

2

H ER NAME WAS Clara and the moment she stepped off the train, she started turning heads. Tall and stately, with black hair, black eyes, and a long black dress. She wore a black hat with a thin black veil that seemed to accentuate rather than obscure her alabaster skin and red lipstick. But it wasn't her beauty that turned heads; it was the haughty aloofness in the way she carried herself. Striding purposefully through the crowd, travelers, porters, and railroad officials stepped swiftly out of her way, glancing at her but then averting their eyes when hers flashed a warning. In her wake a stoutly built man followed. He wore a frock coat, a bowler hat, and a well-trimmed moustache. He had the square jaw, barrel chest and puffy nose of a boxer. He carried a hardwood walking cane with a rounded brass headstock. Behind him, porters struggled with her trunks and luggage. She would be staying for a while.

At the street she approached a waiting carriage. It was a Landau, a two horse enclosed luxury vehicle owned by the hotel to which Clara was heading. A valet held the door open for her. She got in and the bodyguard followed. The porters hurried to load the trunks and luggage into the back compartment as the driver, dressed in a fine suit with a top hat, released the brake, snapped the reins, and proceeded down the crowded street at a brisk pace.

The hotel was called The Annabel Lee Inn and it was the best in town. A wood frame structure, it stood two stories high, its peaked roof overlooking the Genesee valley. It was painted a soft light green, and its windows were edged in cream-colored paint and faced with thin lines of brick red. The inn featured a wrap-around porch with white wicker rocking chairs and tables. The driver pulled up to the carriage-porch on the side of the building, stopped and set the brake. A valet emerged from the hotel and opened the door of the carriage. Clara got out, followed by her bodyguard. She walked up the steps, her black, high button shoes drumming a pattern on the hardwood steps. An attendant opened a large oak door with brass handles and hinges. She nodded perfunctorily as she stepped into the foyer.

Inside, leather chairs were arranged around the lounge, which featured a large stone fireplace, maple tables, shelves, and chair rails. The stairway was also maple and had two stained-glass windows on the landing, surround ed by ornately carved wooden frames. There was cream-colored wallpaper with light blue flowers. She walked up to the reception desk where a well dressed clerk gave her a pleasant smile and asked how he could help her.

"I'll be staying a week, as per my letter, sent to management a week ago," she said. Her voice was clipped and officious. She was used to giving orders. "I'd like two adjacent rooms, facing the square." She placed a heavy gold piece on the desk with an audible clank.

"Yes mam," the clerk said. He turned the registration book around for her to sign. She only used her first name, but it didn't do to question a beautiful woman who was paying in advance with a large coin, the clerk reasoned. He turned and got two keys off a rack, placed them on the counter and rang a silver handbell twice. A bellboy appeared from a back room. The clerk nodded toward the door, where some luggage had been left by porters from the train station. "Rooms 208 and 209," he said. The bellboy nodded and went to the door.

"I like to take buggy rides in the mornings," Clara said. "Can you arrange to have one ready for me tomorrow? Single horse, double seat. About eight o'clock." Without waiting for an answer, she turned and headed toward the large curved and carpeted staircase, her bodyguard following at a discrete distance.

Clara spent the afternoon strolling in the square, where she stopped and watched the medicine show for a while. She bought a bottle of Doctor Mulroney's Elixir on a whim. She visited several shops, where she purchased a few items that caught her fancy. She had tea at a little shop, sitting alone at a table outside and surveying the scene. Passersby noticed her, but a challenging look from the bodyguard, stationed near the door, was all it took to keep them at bay. It was spring, and the day had warmed nicely. Birds chirped, dogs barked, and children played, rolling a barrel hoop down the dusty street with a stick. It was a nice little town, she thought, sipping her tea. Just as I knew it would be.

Dinner was at the hotel restaurant where she took a private table by a window. Her bodyguard stood near the Maître D's station. He made it clear to the man that Lady Clara was not to be disturbed. Anyone wishing to speak with her was to present his card to him and he would confer with her as to her disposition toward the man. The Maître D was tipped well but the tip really wasn't necessary; the bodyguard's threatening demeanor would have been enough to assure his cooperation.

Clara dined on poached trout, fresh spring vegetables, and a glass of white wine. After dinner, she retired early.

THE next day, at precisely eight o'clock, a footman stood next to a gig carriage, the reins of the horse in his hands. It was a two-wheeled, open carriage that was common on the back roads of the region. The bodyguard took Clara's hand to assist her into her seat, walked around the carriage and climbed into the driver's seat. The footman let go the horse and the bodyguard expertly undid the brake and snapped the reins, sending the horse into a light trot. They proceeded down the main street of the city and then out onto a country lane south of town. Wildflowers and budding trees lined the dirt road, and the smells of spring filled the air; flowers, newly ploughed fields, and freshly spread manure.

An hour or so later they reached a small Gypsy camp. There were several four-wheeled, covered Gypsy wagons, brightly colored laundry drying on a line and a large cast-iron pot suspended over an open fire by an iron tripod. The aroma of woodsmoke and the bubbling contents of the pot assailed them as they stopped and climbed down from the carriage. Clara immediately walked over to one of the wagons, opened the door and walked in. A half an hour later, she emerged, smiling, and climbed up into the carriage. The bodyguard climbed up into his own seat and they headed back to town.

Clara spent the afternoon much as she had the day before; she browsed shops, had tea, and walked over to watch the juggler and fiddle player at the medicine show. After a time, Doctor Mulroney recognized her and called her forward.

"My good lady," he announced in a stentorian voice. "Might I do a cursory examination of your beautiful vertex to determine the efficacy of my patented elixir?"

Clara laughed lightly and, to humor the boisterous doctor, stepped up to him, removed her hat and lowered her head for his inspection. He ran his fingers lightly through her hair and, after a few thoughtful exhalations, stood and proudly announced that significant progress had been made. "Her follicles have been cleared and her sebum has been restored. Most importantly, there has been considerable hair growth!"

The crowd seemed unconvinced.

"Is there anyone here who was in attendance yesterday?" the Doctor implored the crowd.

"I was," the man with the slurry voice said. He pushed his way through the crowd. The bodyguard had seen the goings on and had stationed himself close. He stopped the man's progress with a gentle but firm pressure from his walking stick.

"No farther," he said in a deep, rumbly voice. The man stopped but was still able to peer at Clara's hair.

"It's at least two inches longer," he announced. "I swear." Reacting to the pressure from the bodyguard's cane, he backed away into the crowd, which was inching forward to see.

"It's a wig!" someone announced! Hair doesn't grow that fast!" There was a murmur of agreement from the crowd.

"I beg to differ!" the Doctor said forcefully. "My elixir was developed to do just that, among many other things!"

Clara was put out by the doubters. She stepped up to a young boy, who was standing nearby. She bent over and offered her head to him. "Pull my hair," she said. "So that these people can see that it is real."

The boy reached up and took a handful of her hair and gently pulled; then he pulled a little harder, causing Clara to wince slightly. He let go and stepped back. "It's real," he announced, his voice cracking.

Clara gathered her hair and replaced her hat. The doctor handed her another bottle of his elixir. "Another bottle, gratis," he said in a stage whisper. "Keep applying it as before. If you are still in town tomorrow, perhaps I could prevail upon you to return to my humble stand for another examination."

"Perhaps," she said demurely. "I'm beginning to like this little town." People in the crowd clapped politely, taken by this mysterious woman who had appeared as if out of nowhere.

That evening, Clara dined alone again, but now she was beginning to draw some interest. A succession of men presented themselves to the Maître D who then gave their cards to the bodyguard. Each time he pulled a folded piece of paper from an inside pocket and checked it before nodding 'no' to the Maître D. Tonight, Clara chose Chicken Chasseur and a glass of Sauvignon Blanc. After dinner, she again retired early. The next day was an exact repeat of the day prior. A morning carriage ride to the Gypsy camp, a stroll through town and a stop at the medicine show. This time, her hair had grown noticeably longer and, after the requisite examination and proof that it was not a wig, drew considerable attention. The doctor's elixir sold out in only a couple of hours. Joshua and Jason were sent to get more in a rented buckboard wagon.

3

THAT EVENING A carriage approached the hotel and pulled into the carriage-porch at the side of the building. Two bellboys hustled down the steps to assist the occupants. It was an expensive barouche, drawn by two horses, that seated four passengers sitting vis a vis. But this evening it held only one occupant. He was John Osgood Comerford, the real estate developer, investment banker and railroad tycoon who had made a fortune in everything he touched. He was easily the wealthiest man in town and was used to having his way.

He was a man of habit and most evenings, after dinner with his two young children, he would have a whiskey at the hotel's bar while his governess gave the children their music lessons. He was a widower; his wife having died from in a stroke six months earlier. He was usually joined at the bar by several associates who discussed business with him over drinks and cigars. They all had noticed the beautiful lady with black hair who dined alone every night, her bodyguard screening anyone who wished to speak with her. So far, none had made the cut. Tonight, John had a plan of his own. He motioned to the bartender who was idly wiping the bar with a cloth nearby, even though it didn't need it.

"Yes sir," the man said as he set down the cloth. "What can I do for you, Mister Comerford?"

Comerford said something in the man's ear.

"Right away sir," the bartender said. He turned and extracted a bottle of Dom Perignon from a large icebox. He took two crystal champagne flutes from a glass-covered cabinet and examined them for water spots. Satisfied, he walked over to Clara's table. With a quiet word and a nod toward Mr. Comerford, he set the glasses down and opened the champagne.

"I'll need to see his card," the bodyguard said to the Maître D, who was looking decidedly nervous.

"His name is John Osgood Comerford, and I would sooner ask the devil himself for a card than ask him."

The bodyguard raised an inquisitive eyebrow but said nothing. His look made the Maître D even more nervous. The bodyguard was a hard looking man and the bulge in his jacket hinted at a concealed weapon. Weapons were supposed to be checked in the hotel, but, so far, no one had seemed interested in enforcing the rule.

"He owns this hotel and half the buildings in this town," the Maître D said, his voice trembling a little. "I work for him."

The bodyguard nodded, pulled his list from inside his coat, glanced at it and then nodded, once toward the Maître D and then once toward Clara, who nodded back. He stepped back into the recess next to the Maître D's station.

John Osgood Comerford took up a seat across from Clara as if he was supposed to. The champagne had been poured and he raised his glass to Clara, who raised hers in response, although a little haltingly. She seemed shy to Comerford. In his experience he had found that some women were like that, they could be shy to the point of skittishness. Easily spooked. I'll have to be careful with this one, he thought.

"My good lady," he said. "It is not often that a cultured lady such as yourself graces this humble establishment." He drank a sip, and she did too. "Allow me to introduce myself. I am John Osgood Comerford, an entrepreneur and owner of the Annabel Lee Inn, such as it is. Might I ask you as to your accommodations? Are your rooms adequate?"

"Very much so," she said softly. "The meals have been delicious, and the staff has been helpful and friendly. I must say, it will be a disappointment to be leaving. The town has an endearing quality that I have only rarely encountered."

"But must you leave so soon?" John said, finishing his champagne and pouring them each another measure.

"I'm afraid so," she said. "I have been recently widowed; hence my black ensemble. I am in search of a new life, if you will. I have a healthy inheritance and a collection of expensive jewelry, the product of a guilty, cheating husband. But I'm afraid my resources are limited. The only real possessions of worth that I have are my education and musical talents, such as they are."

"And what might they be?" John said, intrigued.

Clara blushed and took another sip of champagne. "I was orphaned at a young age and adopted by a loving couple that insisted that I receive the finest tutors to prepare me for my life. I'm fluent in French, Spanish, Italian and German. I studied literature, mathematics, science, and history. I play classical piano and was tutored in drawing and painting. But I married badly and was left with nothing but the clothes on my back, a few baubles, and a small inheritance. My husband, you see, was shot by a jealous husband. The scandal was too much for me and I left town in search of…well, what, I don't know."

John reached across the table, took Clara's hand, and looked into her eyes. "This is a beautiful town," he said softly. "It can offer you much if you're willing to give it a chance."

She gently pulled her hand away. "I'm not looking for another husband; my last one soured me on the experience. I'm looking for a private school in a quiet town where I can teach and avoid the gossip that drove me away from my home."

John smiled and poured the last of the champagne. "I've noticed that you like to take carriage rides in the mornings," he said, seemingly changing the subject.

"Yes, I do," she said with a laugh. "It's my one indulgence, riding. A fast horse and a light carriage down a country lane is an incomparable experience."

"Who is your driver?" John asked mildly.

Clara frowned. "My hired bodyguard," she said. She looked pensive, as if deciding whether to go on.

John smiled benignly. "You can speak freely with me," he said. "I despise gossip."

"I'm a young woman, traveling alone," she explained. "All I got out of that horrible marriage I have in my possession. Cash money and my collection of jewelry. My husband, out of guilt, indulged me with expensive presents. The money and the jewelry, which I would be loath to sell, will sustain me until I've settled on my new life, whatever that might be. The bodyguard, the man you see standing near the Maître D, is an unconscionable boor but necessary, given my current situation, don't you agree?"

John sat quietly for a time, mulling something over in his mind. Then he said, "Might I prevail upon you to join you on your ride tomorrow? It's been a long time since I saw the countryside from a buggy and your description of your ride has piqued my interest. Plus, I think I might have an idea that might prove to be a pleasant solution to your, shall we say, dilemma. Rest assured that I have no untoward ideas. My proposal will be strictly business, as will be our relationship."

Clara looked at him inquisitively, expecting further details. But John Osgood Comerford played his cards close to his chest, as they say.

4

THE NEXT DAY, if anyone had cared to notice, they would have seen the bodyguard, carpet bag in hand, standing at the train station, waiting to board the westbound train.

At precisely eight o'clock, John Osgood Comerford pulled up to the Annabel Lee Inn, driving a one-horse curricle. It was an expensive, sporty single-axle buggy that was known for its speed, and for its accidents at the hands of inexperienced drivers. A valet held the harness of the horse as John got out and walked up to the hotel's steps. A bellboy escorted Clara down the steps and John helped her up into the seat. He walked back around the buggy, climbed in, and took the reins. He nodded to the valet who let go of the harness. John snapped the reins and drove at a light trot through town. At the outskirts he snapped the reins again and put the horse, a magnificent Cleveland Bay named Danny, into a fast pace. Clara, an enthusiastic driver herself, was amazed at John's skill. They followed the river road, a tree-lined lane that ran for miles past pastures, wheat fields and forests. It was the same road that Clara had taken on her morning rides over the past few days.

After a time, they came to a bend in the road that wound past a large flat space that had recently been used as a camp. Smoke rose lazily from a fire pit, and the grass was still matted where the campers had been. John stopped the carriage for a moment to regard the scene.

"Looks like whoever it was broke camp only this morning," he said. "Gypsies," Clara said. John looked at her inquisitively.

"There was a Gypsy camp here," Clara explained. "I encountered it on my first ride." She looked at John, unsure whether to continue. "Go on," he said.

"Well, if you must know, I have several quirks. One of them is that I like to have my fortune told. I stopped here and asked if there was someone who could do it. There was, of course, that's what Gypsies do. Among other things."

"And what were you told?"

Clara laughed lightly. "That I would have a long and profitable life. And that I would meet the man of my dreams."

"That's what they all say," John said, laughing. "And do you also like visiting medicine shows?"

"Ah, you heard about that," Clara said. "I recognized the, well, let's call him a doctor, even though he isn't. He's a man that my husband did business with at one time. Some sort of financial investment, I think." Clara stopped, clearly upset at the memory. Haltingly, she continued. "It was a scam. Something my husband did to people. He pauperized the poor man, and he was forced to make a living selling snake oil in a traveling medicine show. I could see that he recognized me, so I thought I'd give him a little boost by buying a bottle and then showing up the next day with longer hair."

"Your hair didn't grow?"

"I had it up the first day and then let it down for the next two. It's amazing what you can do with a few bobby pins and someone who's paid to pull on hair gently."

"You didn't drink it? Or put it on your scalp?"

"God no!" Clara declared. "Only the good doctor knows what's in that stuff, but it's probably full of alcohol and laudanum. Very addicting." Clara allowed herself a small laugh. "I've still got a few bottles; would you like some?"

"Not on your life," John said. He snapped the reins, and they continued their ride.

Sometime toward noon, John slowed the buggy and pulled into a copse of trees overlooking the river. "Thought I'd rest Danny a little before we turn back," he explained. He got down from the carriage and expertly unhitched the horse and hobbled it in a little meadow where a small brook flowed. The horse immediately began drinking, making loud sucking sounds.

"I brought a little refreshment," he said, helping Clara down. "I hope you don't mind." He then pulled a blanket and a wicker picnic basket from the back of the buggy. He laid the blanket out and motioned for Clara to sit. When she had, he joined her, the picnic basket between them.

"Just some wine, cheese and bread," he said, opening the basket and extracting a bottle of white wine and two crystal glasses, wrapped in linen. He opened the bottle and poured two glasses. "Sauvignon Blanc," he said, examining the legs in his glass. "I think you'll find it quite charming; I have cases of it shipped from France, along with a quantity of delightful Claret."

Clara nodded nervously but didn't say anything. John could tell that she was worried about his intentions. The situation reminded him of many of the business deals that he had made happen over the years. It sometimes took a considerable amount of patience to get a deal done. Push too hard, and the other party would draw back and begin finding reasons not to sign the deal. He sometimes felt that deal-making was like fly fishing, a hobby of his. In that sport, it was all about presentation. The most realistically tied fly, if cast improperly or retrieved clumsily, would not only fail to hook a fish, but it would also cause it to become skittish. But even a clumsily tied fly, presented correctly, would prove irresistible to the fish.

They munched on cheese and bread and sipped wine in silence, enjoying the day and listening to Danny graze and drink. In their silence the birds and bugs that had quieted during their arrival came back to life, and soon the riverbank was alive with their buzzing and chirping. John poured them each a second glass of wine. Clara sipped hers and said, "this really is good wine, I must admit. You have it shipped in from France?"

"Yes," John said. "Among other things, I run an import export business. I have many business contacts in France, and they give me a price on the wine. Have you ever been there?"

"To France? Sadly, no. My husband was too busy with his business, and his affairs, to travel."

"What was your husband's name?" John asked mildly. "Perhaps I might have heard it in the course of my own business."

Clara immediately stiffened and John realized his mistake. "Please don't ever ask me that question again," she said icily. "I hate the man and his memory. He ruined my life! The worst part is that I trusted him. I now realize that betrayal of a person's trust is among the worst things a person can visit on another. I use my first name now, and no other." Suddenly Clara began softly crying. Gone was the cold, angry woman she had been just a moment ago. John could see that, just below her hard exterior, there was a scared and vulnerable girl with nowhere to go and no one to turn to. He pulled a leather letter case out of an inside pocket and offered it to her.

"What is it?" Clara asked, drying her tears with a linen handkerchief.

"An offer. A way out of your dilemma. A chance for a new life." Clara took the case and opened it. She took out a single sheet of paper and looked at it in bewilderment.

"It's a contract," John said. "I'd like to hire you as a live-in tutor for my children. You'll have your own suite of rooms; a generous salary and you'll share the family's meals."

"A governess," Clara said flatly. The position of governess was widely considered a step down for a woman of substance, nothing more than a glorified household servant. Wiping noses, laundering clothes, preparing lunches until the children were old enough for prep school. Then, no longer needed, the governess would have to seek a similar position elsewhere. John stopped her from saying more by waving his hand as if wiping a slate. "Hear me out. When you read the contract, you'll see that nowhere in it is the title "governess." You're to be a tutor, nothing more. The children are old enough to take care of themselves. You'll tutor them in the core subjects, along with language, art, and music. You have to sign nothing. I have already applied my own signature in front of a notary. If any of the conditions in the contract are not met fully, you may take me to court to seek recompense. But I can assure you, you will never need to. And, if you become unhappy with your situation, you can leave at any time."

Clara read through the contract thoroughly and then read through it again. She dabbed again at her eyes, but this time it was because of tears of joy. She smiled.

"I accept," she said. She offered her hand for a shake and John took it warmly. That afternoon, porters came to the hotel and took her trunk and other luggage away to the Comerford Estate. Later, John drove his buggy up to the front of the hotel. Clara came down the steps and John helped her into her seat. Her hotel bill, she had found out, had been paid by a Mister John Comerford.

5

THE COMERFORD ESTATE was located on a hill overlooking the lush spring countryside. Pastures for Comerford's impressive collection of horses stretched as far as the eye could see, enclosed by gleaming white fencing. In the distance were farmer's fields and patches of woods. A stream ran languidly through the property and then down the hill and toward the town, which could be seen in the far distance. There were several outbuildings, a horse barn, and a coach house. The main residence was built of stone, with gables jutting out from the second floor. Smoke from a large chimney curled lazily into the cloudless blue sky. A pair of well-dressed servants stepped out onto the landing as John helped Clara down from the buggy and escorted her to the stairs.

A sense of intense trepidation overcame her as she went to take the first step. She'd done this before and knew how it would turn out. John was attentive and circumspect in his dealings with her, but she well-knew his real intentions. He was a man used to getting his way, one way or another and, she was certain, he intended to have his way with her. A bottle of expensive champagne sent to her table, a buggy ride in the countryside with a generous employment opportunity. How could she resist? He was gentle and patient in the presentation of his offer and, when she had taken it, he began to reel her in, much as an angler baits, hooks, and plays a fish. Little does he know, she thought, smiling slightly at the irony. I'm not your ordinary fish. She ascended the stairs with a pleasant smile.

CLARA'S initiation into the small world that was the society of the Comer ford Estate was rocky at first. The housemaid, a little snippet of a woman named Mrs. Fitzgerald, known to the family as Missus Fitz, disliked her from the start. She had grey hair pulled back in a bun, a pointed nose, and a tongue that was sharper than any knife. Normally, a governess would work under the direct supervision of the housemaid, but John made it clear that Clara was an autonomous employee who was to be treated deferentially and addressed as Lady Clara. The other servants averted their eyes when she was around, but she could sometimes hear them whispering behind her back. "Gold digger," "trophy wife," and "cradle-robber" were frequently heard, just out of earshot. Oh well, Clara thought. Comes with the territory. Besides, the new hire at any establishment must endure an initiation of some sort. Clara chose to not hear the whispered comments of the staff and simply smiled pleasantly when she encountered them. She knew better than to engage in a household fight, especially at this very fragile moment.

The children were another story. Their names were Jeremy, a towheaded boy of twelve and Anna, a blonde girl two year's Jeremy's junior. They loved their old governess and tutor, Mrs. Potter. She had been dismissed earlier that day amidst many tears from the staff and the children. She was kind, friendly, well-liked, and lenient with the children. "Children learn at their own pace," she often said. "No use pushing them too hard, let them enjoy their childhood while they still have it." She brought cookies and candy to their lessons and gave them frequent and lengthy breaks. Lady Clara, they quickly found out the next day at their first lesson, was nothing like that.

"Let's start by going over your multiplication tables," she said at their first lesson, which was right after breakfast at nine o'clock sharp. "Math gets the brain muscle moving."

Jeremy began haltingly to recite the first table, "two times two is..." Clara cut him off with a sharp look and a shake of her head." No, no, no," she said. "On your slates, both of you. Twos, fives, and tens. I'll wait." The two children scribbled frantically, glancing nervously at their new tutor and at each other. When they finished, she took the slates and examined them. "Tsk, tsk," she said. "Is this only the farthest you've gotten?"

"Yes mum," Jeremy said, his voice shaking. "Mrs. Potter…"

"Isn't here anymore," Clara finished for him. "Now, wipe your slates clean and copy as I dictate."

The two children quickly wiped their slates and held their pieces of chalk at the ready.

"Two times two is four, two times three is six, two times four is eight." She continued that way, her voice clipped and businesslike. After an hour, she stopped and said, "get out your primers."

Jeremy fidgeted a little and cleared his throat.

"Something wrong?" Clara said. Her voice was dry, almost icy, her lips tight against her teeth.

"No," Jeremy stammered. "Sorry mum."

But Anna spoke up, her voice squeaking. "We always take a break between lessons. My brain hurts!"

"That's a good sign," Lady Clara said. "That means it's working. Now, pick up your primers!" she said with a tight, insistent smile. Except for a brief break for lunch, instruction continued like that for the rest of the day.

The children chaffed bitterly under Lady Clara's teaching, but there was nothing to be done; their father would be of no help and Missus Fitz, although she had a clear dislike of Clara, thought that the children needed the discipline. When they complained directly to Clara, she simply said, "You need to be ready for life, it happens faster than you might think. It won't do to find yourselves unarmed in the fight that life in the real world is."

And so, the lessons continued. But the children found that, as the day went on, they became grudgingly impressed with Clara. Her command of the subjects was amazing. When they began working on languages, they found that her voice and inflections were much smoother and more flowing than Mrs. Potter's had been. They tried to mimic her as she ran through a series of general words and phrases in French, Italian, Spanish and German. Their attempts seemed to please Clara and she began to relax a little, even having a bit of fun with some double entendres.

Finally, in the evening, came music, the one thing both children had a passion for. Jeremy loved the piano and practiced whenever he could. John had purchased a rare Chickering, a piano made from ornately carved rosewood and known for its deep, rich tone and beauty. Jeremy's passion was Chopin and Clara smiled as he played "L'Adeau," one of Chopin's most famous etudes. Anna, equally passionate about the cello, played the melody along with her brother. When they finished, Clara graced them with a pleasant smile but said nothing. She took a seat at the piano and played the piece herself. The children were amazed at her facility and looked at each other in awe. They both noticed that Clara had not even glanced at the music. As she finished, they heard someone clapping softly. It was John, standing in the doorway. "Exquisite," he said. He dabbed at the corner of his eye with a handkerchief. "It was one of my wife's favorites."

At dinners, the children, and the staff, got another surprise. Clara was seated at the opposite end of the table, a position formerly taken by John's deceased wife. The first evening Clara had walked into the room, nodded her head hello, and walked over to the seat as if she belonged there. A servant pulled the chair out for her, and she took her seat. The servant pushed the chair in as she did so. Jeremy looked at Anna but didn't say anything. As far as they remembered, no one else had ever sat in that seat except their mother. Their former governess, Mrs. Potter had never dined with them. She always ate in the kitchen with the rest of the household staff.

Every morning, before lessons with the children, Clara would take a buggy ride. She liked to travel up the river road and then circle back through the town, waving to passers-by in a friendly manner. John cautioned her about riding alone, but she allayed his fears by showing him a small derringer that she hid among her clothing. "A woman can never be too careful," she had said at the time.

On Saturday mornings, John insisted on accompanying her on her rides, which she gladly agreed to. He always brought a picnic lunch and a bottle of wine, and they dined along the riverbank while Danny, the horse, grazed. It was at one of these picnics that they first made love.

THE morning was crisp and clear, with a light breeze ruffling the leaves and grass. They were drinking wine and munching on cheese and bread when John spilled a drop of wine on the lapel of his jacket. Clara leaned forward and dabbed at it with a clean linen napkin. As she did, John noticed her musky perfume. Mixed with the smell of the fresh wildflowers that surrounded them, the effect was almost overwhelming. The temptation to lean in and kiss her consumed him. But he was a patient man and to do so would endanger his carefully laid plan. He started to pull away but, as he did, Clara slipped her arms around his neck and kissed him deeply. He kissed her back and soon they were fumbling with buttons and snaps. He remembered that she tasted faintly of licorice.

The encounter left them both breathless and slightly guilt-ridden. John started to apologize but she shushed him. "It's been so long," she said softly. "Since my husband's death I haven't felt the touch of a man, although I've longed for it, and dreamt of it. When I do dream of it, it's always you."

"I think that I've loved you since the first moment I saw you," John said. "But being your employer and many years your senior, I held back from any untoward actions. I haven't felt the comforts of female companionship since my wife died."

"Well, I must say, you made up for it in grand fashion," Clara said with a coy little laugh.

Their secret Saturday lovemaking went on for several weeks until, one morning, John did something very different.

When they arrived at their usual spot, John got down from the buggy, walked around it and helped Clara down. As usual. He unhitched and hobbled Danny, the horse, and spread a blanket on the ground. Clara sat while John got the wicker picnic basket down from the back of the buggy, sat it down on the blanket and then sat down himself. Clara noticed that he had been freshly barbered and was wearing a new suit. He had a white carnation in his lapel.

Opening the basket, John brought out a bottle of champagne instead of the usual bottle of claret. Two crystal champagne flutes were wrapped in linen. He opened the bottle and filled the two flutes. He handed one to Clara and raised his glass in a toast. "To us," he said. They clinked glasses and drank. Then John did something even more unusual. He got up from his sitting position and then knelt on one knee. He pulled a small velvet case from his pocket, opened it, and presented it to Clara. She looked down at one of the most beautiful diamonds she had ever seen. And the largest.

"Clara, will you marry me?" John said. His voice cracked a little as he said it.

Clara looked at the ring for a long time. She had told him she would never marry again, but here was a proposal that few women would have rejected.

John waited for an answer. Too soon? He thought. Am I an old fool who has let a casual affair cloud my thinking? He thought again about the fishing metaphor and wondered if he had tried to set the hook too soon. He was about to close the case, put it back in his pocket and mumble some sort of weak apology. Defeat! He thought. He rarely lost out on a business deal but here he was, losing the biggest deal of his life. He started to pull the ring back when Clara suddenly burst into tears.

"I swore I would never marry again, but I find myself wishing to go back on that pledge. Yes, I will marry you, John Osgood Comerford!"

THE wedding was a small, private affair with only a few of John's business associates joining the immediate family. John's older daughter was away at school and his sister, Ida Mae, sent the invitation back with a terse response to the RSVP. "I will not be attending," it read. "There's no fool like an old fool."

Not much changed after the wedding. There was no honeymoon – John was too busy. The biggest alteration was that Clara moved into John's bed room. Other than snoring in his sleep, and smelling of whiskey and cigars, John wasn't a bad bedmate. And being often tired and, well, old, he didn't require Clara's attentions very often. They did continue their Saturday buggy rides, though. John called them an important tradition that commemorated their love for each other. Sadly, it was on one of their Saturday picnics that tragedy struck.

6

Doctor Tobias Pilcher was having a busy day. It was always like that on Saturdays. At the moment, he was treating a man who had the bad luck of having fallen off a roof he was repairing. His ribs were mashed, and his collarbone was broken. He was in pain and kept taking swigs from a bottle of cheap whiskey that the doctor used as an anesthetic. As the doctor worked, there came a shout from the street. A buggy was speeding down main, driven by a hysterical woman who someone recognized as Mrs. Comerford. Her husband was slumped in the seat next to her. When the doctor saw Clara pull up in front of his office, he called out to his assistant, who was in the back, and he rushed out.

"Doctor, help!" Clara exclaimed frantically. "Help me with John! He collapsed!"

The doctor and his assistant carried the unconscious man into the office and laid him on the examination table. Clara rushed in behind him, urging the doctor to hurry. He felt for John's pulse and shook his head sadly. "I'm afraid he's gone," he said softly.

Clara let out a shriek and began sobbing. "How did he die?" she demanded. "He was just fine, and then he went off to relieve himself in the bushes! I heard him exclaim and then he staggered up to the buggy. I helped him in and asked him what happened, but he couldn't talk!"

"Heart attack, most likely," the doctor said. "Had you been..." he trailed off. The assistant tried unsuccessfully to hide a leer. Clara glared at him hotly but said nothing.

"A man his age," the doctor said, trailing off again. He was feeling John's left leg, running both hands down its length.

"This leg is unusually swollen," he said. He reached for a scissors and cut the pantleg open. He again felt up and down the leg, examining it closely. "A'ha!" He exclaimed "Look at this." He pointed to two small puncture marks just above the ankle. "Snakebite!"

"He was bitten by a snake?" Clara said, now a little less hysterically.

"You said he went off into the bushes to relieve himself," the doctor said. "It looks like he was bitten while he was there. He got a full dose of venom, probably from a juvenile Massasauga, they don't know how to hold their venom back."

"My God," Clara said. "My God."

7

THE FUNERAL WAS a somber affair. John was prepped by the under taker and laid out in his coffin in the parlor of his estate. The children were besides themselves with grief, especially after having lost their mother only a few months before. Clara, dressed in the same black dress and hat that she had worn when she arrived in town, cried softly, dabbing at her eyes with a linen handkerchief. A few of John's business associates had come to pay their respects along with a smattering of acquaintances from town. John's sister, Ida Mae, was there and she could barely contain her anger at John's young wife, who she obviously blamed for John's death.

John's older daughter, a girl in her mid-twenties, returned from her graduate studies to attend. Her name was Alexandra, but everyone called her Alex. Despite almost everyone's advice, Alex was studying law and intended to pass the bar and set up her own practice. "There will never be work for a female lawyer," her aunt told her more than once. "Men just won't accept it; it would be like having a female doctor, or minister, for that matter. Can you imagine a female minister? Oh, no, young lady," she said, tsking with her tongue on the roof of her mouth and shaking her head. "Certain professions are the bailiwick of men, plain and simple. Now, going to law school and meeting a future lawyer to marry, well, that's a different story."

At times like that, Alex simply went quiet and nodded her agreement.

"You're right, Aunt Ida," she would say, to avoid argument. Alex had found, over the years, that some people liked argument, just for the sake of it. Argument was their comfort zone and, unless you were of the same ilk, they would always win, even if their argument had no merit. It reminded her of boys who played knuckles under, a game where two opponents locked the fingers of both hands and then tried to twist the wrists of the opponent into a painful and losing position. The expression "I won't knuckle under to him" came to mean not giving in to someone who was trying to take advantage of another. Her Aunt Ida would never knuckle under to anyone in an argument and, just like a wrestler changing positions during a match, she would change the subject during an argument to gain an advantage. Her arguments weren't logical discussions or debates, they were exercises in willful domination of her counterpart.

It occurred to Alex that, since she was studying law, at some point she would have to argue a case before a judge. Maybe not at a criminal trial - she was working on business and finance law – but at a hearing before an administrative law judge. She realized that she would have to sharpen her skills at argument at some point, the law being fuzzy in many of the cases she had read. But she just didn't want to try and sharpen them by arguing with Ida Mae. The lady didn't play fair, and there was no judge to appeal to. So, she kept quiet. But in her mind, she thought of counters to her aunt's comments, often hours or even days later. She always won her imaginary arguments with her aunt.

Her father's death devastated Alex. Her mother had died only a few months ago, and the grief still weighed heavy on her heart. A cultured, educated, and refined lady, she was the embodiment of everything that Ida Mae thought Alex should become. As a matter of fact, while in discussions with Alex, her aunt often reinforced a particular point by saying: "I'm certain your mother would agree, rest her soul." Of course, her mother being dead, there was no way to verify such a comment, and Alex just had to let it sit there. A respectful nod of agreement was the only way to prevent her aunt from going off on a rant about her mother's qualities and her own lack of them.

But now, with the loss of her father, Alex had the sinking feeling that her aunt might now be right. Her father had encouraged her studies with a shared ulterior motive: once she passed the bar, she would serve as his personal lawyer – he didn't trust lawyers and had been poorly advised by several. A lawyer in the family would introduce the element of trust that was sorely lacking in those that he was forced to use. John Osgood Comerford was an astute businessman but lacked the ability to understand the obliquely worded language of contracts, much of which was written in Latin, a language that he had never had time to learn. Alex had showed a keen interest in the law from an early age. She liked to sit on the floor of his study, leafing through the pages of John's many books, most of which he had never had the time to read himself. He was a collector of expensive books but not a reader of them. But Alex was and soon an idea began to form in his head. He encouraged her study of the law and even hired one of the better lawyers that he used to tutor her. She proved to be an adept and eager student, and, on her tutor's recommendation, she applied to law school. Though she didn't know it, due in part to her shortened name, which could have passed for a man's and a generous endowment to the school by her father, Alex was accepted.

Law school proved to be more challenging for Alex than she had ever imagined. At home, she had read in her father's study and, when she got older and got a tutor, her father set up her own study in a drawing room downstairs. She had an oak desk, a comfortable chair, and shelves for her ever-expanding library. Her tutor, a short, fat man named Chester Howe, had a black mustache that sat incongruously beneath a red, bulbous nose and a jutting lower lip that reminded her of a sausage. He pushed at it with his chin when thinking about questions she asked him saying, "well, well, that's a complex issue" with a lisp as he thought. But he was smart, knowledgeable, and experienced – and he was all hers for the time he was hired to tutor her. In law school she found herself in classrooms filled with other students, all men, or at least boys in the process of becoming men. Her professors, surprised and even shocked at having a female student, looked down their noses at her. She knew that they resented her for taking a seat that rightfully should have been a man's, and a man was the breadwinner in a family, not a woman. It was true that a woman could pass the bar, but employment was unlikely and so it stood to reason, at least in their opinion, that Alex would be depriving a man of a job.

Besides the resentment and outright hostility of the professors and other students, Alex had to contend with living arrangements that were less than ideal. A dormitory room was out of the question, so Alex took a room in a crowded, noisy boarding house that was run by a little snippet of a woman named Blanche Charlap. Alex was the only female boarder and Blanche clearly suspected her of lascivious intent. She watched Alex like a hawk and glared at her if she so much as asked one of the men to pass the peas at dinner. Her room was small, poorly lit, and stuffy. Opening her one window was out of the question, since all the men smoked at their windows and even a slight breeze would bring a torrent of tobacco smoke into her room, along with the smells and sounds of the street below. She would have stayed at the university lounge to study, but Mrs. Charlap had a strict curfew and locked the doors at precisely nine o'clock every evening.

But study she did, and Alex found that she had an affinity for the law. She fairly breezed through her undergraduate studies and found the graduate work not only challenging, but exciting. She was only a few weeks away from graduating and taking the bar when her father died.

Now, with her father deceased, she would have to tap into her inheritance, whatever that might be, to finish up her studies. Her future, as she had imagined it, was now in serious jeopardy.

She had met Clara once shortly after the wedding while on a visit home during a semester break from school. She found her to be cultured, articulate and friendly, but only when John was around. At times when he was off to work, Clara's demeanor changed. She became cold, dismissive, and distinctly unfriendly, retreating to her suite of rooms as soon as she could. Oh well, Alex thought. It must be hard being a trophy wife.

ALEX hated funerals; the macabre display of a corpse in a parlor where burning pots of incense poorly masked the smell of the embalming fluid that forestalled the inevitable necrosis of the deceased. But even more so, she dreaded the ride in the funeral procession. The hearse was a black four wheeled carriage drawn by two black horses. The sides of the hearse featured large oval windows that gave onlookers a view of the coffin, another pointless display of a corpse, Alex thought. The family rode behind it in one of John's favorite carriages, a Clarence. It was drawn by two horses with the driver sitting up front and the family inside an enclosed cab. They rode in an uncomfortable silence, all aware how close Aunt Ida was to a hateful outburst directed at John's young widow. Clara, a widow again after just a few months, kept her eyes downcast on her hands, folded on her lap. Ida Mae made a few bitter comments on what a fool her brother had been to be gamboling about the countryside in a buggy instead of being more attentive to his business. Clara did not take the bait, which left Ida Mae to harumph her way to the burial.

At the cemetery the coffin was carried by six of John's business associates into the Comerford family mausoleum, a large stone structure with the name "Comerford" carved into its marble entrance. Inside there was an open receptacle waiting to become the final resting place for John Osgood Comerford.

An Episcopalian priest intoned a prayer, and the coffin was slid in, making an eerie scraping sound. The door was shut and locked and that was that.

8

Two days later, the family gathered in John's study for the reading of the will. An executor, a thin man with a high-pitched voice and a bad comb-over, intoned the words, "The last will and testament of John Osgood Comerford." The will was simple and short. "I leave all my personal wealth and belongings, including my estate and everything in it, to the love of my life, Mrs. Clara Comerford."

"Impossible!" Ida Mae exclaimed, her voice echoing in the large room. She delivered a hateful look at Clara, who averted her eyes, her hands folded over one another in front of her.

"John would never have left everything to that harlot!" Ida Mae shouted. She looked imploringly at the executor who seemed extremely uncomfortable.

"We spoke at length, after the death of his first wife," Ida Mae explained. She shot another hateful look at Clara and continued.

"His legacy was to go to me, and the children given generous endowments. The estate has been in the Comerford family for generations! He never would have given it away!"

The executor cleared his throat and, as forcefully as his weak voice would allow, said, "Madam, this is the legal will of John Osgood Comerford, notarized and obtained from his personal safe. I assure you that everything in the will is legal, aboveboard, and irrefutable."

Clara suddenly stepped forward, raising her right hand for silence. "I'm as shocked as you are, Mrs. Brown. I think we all are quite aware that John was very much in love with me, as I am...was, with him. His love may have clouded his thinking. I assure you that I never wanted anything more out of my relationship with John than his love. To prove this, I will immediately have a lawyer draw up a legal and binding contract assigning John's legacy to the family in the manner in which you remember it. I only desire two things. One, that I be allowed to stay on at the estate as tutor with the same salary that I have been receiving."

"I can do that," Alex said. "The document will be legal – and binding."

"Good," Clara said. "Please confer with your aunt, draw up the document and I will sign it."

"You mentioned two conditions," Alex said.

"I want an apology from you, Ida Mae, for calling me a harlot."

"I will," the old lady said. "When the document is signed."

Two days later, Clara Comerford disappeared without a trace.

9

Everything leaves a trail, the agent thought as he entered the hotel. Tracking animals was easy; he'd learned it from his father and brother as a child. Of course, it wasn't just tracks in the dirt, it was bent grass, broken branches, and scat. He could tell the size of the animal, whether it was injured and limping and how old the trail was. Tracking humans was much more difficult, especially in a city where no physical tracks would be evident. But humans left trails nonetheless: contacts, sightings, correspondence, and money. This time it was money. His quarry was Little Freddie Cuthbert, one of the last holdouts from Quantrill's Raiders, a Confederate partisan group that operated in Missouri and Kansas during the Civil War. Vicious and bloodthirsty, they terrorized Union sympathizing settlements, raping, killing, and plundering. Known as one of Bloody Bill Anderson's scalpers, Cuthbert had survived the war and had turned up in the Northeast, robbing banks and trains and killing anyone who could identify him. The Pinkerton Agency had agents guarding a mail train with a large payroll shipment. Cuthbert heard of the payroll through an informant and decided to rob the train. Well-named, Little Freddy was the type of person people rarely noticed. He was short and thin and non-assuming, drifting on the periphery of any crowd. He booked a ticket on the train and sat in a second-class seat next to a fat man who was busy cutting into a melon he'd bought at one of the stops. He slurped at the pieces he cut and spat the seeds on the floor in front of him. He offered Freddy a slice, but Freddy declined. "Suit yourself," the man said. He paid Freddy no further mind. As the train slowed at one of the stops, Freddy looked over at the man, who was still engrossed in his melon. "My stop," he said. The man nodded and cut himself another slice.

Freddy walked toward the front of the car and opened the door to the gangway connection, stepped on to it and closed the door behind him. But instead of moving on to the next car he pushed apart the flexible retaining partition and climbed out onto the offside of the train. He scrambled up onto the top of the car and lay flat while the train was in the station. He waited. As the train started up again, he squirmed forward, keeping as low a profile as possible. He reached the mail car and went to the front of it and looked over. Below him was the coal car. He jumped down into it and then crawled up to the open gangway at the front of the mail car. The door was locked, as he knew it would be, but Freddy had acquired many skills over the years and one of them was the ability to jimmy open any door or window he encountered. With the train gaining speed, the big smoke stack belching black smoke and the engine rumbling, there was no way the guards inside would be able to hear Freddy's careful work on the lock. The door came free, but he kept it closed until he could draw his two pistols. He waited for a jolt as the train hit a slight bump in the track, a common thing. When the jolt hit, he shoved the door open with a bang and shot the four guards before they even had a chance to react. He stepped over them, took two large canvas bags full of mail and dumped them out onto the floor. He opened the payroll chest and stuffed the money into the sacks. Before he jumped off the train, he scalped the dead guards, his trademark.

What Little Freddie didn't know was that the bills in the payroll had been marked.

"I want that little weasel found!" Aloysius Cable shouted. He banged his fist on the table for emphasis. The office was filled with every Pinkerton agent in the state. Aloysius was the state director and he had pulled them all from their current cases.

"No stone unturned!" he said, his face reddening and his neck swelling with anger. "No one does that to my agents and gets away with it. No one!"

The agents nodded in unison. Their friends had been shot and mutilated in the line of duty. Cable assigned each one to a zone in the state. Agent Beau Starr drew Western New York. He traveled to Ripley, a small town at the far western part of the state and began his search by traveling eastward. He encountered a marked bill in a hotel called the White Inn in Fredonia, N.Y. As he registered for the night, Beau noticed that a man registering under the name James Frank had stayed for one night during the previous week. The clerk remembered him. "Short little fella," he said. "But he had crazy eyes that darted about nervously. Bought a coach ticket to Silver Creek, as I remember."

Beau tracked Cuthbert through town after town, always one step behind the little man. But eventually, he knew, he would catch up. It was inevitable. He was good at what he did, and this time he had an added motivation, the agents killed had been his friends. In each town Beau went to every tavern, restaurant, and hotel, paying for items or services with a large bill. As the barman or cashier or receptionist dug out his change, he was able to see the money that had most recently been paid.

Now he was approaching the foyer of an old hotel near the tracks of a small town near Buffalo. It was the type of hotel that catered to one-nighters passing through town. The tavern, off to the side in another room, was loud and smoky. A tack piano tinkled in the background, playing one of those saloon songs that had no distinguishable melody. The pianist was banging so hard on it that the notes cascaded together, making it sound more like a series of broken bottles than a musical instrument. Beau walked up to the desk and asked the clerk for a room.

"Yes sir," the man said. "How many nights?"

"Just one."

"Right," the clerk said. He told him the price and turned the book for Beau to sign. He paid him with a gold piece and looked at the bills the clerk gave him for change as if he were counting them. There it is, he thought.

Another marked bill. He looked at the signatures above his and saw the same handwriting he had seen in two other hotels in two other cities. It was a different name, of course. This one had been signed by a certain William Anderson. The space for the clerk to mark "checked out" was blank. The room was 302. He looked at the floor map printed on the wall behind the clerk.

"Can I have 202?"

"Certainly, Sir," the clerk said. He reached back and took a key off a peg-board and laid it on the counter.

Beau walked around to the back of the hotel and looked up. Some of the newer hotels had fire escapes; this one didn't, but its windows were large, and each had a substantial ledge below it. Several windows were open, with men leaning out of them, smoking. Hotel rules forbid smoking in the rooms, but an open window allowed the rules to be bent a little. Good, he thought. The windows won't have been painted shut.

He went up the back staircase to the third floor and walked down the empty hallway to room 302. He listened carefully at the door. There was no noise and no light coming from under the door. Cuthbert was either still out or asleep. He doubted the latter. He walked back down the hallway and took the stairs to the second floor. He went to his room, silently inserted the key in the lock, and opened the door. He pushed it open and swiftly stepped back, but there was no one inside. He walked in, shut the door, locked it, and went directly to the window. As he suspected, the last occupant had left the latch open. He pulled the window up and stepped up onto the ledge. Looking up, he could see the ledge of Cuthbert's window just above him. He jumped up, caught the ledge, and pulled himself up, resting his elbows on it and bracing his feet against the clapboards on the outside of the building. With one hand, he lifted up on the window. It didn't budge. He scrabbled farther up the wall and pushed down on the ledge with his left elbow to give him a better mechanical advantage. He dug his fingers into the soft wood of the sill and pushed upward. Grudgingly, the window moved a couple of inches, which allowed him to work his fingers under it.

He pushed upward and the window rose, squeaking. He wormed his way into the narrow opening, dropped to the floor and rolled. If Cuthbert was in the room and asleep, the noise of the window being opened, the rush of fresh air, and the thump of him hitting the floor would rouse him. Beau drew his knife and waited, breathlessly. The room was dark, and the man would be disoriented. He could only allow Cuthbert to get off one shot. He would miss with the first, but a second shot would be fatal.

But Cuthbert wasn't in bed and Beau breathed a sigh of relief. He got up, closed the window, and positioned a chair where he wanted it. He sat down in it and waited.

LITTLE Freddy Cuthbert sat at a table in the back of a smoky bar, drinking rye whiskey and eyeing the patrons, looking for anyone who might be looking for him. He'd been on the run for so long that he had developed a certain sixth sense that alerted him of a pursuer. He wasn't a thinking man and didn't ponder over the cunning skills that had kept him alive for over two decades, he simply responded to the signs that a hunted animal uses to evade predators. The result was always a dead body left in an alley, scalped, of course. As patrons came and went, he watched each from beneath his hat brim. He had the sense that he was being closed in on by someone, but he had no idea who. One more night in the hotel and then he would move on again. He had money in safety deposit boxes all over three states, so money was not a problem. He traveled light, with just an overcoat and carpet bag. He rode trains from town to town, always jumping off the back landing of the rear car as the train slowed for the station. If the authorities were waiting for him at the stop, he would slip up a side street and register in a hotel under an assumed name. He always paid for more nights than he intended to stay.

As the night wore on and only a few patrons were left, smoking cigars and gambling, Freddy Cuthbert left the bar and walked to his hotel. He entered through a side door and slipped past the night clerk, who was dozing behind the desk. He used the servant's stairs down the hall from the lobby and cautiously mounted them, stopping, and listening at every landing. When he reached his floor he proceeded carefully, checking each door he passed to see that it was locked, his right hand on the pistol inside his coat in a shoulder holster. Finally, reaching his room, he checked the door for the small slip of paper he had inserted in the jam when he left. It was still there. He took out his key, put it in the lock and turned it. Then he turned the knob and quietly opened the door. He stepped into the darkened room and closed and locked the door behind him. He walked over to the lamp, pulled out a match and lit it. The flickering light filled the room with a dull yellow glow. He turned and saw a man sitting in a chair facing him, his arms crossed, and his hands obscured. He let out a low gasp and started to reach for his pistols.

"Don't," the man in the chair said softly. "You've still got a little time. Better to take your chances in court than die here."

Freddy Cuthbert knew that he was caught, and he knew, with a certain ty, that the man facing him was holding two pistols, cocked and ready. He eased his hand out of his coat and raised both hands slightly in a gesture of surrender. "You've got me," he said.

"You can sit," the stranger said. He nodded toward a chair that was facing his. Freddy nodded and keeping his hands in sight, walked over to the chair, and sat down. As he did, his cunning mind searched for an escape. This wasn't the first time he had been apprehended and he had always found a way out of it, his captor lying dead on the floor, his scalp lifted.

"Are you a bounty hunter?" Freddy said, resting his hands on his knees comfortably. "I can pay you double what they're offering. Triple even." The stranger shook his head 'no.'

"Sheriff then? I know what you make. I can pay you a year's salary. All you have to do is report that I escaped."

The agent shook his head again. "I'm a Pinkerton. You robbed a train we were guarding and killed four of my friends."

"Pinkerton!" Cuthbert exclaimed, sneering. "Your men were going to kill me! No trial, just an execution. I had to fight them."

"Did you have to scalp them?"

"I only did that for cover, so that they would think it was renegade Indians. I had no choice."

"No choice," Beau said, anger creeping into his tone. "You've been butchering, raping, and torturing people for over twenty years. You killed and scalped those men for the pleasure of it."

"Were you in the war?" Cuthbert asked. "Do you have any idea what I saw? They captured my wife and sister and put them in a jail that collapsed on them. My wife was killed, and my sister was paralyzed. Jayhawkers, pretending to be agents of the Union. I heard they were laughing as they dragged them out!"

"That's a poor excuse," The agent said. "Men just like you did the same things to my people."

A look of realization came over Freddy's face. He grinned and leaned back in his chair. "You're that half-breed that works for the Pinkertons, Beau Starr. I've heard of you. Word has it that you rampaged pretty much the same way out west. You're wanted in the Territories and Mexico too."

Freddy got a smug look on his face. His eyes narrowed.

"I've also heard that you prefer knives to pistols." He crossed his arms casually and sneered. "You can go to hell if you think you can take me in." With that he reached both hands into his coat, fast as a snake, and drew a pistol in each. But before he could cock the hammers two knives hit him, one in the chest and one in the throat. A surprised look came over his face, but he didn't drop the pistols to clutch at his throat as a normal man would have. He finished cocking the pistols and shot Beau twice before he fell over sideways, dead.

10

IDA MAE BROWN was a determined lady, and she was used to getting her way. She was a large woman, not in stature but in presence. Although slight of figure and somewhat short, she loomed large to any person she encountered. Today she was encountering Aloysius Cable, director the Rochester office of the Pinkerton Agency.

"You mean to tell me, sir," she said, poking a bony finger on the director's desk. "That, despite your advertisements, you have no available agents for the foreseeable future. Tsk, tsk, Mr. Cable," she said, shaking her head sadly. "I thought an agency of your repute would be more accommodating. I guess I'll have to go to another agency." She stood up and turned to leave. "Let's go, Alex," she said to her niece, who was standing behind her.

"Wait just a moment," Aloysius said. It was true that he was short-handed; all his available agents were currently on cases, plus, four of his agents had been killed in a train robbery and another was in the hospital. But he hated to lose a client, especially one so apparently wealthy. She had offered generous terms and would be paying per diem, plus expenses.

"I just had a thought," he said, pursing his lips. "I might be able to persuade one of our agents who has recently retired to take your case."

"That's more like it," Ida Mae said. "We'll be at the Riverview Hotel for one more day. Contact me there if you can accommodate me." She turned and, with her niece in tow, left.

"I'M retired," Beau said. "I told you that. I'm tired of getting shot at." He was lying in a hospital bed, waiting to get discharged.

"This is an easy one," Aloysius said. "No danger at all."

"That's what you always say."

"No, no, no, no," Aloysius said, the words coming in staccato fashion. "This one is different. A young girl looking for her stepmother to bring her to court. All you have to do is accompany her on the search. Use your wiles, find the woman, and serve her the papers. Piece of cake."

"You still owe me for Freddy Cuthbert," Beau said.

"You'll get paid," Aloysius said, examining his fingernails absently. "I just needed to see if…"

"If I was going to live," Beau said, finishing his sentence and giving him a hard look.

"If I paid you and you died, the money would have gone to the State. You have no relatives to leave it to. It would have been a waste."

Beau laughed, then he clutched at his chest wound. He coughed, causing him even more pain.

"You need this, Beau," Aloysius said. "With what I already owe you you'll get a good enough payday to retire for real."

Beau shook his head and managed a laugh. Aloysius was right, he needed a good payday. "Alright," he said. "But if I do this, you've got to pay me what's right. I want a percentage of the payout."

"Percentage?" Aloysius said. "You've got to be kidding."

"No, I'm not," Beau said. "And I want it in writing."

"Since when did you learn to read?"

"Very funny. When do I meet this client?"

"Tomorrow, at the Riverview Hotel," Aloysius said. "Shall we say nine o'clock?"

11

ALEX HATED THE way her aunt stirred her tea. She had the annoying habit of knocking the spoon on the sides of the cup in a loud way as she stirred it, then clacking the spoon on the brim three times – always three times - before setting it down on the plate with another loud clack. But then just about everything her aunt did annoyed her. Not that her aunt hadn't been kind to Alex and her little brother and sister. She had taken them in when their father's estate had been sold to an investor who was currently readying the entire lot of household goods - paintings, furnishing, rugs, beds, and kitchen appliances - for auction. Alex, her funds now cut off, had been forced to drop out of law school and move into a room in Ida Mae's estate. She had no reason to complain. But her aunt was incorrigibly judgmental and never missed a chance to dispense unwanted advice. Alex and the kids were chastised for how they dressed, how they spoke, how they sat and even how they held their silverware. "I swear," she often said. "My brother John, God rest his soul, was more interested in his business ventures than he was in teaching you proper manners."

Alex would have found her own lodgings, but she had no job and no money, so she was currently at the mercy of her aunt. This morning, sitting in the restaurant of the Riverview Hotel, Ida Mae was harping again on Alex's future. Again.

"Your father, God rest his soul, should never have allowed you to go to law school. It was throwing good money after bad. There's no future for a woman in law. It's a man's profession and that's why, in good conscience, I can't continue John's funding of your education; it would be throwing good money after bad. And stop going by "Alex," it's not a ladylike name. Alexandra is much more suited to a woman of class. Find a man, a man of substance, and marry him. Your father had many business associates, one of them might fill the bill. You don't have to love him. Have an affair, or a series of affairs, if he doesn't satisfy your carnal desires. It's what I did, and I never regretted a bit of it. Life's too short. Just look at your poor father, God rest his soul."

Ida Mae stirred her tea again, clacking the spoon as if to signal the end of the issue.

"My father was convinced that I would be the ideal family lawyer. I would have handled the legal aspects of his business deals and he could have rested assured that he wouldn't be cheated," Alex said, a little testily. Conversations with her aunt always put her in a bad mood, and she wanted to avoid any further judgement. "I don't think it's fair to question his judgement so soon after his death."

"I see you're playing your trump card again," Ida Mae said, sniffling and dabbing at her eye with a handkerchief. "Gone so soon, and so suspiciously."

"Suspiciously?" Alex said, ignoring her aunt's crocodile tears. "How can you fake a snake bite? Maybe Clara did take advantage of the situation, but it certainly was no more than a tragic accident."

"I've told you not to say that strumpet's name in my presence," Ida Mae said, stuffing her handkerchief into her sleeve. "She absconded with your father's fortune and sold the house out from under you. You should feel fortunate that I took you in. You could be living on the street, supporting yourself by doing God knows what! You would think that you'd be a little more grateful to your poor old aunt." She took out her handkerchief again.

"Spare me the histrionics," Alex said. "And let me inform you once again that whatever Clara did, although despicable and immoral, was not illegal.

Even if you find her, and I doubt you can, you won't have a leg to stand on in court. The will was signed and notarized. I must advise you, as a lawyer, that the wild goose chase you are suggesting will be throwing good money after bad."

Ida Mae's eyes narrowed angrily. "Using my own words against me is beneath you. And you're not a lawyer."

"Yet," Alex said. She was about to say more but the Maître D was looking at them nervously, their voices having risen to an uncomfortable volume. Alex was angry with herself for having engaged in an argument with her aunt. She knew better. Ida Mae raised her shoulders slightly, which re

Minded Alex of a rooster puffing its hackles up before a fight. She knew she was in for a public tongue lashing that she had no way of stopping, short of fleeing the scene. But, just as her aunt inhaled for the tirade, the front door opened, and two men entered the hotel lobby, distracting her. One was short and fat, the other was loose limbed and tall. They were dressed in grey three-piece suits, white shirts, and short silk ties. Both men wore bowlers. Must be some kind of Pinkerton uniform, Alex thought to herself. The taller one was limping slightly and had his left arm in a sling. They approached the Maître D, who seemed relieved to have the argument interrupted. He nodded toward their table and the two men approached, the short one leading the way.

"Ah, Mr. Aloysius Cable," Ida Mae said in clipped tones. "I see you've found a way to accommodate me after all. Is this your agent? He looks injured. Is he up to the task?"

"Very much so," Cable said. "I can attest to his fitness and skill." He introduced Beau to Ida Mae and Alex. Ida Mae gestured for them to sit.

"Starr, that's a strange name," Ida Mae said as they sat."

"Yes, Aloysius said. "Beau spent some time with the Indians as a youth." Ida Mae shot him a hard look. "Does he speak English?" she said. "Or does he need you to interpret for him?"

Aloysius shook his head slightly. The woman was direct to a fault. He looked to Beau, who spoke softly.

"I was raised by my Arapaho family. That's where I learned to track."

Ida Mae harrumphed. "Little good tracking skills will do you here in the civilized east. I doubt you'll find many horse prints on the cobblestones."

Beau ignored the insult. "Everything leaves a trail; you just need to know what to look for."

"Beau recently captured one of the most notorious outlaws in the country," Aloysius interjected quickly. He felt the conversation was going sideways and he needed to right it. "He tracked him by following a trail of stolen money that had been marked."

"I read about that," Ida Mae said. "A bank and train robber and cold-blooded killer. The account said he was one of Quantrill's raiders and that he scalped his victims. But captured is a misnomer. I believe the account said he was killed."

"True," Beau said. "I killed him as he was shooting me."

"Certainly justified," Aloysius interjected. "Cuthbert was declared an outlaw anyway. Wanted dead or alive."

"Well, this news is reassuring. Anyone who can apprehend a notorious criminal must have considerable skills. You may do after all, Mr. Starr. You and Alex can start immediately, that is, if you feel fit enough."

"No need to involve your niece," Beau said. "If Clara can be found, I'll find her. Besides, I prefer to work alone."

"Unacceptable," Ida Mae said. "Alex will accompany you in your quest as an agent of the family. There's a lot of money involved, and I don't want someone to find it and then disappear himself." She looked at Aloysius. "I thought I made that clear yesterday, Sir."

"You most certainly did, Madam," Aloysius said. He turned to Beau. "Having a young lady along might be a good cover for your search." Beau gave his boss a long look and then turned to Alex who, up to now, had been silent. "What are your thoughts?" he said.

"My thoughts?" Alex said. "I think it's a wild goose chase and I've made that very clear to my dear aunt. But, as you might have surmised, she is a very, shall we say, insistent woman. I'm ready to give it the old college try if you are."

Beau nodded toward Aloysius, who looked relieved. The charges the old lady would accrue for the duration of the case, however long that might be, would be considerable. It could take a while until the young lady concluded that Clara had indeed disappeared and decided to drop the case. In his experience, a person who went missing of their own volition usually stayed missing. He had handled many missing people's cases, and few had ever panned out.

"Tell me everything you know about Clara Comerford," Beau said.

It only took the ladies a few minutes to fill the agents in on the scanty knowledge they had of Clara. Alex had been away at school and Ida Mae had studiously kept her distance. Most of the information they had had been gotten second hand. Clara had come into town and booked a room at the Annabel Lee Inn, which John owned. John had noticed her and persuaded her to tutor his children. She moved into the house. Eventually John proposed to her, and she accepted. Then there was the wedding, which neither Ida Mae nor Alex attended. Finally, there was the tragic accident and death of John, the funeral, and the reading of the will.

"She promised to honor the conditions of the original will," Alex said. "There were witnesses. I was in the process of drawing up the papers with my aunt's guidance."

"Two days later, she vanished," Ida Mae said. "Like a ghost, she was gone."

"Who took her to the train station?" Aloysius asked.

Alex and Ida Mae looked at each other and shrugged.

"It would be a long walk, with luggage," Aloysius said. "She must have summoned one of the drivers. He would have driven up to the house and helped her with her luggage. Members of the staff would have noticed."

"No one said anything at all about her departure," Alex said, a curious look on her face. "It does seem odd, now that you mention it. The staff didn't like her much and didn't miss a chance to gossip about her. You would think I would have heard something."

"Perhaps she was picked up by someone," Beau said. "If she has an accomplice, he may have come for her sometime during the night, when no one would notice."

"Her fleeing implies guilt," Aloysius said. "She could have stayed and been mistress of the estate and had a comfortable existence. Classic behavior of a con artist. She hunted John, enticed him with her feminine wiles and captured him. She got him to change his will and then, when he died, collected on the will, and skipped town."

"Then it's a fait acompli – a done deal," Ida Mae said. "Find her and bring her before a judge. He'll rule in our favor."

"Not so fast," Aloysius said. "I said that her behavior implies guilt. It doesn't prove it. It's a free country. People can go where they will. But if she has an accomplice, that will make a much stronger case for you. We must consider the idea that this may have been a one-time thing, you know, a young lady comes to town and digs some gold. He's an old man. She stays with him until he dies and then inherits everything. Shady, immoral but not illegal. We must find out which of the two possibilities we're dealing with. If it was a conspiracy, then we take her to court and win. But if it's not, we'll have to drop the case."

"I see," Ida Mae said, a thoughtful look on her face. "Thank you for your honest assessment, Mr. Cable. Where do we start?"

"Let's take it back to the beginning," Aloysius said. "How did she arrive in town?"

"She arrived on a train," Alex said. "On a Saturday."

"Alone?" Aloysius said.

"I don't know," Alex said. "I wasn't in town that day, or that week, for that matter." She paused for a moment, furrowing her brow, considering something.

"Miles Jennings, the Maître d at the restaurant, was a close friend of fathers. He was a pall bearer at his funeral. While we were talking, he mentioned Clara's arrival at the hotel. He said that she had a bodyguard with her. I thought nothing of it at the time and, frankly, I'd completely forgotten about it until just now. Miles said he was a big man and was a little threatening. Said he was glad when the man left."

"Sounds like one of our guys," Beau said, smiling. Pinkertons were supposed to look threatening.

Aloysius shook his head. "Not one of ours, but there are plenty of private agencies around now days. Could have just been a temporary hire, a precaution taken by a woman traveling alone. Or he could be the accomplice we're looking for." He stopped for a moment, looking around at the group.

"If it is an accomplice and he's part of a conspiracy, they'll be very watchful for someone on their trail. Clara will be a lot harder to find."

Ida Mae turned to Beau. "How do you plan on starting?"

"To find where she's going, we need to see where she's been. I think we should start at the Comerford estate. It's where?"

"Geneseo," Alex said. "About thirty-five miles south of here."

"There's a southbound train leaving in a couple of hours," Ida Mae said.

"I'll see you at the station," Beau said. He nodded once to Aloysius, who nodded back.

12

THE TRAIN RIDE may been only thirty-five miles, but it was made interminable by the dozens of little whistle stops along the way. It seemed that, just as the big, coal-fired engine got up to speed, the whistle would sound and steam would be released, slowing the big beast until it stopped at another small town. It was a large steam-engine train built by Horatio B. Brooks at the Brooks Automotive Works in Dunkirk, New York. A large, fire-tube boiler set horizontally on a set of large wheels and smaller bogeys, it was fired by coal, shoveled into a firebox that heated water into com pressed steam. The steam drove the pistons, which then pushed and pulled connecting rods that applied torque to the driving wheels. The steam also operated the whistle and brakes. It was a state-of-the art locomotive that pulled several dozen cars; there was a coal car, a mail car, several freight cars, and then the passenger cars: third class, carrying a mass of people crowded together, standing, or sitting on uncomfortable benches, like steerage on a ship. Second class was a little roomier and featured padded benches in booths. At the very end were the first-class cars. The Pullmans. Invented by George Pullman, from Brocton, N.Y., they were the latest in comfort for their high-paying passengers. There was a dining car, several sleeping cars and, at the very end, a lounge car. It had ornately carved Cu ban mahogany, a curved, gilded tin ceiling, and an observation deck on the back. It was in this car that Ida Mae, Alex, and Beau sat.

Ida Mae had been brought a pot of tea by a steward and was stirring it with a silver spoon, holding forth on the state of the American economy.

Alex was taking notes from a book and seemed decidedly disinterested – she'd heard it all before. That left Beau to bear the brunt of Ida Mae's lecture. "People talk about America being an egalitarian society, where everyone has equal opportunity. Rubbish, I say. Some have risen above their station, of course; Andrew Carnegie and Joseph Pulitzer are examples. But most, like J.P. Morgan, J.D. Rockefeller and Cornelius Vanderbilt came from wealthy families. To the manner born, as they say. Good breeding, a disciplined, moral upbringing, and an advanced education. Those are the hall marks of American leadership. They built businesses. They were driven. They had purpose, and that's why civilization is triumphing over savagery. Savages have no purpose."

Alex looked up from her book and fixed a hard look on her aunt. "I think that Mr. Cable explained that Mr. Starr's family was Arapaho, Aunt Idie. You might want to consider an apology."

"I'll do nothing of the sort, young lady! And don't call me that name, you know how I hate it!"

She stirred her tea thoughtfully and then addressed Beau in a softer tone, "I'm sure you understand that I meant no offence. I was only speaking in general terms. I'm sure that, in your culture, without the use of advanced tools, it was a struggle to just get the basics in terms of food, clothing and shelter. But it must be an idyllic life, gamboling in the wilderness with no responsibilities other than to eat, sleep and procreate. In our society we must prove ourselves worthy in order to achieve success."

Beau let the additional insult go. He was an employee, on a job, and it didn't pay to argue with a client. But, as he sat, stoically enduring his client's comments, he thought back to the time when he had to prove himself. He could still remember the smells of the tipi.

IT was cold on the ground, even in his blankets. The smells of wood smoke, dog, horse and hide were strong in his nostrils. They were familiar smells and comforting. Smells of home. But still he was nervous. He was wide awake and had been all night, pensive, worried and a little scared. He tried to screw up his courage. Tried to be brave. But still the thought of a mistake or, worse yet, a lapse of concentration or resolve terrified him. But he was excited too, and his heart beat as fast as a rabbit's. It was to be his first hunt.

He could hear his brother's breathing next to him and worried that he might wake him. But he had to check one more time. His bow was tightly strung, and the handmade bow, made of Osage orange wood wrapped in sinew and backed with rattlesnake skin, creaked slightly as he tested the tension. He checked his quiver of arrows. They clacked together slightly as he did so.

"Stop doing that, Cries" his brother said, using the first part of Cries Seeing-His- Blood, his little boy's name. He had gotten it when he was very young. He had cut his forehead when he tripped and fell during a race. He bled like a stuck Prairie Dog and the salty blood had caused his eyes to water. He hated the name, but his father had yet to give him his man's name.

"You're keeping me awake," his brother said. "You've checked them enough! Go to sleep!"

I can't, he wanted to say back, but he'd already said it several times. Who can sleep the night before his first hunt? He peeked out from under the hide covering of the tipi but saw nothing but the brilliant stars that lit the grassy plains like a million distant candles. His mother called them stars in her language and told him that the ancient Greeks thought they were distant suns, something his brother and the other boys ridiculed him for saying. They knew them to be the council of all the great chiefs of the past, placed there by Wahanda. His mother called the great circle of chiefs the Corona Borealis and its center star, the star that does not move, Polaris – the North Star. But whether they were stars or chiefs, he could read them as well as anyone, and they told him that dawn was still far away. A long wait, with much to ponder. He thought again about his recent initiation.

A boy entering manhood was given a mouthful of water and sent on a long run during the heat of mid-day. There was no water at all on the course, which had braves stationed along the way. To swallow the water was to fail. He had run the course and spat the mouthful of water out at the end, to the satisfaction of the many onlookers. The men cheered and the women ululated. He was given a skin of water to drink, which he gulped down thankfully. Then, later, amidst much pomp and ceremony, he was suspended from a pole by rawhide thongs attached to two bone skewers that pierced the skin and muscle on his chest. He hung there until his weight tore him loose. To cry out or show pain was forbidden. He had passed that test too. But now, in his mind, came the real test: his first hunt with the braves of the tribe. He worried that he would dishonor himself in front of the others. He knew that his father would be watching him closely. He lowered the hide flap and checked his equipment again, this time more carefully. He lay back down and dreamed of the hunt.

A sharp kick to the ribs woke him. He opened his eyes and looked up at his brother, who was laughing at him. "Get up, or you'll miss the hunt," Little Otter said. Cries scrabbled to his feet, grabbed his bow and quiver of arrows, and staggered toward the open flap on the tipi. In his haste he lost his grip on his quiver and his arrows clattered out onto the dirt floor. His brother laughed again and left him to gather his arrows and head out on his own.

His father, Yellow Bear, the tribe's chief, gave him a stern look as he headed toward the horse corral; most of the other braves had already caught their horses and were mounted, checking their gear. Cries whistled softly and his horse, a small but nimble pinto named Rabbit, snorted, and came to him, shaking his head and whinnying excitedly. He knew what an important day this was. Cries leapt up onto Rabbit's back and took the raw hide reins in his hand just as Yellow Bear gave the signal to move out. The braves whooped and the women and children ululated. He saw his mother standing next to the tipi, her blonde hair flowing in the breeze. She smiled at him and nodded her encouragement.

The group of twelve hunters galloped off in a cloud of dust. After the initial exciting charge, Yellow Bear gave a signal and the hunting party slowed to an easy trot. Signs of the herd had been spotted some miles away, and it was moving north, away from them. Little Otter rode beside him, clearly as excited as he was. Although he was a couple years older, the hunt was still something that got his blood up. Of course, the same could be said for the rest of the group, it was what they were bred to do. Like hawks hunt rabbits and panthers hunt deer, the Arapaho hunt buffalo. Their entire way of life depended on the big, shaggy animals who were used for their meat, their hides and even their bones. Nothing was left to waste. It had always been that way.

The hunting party soon came upon the tracks of the big herd and scouts reported that it had passed there only a few hours ago. They halted for a brief rest and checked their weapons and their tack. They drank water from leather skins and chewed jerky. After a while, Yellow Bear signaled to the group and they proceeded onward in silence, the only sound was the light clomp of the unshod horses' hooves and the creak of rawhide and leather.

The sun was high in the sky when they sighted the dust cloud of the herd. Yellow Bear signaled for the group to fan out and prepare to give chase. When the buffalo realized they were being pursued, they would stampede. Little Otter smiled at his little brother and signed "good luck." The group urged their ponies forward at a light trot.

They were only a few hundred yards behind the massive herd when some of the buffalo in the rear noticed them. They began to run. The hunting party broke into a gallop, issuing war cries as they urged their ponies on. The dust kicked up by the herd soon engulfed Cries and he was blind Ed. He lost sight of Little Otter and the rest of the hunters. Rabbit plunged ahead into the rear of the herd and Cries found himself riding alongside a large bull. He readied his bow and, steering with his knees, nocked an arrow and fired into the side of the big beast's neck. The arrow went straight through. It didn't seem to affect the animal at all. He nocked another arrow and fired, then he fired a third and a fourth. The buffalo plunged on, oblivious to any injury. He still had a dozen arrows in his quiver, and it looked like he was going to have to use them all. He was reaching back for another when Rabbit jumped a small mesquite bush. The action caused the quiver to slide forward off his shoulder and onto his elbow. Before he could do anything, he saw his remaining arrows tip out of his quiver and clatter toward the ground. No arrows! And the big bull buffalo was still running next to him, unfazed by the arrows that were protruding from his hairy mane. Cries had one shot at redemption. He leapt from Rabbit's back and onto the charging buffalo, gripping its mane with his left hand as he UN

Sheathed his knife with his right. He leaned over and around to the side of the animal and plunged the knife into its neck to the hilt. He worked it back and forth, desperately clinging to the shaggy beast below him. He could feel its muscles and tendons expanding and contracting as it surged on. He became one with the animal, a sweating appendage breathing hot air into the rancid, tangled fur. The boy was spattered with foamy, hot blood that smelled and tasted metallic. But still the animal ran on.

Suddenly, without warning, the bull buffalo pitched forward onto its collapsing front legs. Cries was thrown into the mass of stampeding buffalo. He managed to stand for a moment, and he looked desperately for Rabbit, but the pony had been swept away with the herd. He was jostled and banged and knocked to the ground several times, but he somehow came back to his feet. Then, in one fluid motion, he felt himself lifted by the back of his shirt and thrown across the withers of a horse. The rider was laughing, and he recognized the laughter as his father's. Humiliation! He had lost his quiver, his bow, and his pony. He had expected to be trampled to death – it would have spared him the shame he would now have to face.

His father eased his horse out of the stampede and turned back the way they had come. The dust was just settling as they arrived at the killing ground. He looked up from his perch and saw the hunters wandering around the churned ground and identifying their kills by the fletching's on the arrows protruding from the downed beasts, some of which writhed painfully, trying to struggle to their feet. It was a scene from time immemorial, hunters butchering their kills as they always had, and always would.

His father reached the large bull that had thrown his son. It lay on its side, eyes staring vacantly and tongue lolling out of its bloody mouth.

"Good kill," his father said. He threw his left leg over his son's body and dismounted. Cries slipped down himself, hanging his head in shame as he regarded the dead buffalo.

"You picked the biggest bull you could find and split the herd, making it easier for the rest of us," his father said, taking his son by the shoulders. "Then you pounced on the bull and killed him with your knife, a feat I have never seen done, even by experienced hunters. Most would have let the beast bleed out."

Cries noticed several hunters approaching, regarding him with respect, not the derision he had expected. Little Otter came forward, leading Rabbit and carrying his bow and quiver full of Cries' fallen arrows. He shook his head and smiled.

"Cries-With-Blood-on-his-Face is no more," his father announced to the growing crowd. "He pounced on the big bull like a mountain lion. We shall call him "Boh'oohoox, the Mountain Lion."

The boy's heart swelled with pride. His friends showed a new respect toward him and were already using his new name, "Boh," as they crowded around him, congratulating him. His father smiled as they rode back to the village.

13

The jerking of the stopping at the platform brought Beau out of his memory. He looked around and found himself again in the lounge car of a train. Ida Mae had been talking non-stop and he had been nod ding his head, feigning interest. It was a trick he had learned when he was young: pretending to be interested in something while his mind drifted away.

"I hope you understand my point of view, Mr. Starr," Ida Mae said in conclusion. Out of the corner of his eye he saw Alex roll her eyes. He sup pressed an urge to laugh. Mustering all the sincerity he could, he said, "Of course."

"Good," Ida Mae said, pleased with her commentary. "Shall we?" she said, standing. Alex and Beau stood and headed for the exit. The three of them worked their way through the crowd on the platform, two porters following behind with the ladies' luggage. Beau himself only had a modest leather satchel, in which he kept his casual clothes and a few personal items. He was wearing a wool three-piece suit with a white shirt and a short black tie. He preferred to wear his casual clothes when he could but traveling with ladies of substance required that he dress accordingly. On his head he wore a black bowler hat that he had acquired when he first joined the Pinkertons. It seemed to be part of the uniform in these parts, but he much preferred a simple bandana, tied at the back, for a head covering.

As they passed the ticket booth, Beau excused himself and walked over to it. As he was inquiring about hotels in town, Ida Mae approached. "No need to find a hotel, Mr. Starr," she said. "I've got a large estate with several guest rooms. You'll be staying with us when not away on your search. I'd like to keep you close to discuss your findings." Beau could see no way to say no, so he said yes. He followed the two ladies out to a waiting carriage, handed his satchel to one of the porters, who were loading the ladies' luggage into a covered rack on the back, and climbed in.

"This is a Landau, Mr. Starr. It was a favorite of my husband's, poor soul. Many people think me a widow, yet my husband is still alive. An unfortunate accident left him with severe brain damage, I'm afraid. He's now not much more than a vegetable."

"I'm sorry to hear that," Beau said. He had seen many braves injured like that, so badly broken that there could be no recovery. Someone, usually the chief or the shaman, dispatched the man to end his suffering. His uncle had died that way. He received a blow to the head from a club during a battle and had been knocked from his horse. His neck was broken, and he couldn't move his arms or his legs. He had been brought back to the village, where the shaman, after putting a weapon in his hand and reciting a prayer, dispatched him, insuring him of a warrior's death. That a man was left to linger with no hope of recovery was abhorrent to him. But it was the way of the Whites.

THE Brown estate was on a hill overlooking a lush valley near the Genesee River. Apple peach and pear orchards stretched out below it, along with rows of grapes and fields of wheat. There were miles of white fences behind which dozens of thoroughbred horses grazed. Cattle could be seen in a large pasture next to a large barn, painted red. The main house was a two-story brick structure with tall windows on both floors, several gables jutting out from the red tiled roof and white marble steps leading up to a large landing. A columned portico led to the front entrance which featured an oak door with brass fittings. A porch fronted by a wrought-iron balustrade jutted out from both sides of the door, running the length of the front of the house. The carriage pulled up to a covered carriage porch on the side of the building. A valet opened the door of the carriage and assisted the ladies down and then up the stairs. Beau followed them inside to an opulent foyer where leather chairs, sofas and tables were arranged throughout. It reminded Beau of the foyer of a grand hotel, but without the reception desk.

"Your things will be sent up to your room, Mr. Starr," Ida Mae said. "I suggest you freshen up before dinner. It's served at precisely six o'clock." He thought her tone was a little dismissive. He thanked her and followed a valet up the stairs. They walked down a long hallway past several doors until they reached one at the far end. The valet opened the door and gestured for him to enter. He thanked the man, tipped him, walked into the room, and closed the door.

There was a bed, a dresser and a nightstand with a porcelain bowl, a bar of soap, a pitcher of water, and a towel on a hook. Beau took off his coat, his vest and his shirt and washed up. He didn't need to shave. He took a fresh shirt out of his satchel, dressed, and sat cross-legged on the floor. He grasped his spirit stone and softly chanted. His spirit stone was a crystal that he had gotten on the last day of his initiation. The old sachem of his tribe, One Ear, had told him to fast for four days. At dawn on each day, he was to run to the river and swim to the bottom of the deepest hole. On the last day he was to grasp the gravel on the bottom and bring it back to the old man. He had, and One Ear had found the crystal after poking around in the small pile of gravel Beau had brought him.

"This is your spirit stone," he said. "Keep it with you at all times. When you have an important decision to make or when you are starting a new journey, consult it. It will center you and help you to make the right choices."

Now, Beau hoped that he had made the right choice in taking the case. It was an easy job, paid per diem plus expenses and he would get a decent percentage of the settlement - if they found Clara Comerford and the judge ruled in the family's favor. And he did need the money, but not to retire.

He needed the money to finance his own, personal search for the man who had caused him to leave his homeland on the plains.

When he had first come to the northeast, Beau had nothing but the clothes on his back and a few dollars. He quickly found that a few dollars didn't go far in the crowded, civilized region. His mother had taught him English, and white-man's manners and mannerisms, but they only allowed him fit in, not get paid. His real talents were what he had learned on the plains: hunting, horsemanship, fighting and tracking. His ability with horses got him odd jobs at stables, but those jobs usually amounted to shoveling manure and pitching hay. But he was able to earn room and board, and stables were good places to pick up information. He had seen the man once, from a distance, leading his gang into a hacienda in Juarez. He was tall, barrel-chested, and had black hair with a white scar running down the side of his left cheek. But more than his physical appearance, the way the man carried himself conveyed a sense of malevolent arrogance that seemed to strike fear in everyone he encountered. Someone like that you never forget, try as you might.

Beau found out later that the man was likely headed to New York State, where his brother lived. Beau traveled to the region and began his search. He asked around discretely, at stables, hotels, taverns, and train stations. A man matching that description had been seen here and there, but always many days ago. He didn't seem to stay in any one place long.

Then one day he had a piece of good luck. Two Pinkerton agents were boarding their horses for the night in a stable where Beau was working. He approached them casually as he was taking care of the horses and described the man he was seeking. "He owes me money," Beau said. They told him a man of that description had been seen in Rochester in the company of a beautiful woman.

"Obviously a hired bodyguard," the one man said. "The woman was too high class to be married to a rough looking sort like him." His partner laughed and took a long, appraising look at Beau. "What of you, sir," he said. "You have the looks of a fighter, not a stable boy." It was true. Beau had sustained a few cuts from hunts and fights, and they stood out on his ruddy, hairless face. "I lived out west for a time," he said simply.

"Were you a scout?"

Beau took a moment to answer. He didn't want to reveal his identity, or the identity of the man he was after. Word might spread. The last thing that Beau wanted was for the man to discover he was being trailed. The man would turn hunter, making him doubly harder to find, not to mention that he himself would become prey. Beau had no intention of being ambushed after having come so far.

"I did a little scouting," Beau said a little ambiguously. "Mostly as an assistant. I was young," he added.

"Did you work for General Crook at all?" the man said.

Beau shook his head no. "I knew of him, of course. Everyone did. But I never worked for him."

Beau remembered the legendary General and had even seen him once, at a distance. He remembered that the general wore a canvas suit and a pith helmet. He was fair to the Indians and had made friends with the Shoshone and Crow. The trouble the general had was that the different Indian tribes had grievances against each other, dating back for generations. Making friends with the Shoshone and Crow made the whites enemies of the Sioux, who hated the Shoshone and Crow. They finally came together under Crazy Horse at the Greasy Grass. But, by then it was far too late to present a united front against the white incursion. It was probably too late many years before.

"Our director, Aloysius Cable, was an officer with Crook," the man said. Beau adopted a casual look of interest. "I would like to meet him some time, maybe he knew some of the people I knew."

The man pulled a card from his pocket and handed it to Beau. "You should look him up," the man said. "If you were a scout, he might be interested in hiring you. It would be a whole lot better than shoveling shit," he added. He and his partner shared a laugh and left. A few hours later Beau was on a train to Rochester.

The first thing that Aloysius Cable said to Beau when they met in his office was hello, which surprised Beau greatly. It wasn't the greeting that surprised Beau, it was the language that Cable used: it was Arapaho. He also used the slight hand gestures that indicated a peaceful meeting. Beau re turned the gesture and greeting but was puzzled. How did the man know that he was Arapaho? Cable invited him to sit, and he sat himself. As he sat, Beau took in the room. Every bit of it, from the wooden desk and chair to the neat filing cabinets lined up along the wall and the pictures of presidents on the wall bespoke a certain military bearing. Cable himself dis played a dress and bearing of a life spent in the military. He wore a gray wool three-piece suit, with a starched white shirt and short silk tie. His hair was white and close-cropped, and he wore a trim white mustache. Aside from a sizeable middle-age paunch and a gin-blossom nose, everything about him was military.

"You are surprised that I speak Arapaho," he said, his hands neatly folded on his desk.

"I'm more surprised that you know I'm Arapaho," Beau said. Cable smiled.

"I spent a lot of time out west a few years ago, campaigning under General Crook. I got to know the various indigenous groups quite well. The Arapaho are a proud people, and the men carry themselves a certain way. So do the Shoshone, Crow, and Sioux, but each group has its own distinctive way of walking, talking, dressing and, well, looking? As you walked in the room, you might as well have carried a sign that identified you as Arapaho." Cable smiled again and opened a small, wooden humidor and extracted two cigars. He snipped the ends of each and handed one to Beau. He lit them both with a large sulfur match and puffed lightly, sending a fragrant cloud of tobacco smoke into the air. He looked at the cigar for a moment as if he was about to ask it a question. Then he looked back at Beau. "You have mixed blood, I see. Your mother was white, I assume?" Beau nodded.

"She was captured as a young girl by another tribe and then traded to my father's. I don't know much about the particulars, but I know that they both fell in love so deeply that she resisted all efforts of repatriation. Her family had evidently been killed, so she had no one to go back to. She was welcomed into the tribe and fully embraced the Arapaho culture."

"I've heard of several such cases," Cable said. "The most famous one was Quannah Parker. His mother was white too. He's an important leader of his people now; and he kept his braids."

Beau was a little stunned by the comment and he wondered what Aloysius Cable's point was. The man didn't strike him as a person who talked idly, without considering his words or their meanings.

Then he realized that it was a test. Cable was trying to ascertain his mettle. Cable wanted to know if Beau would react angrily or maintain his composure. Part of the process, Beau reasoned.

"My people are all dead," Beau said softly. But he looked Cable in the eye when he said it. "I came here to find the leader of the gang that killed them."

Cable drew on his cigar thoughtfully. "Who is this man you're seeking?" He said.

Beau described the man, the image burned in his mind. Cable blanched. "A white scar on the left side of his face?" he said. Beau saw that the man's demeanor had changed drastically. Cable got up and walked over to a short table that contained a decanter of whiskey and two glasses. He poured himself a liberal quantity, quaffed it, and poured another.

"I know the man you're seeking," he said, his back to Beau. "He is known as Quint. I served with him during the war and then out west." He turned and faced Beau, the whiskey glass in his hand. "He once swore that he would kill me if he ever saw me again."

Cable looked down at his glass, regarded its contents, and drank the whiskey off. He looked nervously at Beau, but then visibly composed himself. "I'm sorry, I'm afraid I've forgotten my manners." Without asking, he poured another glass and handed it to Beau. Then he poured another mea sure for himself. He walked back to his desk and sat down heavily. "Quint was a gifted, talented, and intelligent officer. We attended the Point together and served in the Mexican War. He was brilliant, decisive, and inspiring. His troops worshipped him. But then something happened, I think it was during the war. We were with Stoneman, chasing the rebel cavalry all over the South. The Rebs were better horsemen than we were, and better mounted. He was on an extended reconnaissance with forty men under his command. The Rebs attacked and his troop was cut to pieces. He managed to break free with a dozen men and make it back to our lines, but he lost the rest and was badly wounded himself." Cable paused, relit his cigar and took another sip of whiskey. "They called him a hero, gave him a medal, and sent him home to recuperate. But I think the biggest wound he received was to his pride. I'm sure that he felt he had blundered into the ambush and gotten his command slaughtered. I would have felt the same way. The medal would have been a slap in the face. I didn't see him again for several years until, quite by chance, he was posted to my command out west during the Indian campaigns." He paused again and shook his head sadly. "He was a changed man; he had become bitter and resentful. He was insolent and insubordinate. But worse, he developed an abiding hatred of the Indians. Instead of trying to make peace, as General Crook had encouraged us to do, he led his troops on a campaign of attrition. I questioned him about his methods, and he said: "The Romans made a desert and called it peace." Shortly after that, I was forced to strip him of his rank and cashier him. It was then that he said he would kill me the next time that he saw me. I heard that he formed a band of Comancheros and made a living slaughtering Indian villages and selling scalps."

"My village was one of the ones he raided," Beau said. "I caught up with his gang, but he had slipped away. I was told that he was heading to New York State to find his brother. That's why I'm here. And that's why I cut my braids."

Cable nodded and drank off his whiskey. He had thrown the comment out to see Beau's reaction. It had worked. Cable knew, from long experience with indigenous groups that pride in their culture ran strong. If Beau had cut his braids and left his homeland, there must have been a very compelling reason. He had found out, but the knowledge was shocking. Quint was a dangerous man, and to have him loose somewhere near was troubling. "I advise you to take caution in your search for Quint," Cable said. "He's a psychopathic killer and if he finds out you're looking for him, he'll turn hunter. You'll have to always watch your back."

"I'll find him," Beau said. "It's my only purpose."

Cable hired him as an agent, and Beau traveled the length and breadth of the state, doing the jobs Cable gave him but all the while searching for Quint. But now, sitting in his room at the Brown estate, Beau realized that had come no closer to finding the man than the first day he had set foot in New York.

DINNER at the Brown estate was a formal affair and there were several courses, each paired with an appropriate wine. The children, Jeremy, and Anna were excited to have a guest, and were beside themselves. There had been a lot of grief in their lives in the past year. Their mother had died suddenly, leaving their upbringing to Mrs. Potter, the governess. But then she had been dismissed and replaced by Lady Clara, who quickly assumed the position their mother had once had. Then their father had died and Lady Clara, who they had come grudgingly to like, had disappeared, and left them homeless. Aunt Idy, as they called her behind her back, had kindly taken them in, but life around the Brown estate was decidedly less fun than their own home. Their aunt, Grand Aunt, as she insisted on being referred to in her presence, was a harsh disciplinarian and insisted on proper manners and speech. But they were used to a more lenient lifestyle and, despite their aunt's constant chiding at their manners and comportment, they ignored her whenever they could. The new guest was just too much of a temptation for their curiosity.

"Hazel says you're an Indian," Jeremy blurted, referencing the house keeper, Hazel Smith. She was as old as Ida Mae and had been with the Brown household as long as anyone could remember.

"Indians are red," Jeremy continued. "Why aren't you read?" Ida Mae shot a hot look at the boy, but Beau, toying with his dinner, laughed.

"Ruddy would be a better description. I'm lighter skinned because I'm half White. My mother was a young girl when she was taken in a raid. She told me that at first her only desire was to escape, but escape was impossible, out on the endless plains, so she had no choice but to stay, hoping to be rescued. But gradually she came to be accepted by the tribe. She fell in love with one of the warriors, and they were married. He was my father, and he taught me everything about riding, hunting, tracking, and fighting, as he did my brother. My mother taught me English, reading, writing and arithmetic, and manners." He looked briefly at Ida Mae. "White manners," he added.

"What happened?" Anna asked, intrigued. "Why did you leave?" A pained look came over Beau's face. He grew silent and looked down at his plate.

"Anna!" Alex said.

Beau looked up and shook his head. "She asked sincerely, and she is due a sincere explanation," he said, his voice quavering ever so slightly. "There was a raid. A group of Comancheros attacked my village just before dawn. They silently killed the guards. My father and the other braves were taken completely by surprise. The tribe fought hard, but they were outnumbered and overwhelmed. Everyone was killed."

An image exploded in Beau's head. It was dawn in his village. The air was filled with smoke and screams and the sound of gunfire and the triumphant whoops of the attackers. He saw the faces of his mother and father and brother. He saw Morning Star running, screaming his name for help. He saw the faces of the attackers, grinning and waving bloody scalps like pennants. It was an invented memory because he hadn't been there. He began sweating; his heart raced, and his breathing quickened. He realized that everyone was looking at him strangely and he fought back against the memory, calming himself.

"How did you escape?" Jeremy asked. "How did you survive?"

"I wasn't there," Beau said, wiping his forehead with a napkin. "I was away, on a vision quest. I found them when I returned."

"What's a vision quest?" Jeremy asked.

Beau regained his composure and managed a slight laugh. "In our culture, a young boy, about your age, goes off into the wilderness alone. He fasts and prays until a dream comes to him. In it, the spirits reveal to him his destiny, his purpose in life."

"What did you see?" Jeremy asked. "What was your purpose in life?"

"I thought it was to take my place in the tribe, to be a hunter and a warrior, but when I returned, I found that I had no family and no tribe. I was alone and had nowhere to go, so I drifted around for a time. Then I came east and joined the Pinkertons." He stopped and looked around again. He smiled. "Now, here I am, using all my skills to find a missing widow." Everyone laughed, the adults a little nervously. The children exchanged looks of wonderment. They'd never been around someone with so much adventure. They clearly wanted to ask more, but a stern look from Ida Mae forestalled them.

"If I was in my native dress right now, I'd be wearing my hair long and braided on two sides," Beau said lightly. "I would have on a leather loin cloth and moccasins and war paint on my face." He made as if to yell a war cry but then stopped, laughing. The children squealed with delight, drawing another look of disapproval from Ida Mae.

As he laughed, Beau's face softened. Alex suddenly realized that he was a lot younger than he appeared. The hard countenance of the veteran Pinker ton detective melted away, leaving behind a young man not much older than Alex herself.

"How many years ago did the raid occur?" she asked mildly, as if just making small talk.

"Let's see," Beau said, rubbing his chin thoughtfully. "I think it was around ten years ago. Maybe eleven." He paused for a moment. "Sorry, I've never been asked that question before. Yes, I think it was eleven." Alex did the math. Jeremy was twelve.

After dinner Ida Mae, Alex and Beau went to Ida Mae's drawing room; it was the room where Ida Mae spent most of her time, receiving guests, reading, and writing letters. She called it her salon. There were family poor traits on the mahogany paneled walls, leather chairs, a fireplace, and a baby grand piano in the corner. A deep brown carved table held decanters of various spirits and wines and there was a shelf with crystal wine glasses, brandy snifters, and cut-glass tumblers. Alex got three tumblers down and poured a measure of deep brown liquor into each. The discussion revolved around what strategy they would use to find Clara, and she was worried.

"Whiskey?" she said to Beau and handed one to him without waiting for a response. This is going to be a trial, she thought. The agent would have his ideas about how to proceed with the search, and his experience and knowledge should see them through. But Ida Mae was a notorious micromanager and Alex wondered how Beau would respond to her directions. She felt that a clash was inevitable and hoped she could mitigate a crisis that might end up with the Pinkerton agent walking out the door – or being sent out of it by Ida Mae. She handed a glass of whiskey to her aunt who took it and said, "Of course you would select my most expensive bourbon." She looked at the whiskey appraisingly and held the glass up in the gesture of a toast. She took a sip. "Well, at least you've got good taste – at least in whiskey."

The three sat down in leather chairs, facing the fire. They sat in silence for a while, each waiting for someone else to start the conversation. Finally, Alex spoke up.

"Train stations," she said. Ida Mae looked at her questioningly. "Clara was most likely dropped off at the train station. We know that much. Someone, the Ticketmaster or one of the porters, would remember someone like Clara. A ticket to where? One of them might remember. Then we go there and try to pick up her trail."

Ida Mae nodded her agreement. Beau said nothing.

Ida Mae looked directly at Beau. "Well, speak up, young man. You're the professional here."

Beau set his glass down and looked at Ida Mae. "My agency has investigated hundreds of cases like yours," he said softly. "What appears to the untrained eye as a causal relationship that grows into something more is often carefully planned, choreographed, and played out? How did Clara manage to catch the eye of the most wealthy and available man in town, romance him and then marry him? Why was she so quick to abscond with her inheritance?" He paused for effect and took another sip of whiskey. "Everything about the will is legal. She could have stayed at the estate and been the mistress of it. The fact that she ran implies that she's a serial grifter. A con artist. We must assume that everything she did with John, she did before, and will do again, and she won't be easy to find."

"So how do you propose we go about the search? Alex said.

"I agree with you, Alex. We go everywhere she has been seen and try to find some clue to follow. But we don't start with where she was last seen, we go to where she was first seen after John's death. We go to the doctor who treated him."

14

DOCTOR TOBIAS PILCHER's office smelled strongly of formaldehyde, sawdust, tobacco, and whiskey. When Alex and Beau entered, the good doctor was in the process of setting a young boy's leg. He'd had the unfortunate bad luck of being run over by a wagon and was screaming in agony. His mother cried and his father, who had been driving the wagon, tried to comfort his wife. The doctor's assistant had the boy pinned to the table by the shoulders and was trying to keep him still as he writhed in pain. The doctor had a medieval looking contraption strapped to the boy's leg and was turning a device whose purpose was to stretch the leg enough to reset the bone. He was sweating profusely and paused from time to time to wipe his face with a soaked towel and catch his breath. Finally, with a loud pop, the leg went back into place. The boy passed out from the pain and the doctor staggered backwards, steadying himself with the back of a chair. Winded, he accepted a half-empty bottle of whiskey from his assistant and drained it in one long gulp. He finished the job by strapping long splints on either side of the boy's leg and then tying them in place with stout twine.

"Oh, thank God," the mother exclaimed, almost fainting herself. Her husband steadied her. She turned and looked up at him. "You should watch where you're driving!" she exclaimed hotly. "Get your hands off me and help Little Jimmy to the wagon."

The father complied with the help of the doctor's assistant, the boy whimpering as they went out the door toward the wagon. The boy's mother smoothed her dress and clutched her purse. "How much?" she said. The doctor told her, and she fished in her purse for a moment and pulled out some bills. "Here's half," she said. "I'll get the rest to you as soon as I can."

The doctor took the bills and said, "I understand, Mrs. Willy." She nodded once and then looked at Alex and Beau for a moment and walked out.

The doctor shook his head sadly. "Add what they owe me to their outstanding bill," he said to his assistant as he returned from the wagon. He wiped his hands on his apron and looked at Alex and Beau. "What can I do for you?" he asked, giving Alex an appraising look. She ignored it.

"I'm Alexandra Comerford and this is my associate, Mr. Starr. A while back you treated my father, John, who had collapsed during an outing with his wife."

"Yes, I remember," the doctor said. "Snakebite, as I recall."

"Yes, that was your assessment," Alex said. "What can you tell me about the circumstances?"

"Nothing to tell," the doctor said, looking a little tired, and a little thirsty. "Your mother drove him here and said they had been picnicking. He went into the bushes to relieve himself, cried out and staggered back to the buggy. She drove him here and we brought him into the office and put him on the table. I saw that he was not breathing. I checked his pulse and he had none. He was dead. Upon an examination postmortem, I noticed that his left leg was swollen. I cut his pants open and noticed fang marks on his upper ankle, just above the boot."

"Isn't it unusual for an adult male to die from a snakebite so quickly?"

"Yes, unusual but not without precedent. I was told at a conference last year that a man had died from snakebite in Utica. The doctor also thought it unusual, but others attested to it often being the cause of a heart attack. That may have been the case with your father. Hard to tell."

"This doctor in Utica," Alex said. "Do you remember his name?"

"Yes, I do, the doctor said with a laugh. "Because it was so unusual. His name is Doctor Boyle."

Alex wasn't impressed by the joke. "Thank you, Doctor," she said. She turned to Beau. "I guess we're going to Utica."

15

THE NEXT MORNING a coachman drove Alex and Beau to the train station where they caught the nine o'clock local to Utica. The engineer blew the whistle and the train chugged forward, belching black smoke into the clear blue sky. They passed farmsteads, pastures, wheat fields and orchards as they sped along the countryside. As they rode, the topic of tracking came up. Alex was curious about the technique.

"When an animal, or a human, moves, the environment surrounding it is changed," Beau said. "With an animal, there are tracks left in the dirt, small pebbles are displaced, grass is bent, and small twigs are snapped. Moss and lichens are smudged on rocky ground and, if your quarry has taken to a small brook or swamp, the water is muddied and settles differently than the patterns in the mud and silt nearby. A good, trained eye can tell how long ago the quarry passed by and whether it was traveling fast or slow."

"What about a human quarry traveling on a train like this, or in a coach or on a horse? What about the city, with its crowds of people and cobble stoned streets?"

"A ticket must be purchased, a coach or horse leased. Meals are eaten and rooms are rented. Porters, drivers, desk-clerks, and waitresses interact with the person. The memory is tucked away in their subconscious and only emerges if the right questions are asked at the right time, and in the right way." Beau laughed a little and shook his head. "Like the kids did at dinner yesterday. I've never been asked about my past before, and my memory was triggered. I got a little carried away. Sorry."

"Don't be sorry," Alex said. "It was refreshing to hear someone talk about his past so openly."

"Well, my past is something I'm not proud of; at least the part that came after the raid. I did love my Arapaho family, though and I hate the men who took it from me."

"I understand," Alex said. "I guess I feel the same way about Clara. Even if my father's death was an accident, it seems clear to me that she cultivated my father's affection to enrich herself."

Beau looked at the sad young lady and regretted his comment about chasing widows.

"I'll do my best to find her," he said reassuringly. "After that, it'll be up to you and the court to bring her to justice."

16

Utica is located on the Mohawk River in Central New York. Once known as the "Gateway to the West," it was a rail center with dozens of factories, manufacturing everything from textiles to plows. The fertile fields outside the city produced livestock, grain, and fruit. Alex and Beau descended from the train at the central station, a busy, bustling place. People, carrying packages, carpetbags and suitcases jostled their way to and from the train. Alex and Beau made their way through the crowd and proceed end down Genesee Street, seeking an unfortunately named "Doctor Boyle." They found his office in a large building overlooking a tree-lined park. He was busy and they had to wait in the reception room for over an hour. Finally, the receptionist, an efficient lady with her hair in a bun, ushered them into the doctor's office.

"Mrs. Hutchins tells me that you want to know about a man who died of snakebite a while back," the man said. He was unusually tall and thin and had a protruding Adam's apple. He reminded Alex of Ichabod Crane of "The Legend of Sleepy Hollow." Her mother had read her the story every Halloween, and she was still terrified of dark, stormy nights in the country.

"Yes," Alex said. "My father died of snakebite recently and I was told that you had a patient who had a similar accident."

"Yes, I do remember the man, it's not often that you treat snakebite any more. I had an office on the outskirts of town at the time and two farmhands brought him in. They said he was inspecting the field when he cried out and collapsed. They put him in their buckboard and drove to my office. Sadly, he was dead when he arrived. I examined him and saw that his left leg was swollen. I cut his pants away and saw the fang marks and realized that he had been bitten."

Alex shot a surprised look at Beau, but his face was impassive. He almost looked bored. She turned back to the doctor. "Do you remember his name?"

The doctor gave a short laugh. "Of course I do. He was the richest man in town at the time of his death. His name was William Clifton. Had a huge estate just west of town."

"Does his family still live there?" Alex said.

The doctor shook his head. "I heard that they sold the place and moved out of town."

"Any idea where they moved?"

"No idea. Big house though. An estate overlooking the river."

"You don't happen to know the address, do you?"

"No, I don't, but you can't miss it if you head west on the Seneca Road. About five miles."

Beau suddenly stood, an easy practiced movement. As he stood, he put light but insistent pressure on Alex's elbow. Surprised, she stood also. The doctor followed suit.

"We don't need to see the house," Beau said with understated finality. "We were just curious about the coincidental nature of the two unfortunate events." He shook the doctor's hand with a friendly smile. "You've answered all our questions."

Alex turned a questioning look on Beau, but he met it with a smile "Shall we?" he said, offering his arm to Alex. With a "good day, Doctor," he gently turned Alex toward the door.

"Why did you pull us out that office so abruptly?" Alex said as they stepped out onto the crowded street. A babble of voices, the creaking and clanking of harness and the clop of horse hoofs on the cobblestones filled their ears. "I had more questions," she said, shouting a little above the din and with just a touch of anger. "I had more questions," she said again, more softly but more firmly.

Beau smiled his inscrutable smile but didn't say anything. He turned and began casually walking up the street. Alex had to scurry to catch up. She wanted desperately to grab him by the elbow, stop him and demand answers. But somehow his demeanor dissuaded her. She walked briskly next to him; her lips pursed.

"That's better," he said softly. "If you cause a scene, we'll be noticed. We don't want that."

Alex smiled and adopted his casual tone. "And who would notice us?" She took his arm, jokingly. "A couple, out for a pleasant stroll and taking in the sights."

"No one, probably," he said. "But in this business, you can't allow probably. I know you had more questions, but you'd already asked too many." Alex looked at him quizzically.

"People like to talk, and they will prattle on if you allow them. But too many questions make a discussion an interrogation. They become defensive and they watch their words. The good doctor had already given us all that we need."

"And what is that?" Alex said.

Beau smiled again. "You tell me."

Alex felt anger rising in her breast. You work for me, she wanted to say. She was getting a little tired of his manner. She wasn't a little girl, she was a highly educated young lady and this…well, this rough-cut private eye was beginning to annoy her. She simply needed to find Clara and demand satisfaction for what she'd done to her family. If she was somehow involved with the death of William Clifton as well as her father, then direct action was called for. Sleuthing around and not asking questions that needed to be asked didn't seem to be producing results. She looked at him and noticed a raised eyebrow. He was waiting for her answer.

"Alright," she finally said. "William Clifton died of a heart attack due to snakebite and his family subsequently moved away. That's not much." Beau smiled benignly at Alex. Intelligent? Yes. he thought. Educated? Highly. Spoiled, empowered, and privileged? Like most of his clients. People who could afford to pay the agency per diem plus expenses and then a percentage if a settlement was reached. Not her fault, he thought. She didn't even realize it. She put on a bold front but having lived a sheltered life, he was worried that she might not hold up to the kind of investigation it was going to take to find Clara Comerford.

"We got a name, Clifton," Beau said. "And we learned that he died under similar circumstances as your father. We know that he was rich and that his family moved away after his death. Why? The doctor certainly didn't know. Nor did he know the identity of the farm hands who brought Clifton in. Any more questions might have piqued his interest in our motive. As it is, we were just two people looking into a coincidence out of curiosity. Nothing more. He will forget us."

"We did get the address," Alex said tersely. She didn't like to being talked down to, although most of the men she encountered did it to her on a regular basis. Professors and other students at school invariably did. Men with inflated egos didn't relish the thought of being shown up by some smart ass girl. They tried to put her in her place and keep her there. It had been a struggle, but she had prevailed. She certainly didn't intend to let a hired private eye get away with it.

Beau laughed, his blue eyes twinkling. Alex was more thin-skinned that he had thought. He could see that her ire was up and that she was ready for a fight. He thought of a quote from Sun Tzu: "He will win who knows when to fight and when not to fight."

"What are you laughing at?" Alex demanded. It unnerved her that he had such a disarming manner about him. She was ready for a fight, and he wasn't being triggered. To further frustrate her, he didn't answer. Then she realized why he was laughing. The location of the estate of the richest man in town would be no secret. She shook her head and laughed.

"I take it we're going for as buggy ride to the Clifton Estate," she said.

"Unless you'd prefer to walk," Beau said with a smile.

17

Beau got a surprise when they arrived at the Clifton estate. The estate was supposed to be abandoned, but there were acres of well-tended orchards stretching up the gently rolling lands over-looking the Mohawk River. Fields of wheat and corn waved in the gentle mid-day breeze, the sun lighting the scene like a Tuscan frieze painted by some Renaissance artist. Rows of grapes followed the contours of the hills and lengths of white fencing enclosed a herd of horses which grazed on impossibly green fields. A grain silo stood at attention in the distance and smoke curled up from a smokehouse that was located near several buildings and a large barn. Beau looked over at Alex, but her face registered no surprise. He realized that she had probably never seen a run down, dilapidated estate, with its fields overgrown and its fences broken. It took a number of workers to keep up the fields and fences of a large estate; to her, workers were probably just a part of the landscape.

The roof of the main house could be seen beyond the fields on the river side of a tree-covered hill. Beau drove the rented buggy toward the lane that led to it. The massive, filigreed wrought-iron gate was rusted, and one side was off its hinges. Beau stopped the buggy, got out and pulled the creaking gate open. The lane beyond it was unused and overgrown. He walked back to the buggy and got in. Looking over at Alex, he shrugged and snapped the reins without saying anything. They rode slowly, Beau negotiating the unseen roadbed, now covered with grass, weeds and underbrush.

The house itself was another surprise. It was extensive, its roofs sporting several stone chimneys. The tiles that were once in neat rows were covered with rotted leaves, broken branches, and other detritus. Weeds had sprouted from the gutters, some of which hung at crazy angles, covered with green mold. The walls were thick grey stone that stood like the run INS of some medieval castle, but the doors and windows were broken and smashed, and birds flitted in and out of the openings, some carrying nesting material. A raccoon chittered out from its nest as they approached the main entrance and squirrels stared brazenly from the branches of two large oak trees that flanked the once magnificent carriageway.

Then Alex said something that indicated that she had noticed the dichotomy of the well-tended fields and the run-down main house. "The damage to the house was intentional," she observed, shaking her head. "Someone doesn't want the estate sold. Windows don't break themselves and doors don't jimmy themselves open." She looked over toward the smokehouse and other outbuildings. The workers there had stopped working and were staring up the hill at them. "I'm surprised the building wasn't burned down for the insurance," she added. "Those workers may know why."

Beau snapped the reins and headed toward the outbuildings. After a time, they arrived at the barn, where the workers who had been staring at them stood in a cluster. They looked up when they saw the buggy and one of them shouted something indistinct toward a small house that lay beyond the barn. An old man with a grey beard and nappy white hair came out. He waved. Beau pulled the buggy up to the house, followed by the workers. Beau stopped, got down and circled the buggy to help Alex down, the gentlemanly thing to do. But before he got there, she had hopped down and was heading toward the old man, her leather brief case tucked under her arm in a business-like way.

"Alex Comerford," she said, extending her hand to the old man. He took her hand lightly, clearly surprised that a woman would offer to shake an old black man's hand. His hand was wizened and rough from years of hard farm work. She shook it with a smile.

"Amos Pilchard," the old man said. "I and my boys crop these lands. We worked for Mr. Clifton for many years."

Amos invited them to sit on the porch. He seemed nervous. A comfortably heavy woman appeared with a pitcher of what looked like cider on a platter along with four glasses. She was wearing a cotton dress, a white apron and had her hair covered with a white scarf.

"I'm Dottie," she said with a pleasant smile. "I've been stuck with this old geezer for nigh on to forty years. No turnin' back now," she said with a deep laugh. They appeared to be ready for company and Alex realized that they must have been seen when they drove up the long lane to the estate. Dottie gestured toward several well-made chairs and a settee. Alex and Beau sat, each accepting a glass of cold cider. A few younger children could be seen peeking out from behind curtains.

"Well, I 'spose y'all come out here lookin' to buy the estate, like all the others that come out here lookin'," Dottie said with a smile. Her teeth were large and white, and her eyes sparkled when she spoke. Amos sat mutely, used to letting his wife do the talking.

"What happened to it?" Alex said. "It looks like it's been neglected for some time."

"Mr. Clifton died, and the family moved away," Dottie said. "A man bought it but then left. Don't know why. Bank's waiting on a second buyer." She took a long sip of cider and smacked her lips. "Don't no one want to buy it, though? The shape it's in."

"How did the windows and doors get broken?" Alex said. "It looks vandalized." She noticed that a couple of the boys looked nervously at each other when she said it.

Dottie looked to Amos, who shifted in his chair and cleared his throat. "Miscreants done it," he said unconvincingly. "Come by at night, drinking and carousing. Smashing windows and raising hell. Had to put fires out a couple of times too. Isn't nothin' a black man would dare do about it, though." he added weakly. Dottie gave him a hard look.

"The good Lord knows and there will be a reconin' on Judgement Day.

Caint hide nothin' from the Lord," she said, her voice rising. Amos looked down at the floorboards. The boys shifted away slightly, and the kids disappeared from their hiding places.

"We're not interested in buying the property," Beau said softly. "Nor are we interested in finding who did the damage to the house. We came seeking information on the death of the original owner, Mister William Clifton. I heard that Mister Clifton died of a heart attack as the result of snakebite." He looked over at Alex for further explanation.

"Yes," she said. "Do you encounter many venomous snakes here?"

Amos spoke up, "Ain't never seen a rattler around here. Not even a Copperhead. Ole man Clifton wasn't even around here when he was bit. He was on a buggy ride with that young wife of his. Used to see her all the time, ridin, 'cross the fields. Don't see what she saw in that ole man, 'cept his money."

Dottie shot a hot look at her husband. "Don' you be judgin' Amos Pilchard!"

"You know it's true," Amos said. "Disappeared with the family inheritance, I heard. Left the family without a plug nickel!"

Alex and Beau shared a look.

"The two men who took Clifton to the doctor," Alex said. "Were they your sons?"

Amos shook his head. "Don' know nothin' 'bout them. Never seen them before or since. Just heard it was two farmhands brought him in."

"Thanks for your time," Beau said, rising. Alex bit her lip and rose also. She also thanked them and followed Beau to the steps.

"Detective came snoopin' 'roun here sometime after Clifton died. Asked a lot of the same questions you did. Big man, bowler hat, mustache. Never saw him agin."

Alex noticed that Beau's eyes opened wide in surprise – or shock, she couldn't say which. It was only a momentary thing, fleeting, like the shadow of a nighthawk passing the full moon. It disappeared as quickly as it had appeared, but it remained indelibly etched in her mind, like the flash of light from a photographer's pan. They walked out, climbed up into the buggy, and drove away. They rode for a long time without speaking. Beau drove the buggy into town and left it at the livery stable where he had rented it. He paid the liveryman with a silver coin. Alex and Beau walked down Main Street again. Beau still hadn't spoken and seemed to be consumed with some sort of quandary. Alex had learned by now not to press him.

"Can you at least tell me where we're going?" she said, trying to keep her tone light. He smiled, regaining his former character.

"To the bank," he said.

The properties agent at the bank was a short, sweaty man with a bald pate, a bad shave and even worse breath. He invited them to sit and sorted through a pile of rumpled papers, like a monk searching among a pile of manuscripts. "Let's see, let's see," he said, shuffling the papers. He glanced up at a large wall clock near the big double doors where people bustled and bumped, trying to get their business done before closing time.

"Ah, here it is," he exclaimed. "Clifton." His beady eyes shifted over the document. He shook his head and tsked. "Now I remember. Total loss for the bank. The estate was sold through an intermediary who then sold it to a …" He squinted at the page. "A certain Doctor Douglass who then leveraged the value of the estate for a loan with the deed as collateral. Needed the money for upgrades and machinery, he said in his application. Boiler plate stuff, really. It was given to a new hire who reasoned that, since the man was inhabiting the residence, there was no risk." The man laughed and wiped his sweating forehead, stealing another glance at the clock. "The good doctor made two or three payments and then disappeared. No trace. The young agent lost his job over it."

"No trace?" Alex said. "No forwarding address? Nothing?" The agent shuffled the documents again, obviously in a hurry to conclude business and get to a bar. "No, no trace. The bank hired a detective to find him, one of your Pinkertons," he said, glancing at Beau. "Found nothing. The place is a shambles now, vandalized, and irreparable. We can only hope for lightning," he added, looking as though he immediately regretted his words.

He cleared his throat and tapped the stack of documents on the table to straighten them – and to indicate that the meeting was over.

Beau stood, turning to regard the clock, which was nearing five. He looked down at Alex, who stood and nodded, thanking the agent for his time. As they turned to leave, Beau turned back for a moment.

"The Pinkerton, the detective you hired. Do you remember his name?"

"No," the agent said, rising himself and rubbing his sweating bald head. "He flashed his ID at me, but I didn't notice it. He had a sort of menacing way about him. I was glad to see him leave."

Alex again saw another fleeting look pass across Beau's face. He banished it and they went out the door and walked to the train station in silence.

18

IDA MAE BROWN was stirring her tea with a series of aggressive clinks of her spoon, indicating that she was displeased. Alex and the Pinkerton had jaunted off to Utica on a whim, the whim being a coincidental snake bite injury. In her view, they should have been traveling on the main rail line, checking for clues of Clara's whereabouts. A woman of her stature and, well beauty she had to admit, would be noticed. Train tickets, meals, hotel rooms and per diem charges paid to the Pinkerton agency were only justified if progress was being made. She was dubious about the trip to Utica. She tapped her spoon three times on the rim of the cup and set it down with a sharp clink. A report was in order.

Alex cleared her throat. She knew that her aunt liked to make people feel nervous; it gave her an edge. But knowing that didn't help. Her aunt had made her feel nervous since she was a child, but now, living in the same house, and being beholden to the old woman, she was especially vulnerable to her aunt's criticisms. Now her aunt was sitting imperiously, like some sort of potentate, expecting answers from her minions. She tried to shake the nervousness she felt but couldn't seem to banish it. She cleared her throat again and looked over at Beau, but he sat impassively, as usual, waiting for her to take the lead. She began softly, hoping her aunt wouldn't notice her nervousness.

"The doctor told us of a man who had been snake bitten and died, much like father," she said. "We went to the man's estate and found it dilapidated and overgrown. Sharecroppers had kept up the fields and livestock and, with no owner to share it with, kept the full share of their labors. I suspect that some, or all, of the damage done to the house was done by the share-cropper and his boys to keep potential buyers at bay. We checked with the bank and found that the estate had been sold through a third-party investment firm and purchased by a certain Mr. Douglass who then borrowed a huge sum against it. He then defaulted and disappeared." She looked over at Beau. "Did I leave anything out?"

Beau smiled. "Quite a bit," he said mildly. "And you included as lot of information that's not relevant to the case."

Alex felt her face go red. Here we go again, she thought. Beau's condescending attitude was getting under her skin, but she refused to let him know it. But her aunt did notice.

"Mr. Starr is the professional here. And we...I am paying him well for his expertise. I'm certain that he'll enlighten us." She turned her gaze on Beau. Her expression was one of expectation.

"Two farm workers took Mr. Clifton to the doctor's office. The share cropper told us that Clifton and his wife had been on a buggy ride. Those two farm workers are likely part of Clara's team, along with the mysterious Mr. Douglass."

"That's right," Alex said, forgetting her self-righteous pout. There were details she had missed.

"A team of four, or more," Beau continued. "Bilking wealthy business men's families out of their inheritances. There must be others; we have to find similar instances to determine a trail that will lead us to them."

Ida Mae had a pensive look on her face. She took a sip of tea and set the cup down.

"The name Clifton seems to ring a bell," she said. "I think I heard Jacob mention the name several times. I wish we could ask him," she added. A sad look came over her face for a moment. Then she continued. "Jacob and John did a lot of business together. Perhaps Clifton was one of your father's business associates as well. He had many. I think you should go through your father's papers to see what names come up."

"His papers are locked up in his office," Alex said. "When the house was sold, his office was sealed. To get them would require a court order."

Ida Mae stopped her with a wave of her hand. "It would surprise me to find that Mr. Starr is unfamiliar with surreptitious surveillance and the obtaining of important documents that might provide clues to a case."

Again, Alex saw the smug smile. She looked over at Beau, whose only response was to raise his eyebrows slightly and clear his throat. "We'll have to go at night."

19

The house, dark and ominous, loomed over the neglected fields in the pale moonlight. It stood like some abandoned medieval castle, its pea's ants, and knights long dead and forgotten. Alex knew every trail and path by heart, having grown up there, but she was amazed at how silently Beau moved through the woods. He had coached her before they left. "Point your toes in slightly and sweep as you step forward. Sweep with your arms as well. You'll sweep away branches and twigs that would snap if you stumbled onto them. A clumsy person might as well have a brass band walking along with him. And if you must look directly at a light, keep one eye, always the same one, closed. Night vision takes a while to develop but can be ruined in an instant. Use your peripheral vision. Looking directly doesn't work at night."

It irked her to be lectured but Beau did seem to have considerable skills, she had to admit. Occasionally she would turn to look if he was still there, he was so quiet. But she couldn't help but be troubled by his need for quiet, and secrecy. Did he really think that someone was watching the house?

Watching them? It occurred to her that the banker had told them that a Pinkerton had investigated the case in Utica, but Beau insisted that Aloysius Cable had told him of no such case. Had someone been posing as a Pinkerton to prevent a real investigation, or had he been intent on cleaning up after the scam? She had never liked the dark to begin with and now she felt a certain trepidation mounting in her as they got closer to the house. An owl hooted and something scurried in the brush, giving her a start. She gasped and stepped on a twig, which snapped loudly in the still night. She knew that Beau was right behind her and was probably shaking his head in annoyance. A feeling of paranoia washed over her, and she chided herself for the little noises she made. Forcing herself to move more slow lee and carefully, she slowed her breathing and her pace. As she got quieter in her movements, the woods seemed to come alive. The scuffling's and snuffling's of night creatures got louder as they proceeded, unnoticed. There was the smell of pine and rotting humus from the forest floor. Trails she had trodden her whole life on bright sunny days now became fraught with danger and intrigue. She led on and Beau followed, a ghost behind her.

They slipped silently across the open space between the woods and the house, the only sound was the brushing of grass against their legs, soft and insistent, like a sheet being pulled from a bed. Alex led Beau to a back door near the kitchen used for deliveries. The front door would most likely be chained and locked and would be far too visible. The delivery door was bolted from the inside, but Alex remembered a window off the pantry whose latch was broken. They walked around to the rear of the building and found the window. Below it was a jumble of weeds and discarded wooden boxes and bottles. The window was high up, so Beau gave Alex a boost. She grabbed the ledge below the window and scrabbled up so that she could stand on Beau's shoulders.

The wood frame of the window had swelled in its tracings, and it took considerable effort to force it upwards. When she had it three-quarters open, she squirmed through it. There was a dusty shelf filled with canned goods on the inside. She carefully pushed them aside and clambered onto the shelf, walking on her hands until she could bring her knees through the window. The shelf bowed under her weight, and she hoped that it wouldn't give. It didn't, and she was able to turn sideways and swing her legs down to the floor. She felt her way carefully through the darkened pantry to the kitchen, went to the delivery door and unbolted it. She opened it and Beau silently slipped inside. He said nothing.

Houses, especially old ones, have lives of their own. They breathe, creak and groan with the invisible air currents that well up from the bowels of the basement or invade through miniscule cracks where the caulking has crumbled. Rodents, squirrels, and birds inhabit the walls, sub flooring and eaves. Their scamperings and flutterings, along with the brushing of leaves and branches of the trees and bushes that surround a house seem to make it a living thing.

The two intruders made their way through the darkened rooms, the floorboards creaking with their passing. They reached a wide, carpeted stairway that led to the upstairs rooms; if there were any papers with her father's business associates listed, they would be in the study.

The downstairs rooms were dark, but the curtains on the tall windows were tied open, letting in a small amount of ambient light provided by the stars and a half moon. Upstairs, the curtains were closed, making the hall way ink black. But Alex had lived in these halls and rooms her whole life. She could negotiate them blindfolded which, in effect she was now. That Beau was able to follow without being led was a surprise. The only evidence she had of his presence was his soft and controlled breathing.

When they reached the study, they found that the large oak doors that usually stood open had been closed and locked. Beau produced a small metal instrument that glinted in the light of a match he had struck with his thumbnail. The smell of sulfur was strong as he handed the match to her. "Hold this," he said in a whisper. By the time the match burned itself out, he had sprung the lock. He twisted the doorknob and opened one side of the double-door. Lighting another match, they slipped into the room.

The study was exactly as Alex remembered it. There were hardwood bookshelves filled with encyclopedias, legal texts, histories, and novels. There was a large oak rolltop desk, now closed, a hardwood swivel chair and two brown leather sitting chairs, facing each other across a carved ivory chess set on a polished wood board of alternating dark and light brown squares. There was a table on which sat several decanters of whisky and some cut-glass tumblers. The room still smelled of whiskey and cigars. For a moment, Alex was overcome with grief at the memory of her father.

Beau closed the door behind them and lit a kerosene lamp. The room was bathed in the soft yellow glow of the flickering wick. Alex suppressed a sniffle and dabbed at her eyes with a kerchief, hoping Beau didn't notice. She opened the rolltop with a key her aunt had given her and began rummaging through the drawers of the desk. She found nothing of importance. She turned her attention to the safe, hidden behind a large painting. Her aunt had given her the combination. She turned the knurled knob and heard the wheels in the wheel pack turning. At the last number, the lock bolt disengaged with a metallic click and the bolt work was freed. She turned the lever and opened the heavy metal door. Inside, she found, among a jumble of papers and bills, a large, leather-bound ledger book. She withdrew it and opened the heavy cover. She ran her finger down a list of transactions. She stopped on an entry marked "Clifton, William L." She showed Beau. He nodded. "This is what we came for," she said, closing the cover. She closed and locked the safe. They left the study, but not before Beau had meticulously returned everything in the room to the state in which they had found it, an action that Alex found curious. "It's best not to leave a trail," he said without further explanation. They retraced their steps through the old house. In the kitchen, Beau slipped out the delivery door and Alex closed and bolted it. She then went into the pantry, climbed up on the shelf and squirmed out the window backwards, feet first. Beau caught her feet and placed them on his shoulders. Alex moved the canned goods back where they had been on the shelf and then closed the window. She allowed Beau to help her to the ground. They walked back into the woods, found their tethered horses where they had left them, mounted, and rode off, the ledger book firmly clasped under Alex's arm.

20

IDA MAE SAT in her chair with the ledger in her lap. Her cat sat next to her on some cushions, like a vizier attending a grand potentate. Alex and Beau sat before her, supplicants seeking a judgement. Ida Mae held up a piece of parchment upon which was written a list of names and addresses in elaborate cursive.

"These are your father's most prominent business associates," she said, waving the sheet slightly to dry the ink. "You'll have to do bit of traveling, I'm afraid. They're spread out all over the state."

Alex nodded. Beau sat impassively; his eyes focused somewhere beyond the scene before him. Ida Mae handed Alex the list, reached down and retrieved a leather money bag.

"I trust this will sustain you on your journey. Transportation, lodging and meals. Leave no stone unturned. We must find this Clara person and bring her to justice. It's not so much about the money anymore. Doing harm to our family is something I will not tolerate. Nemo me impunelaces-sit – no one attacks me with impunity."

"The ledger should be returned to your father's study," Beau said, looking directly at Alex.

"Nonsense Mr. Starr!" Ida Mae exclaimed, holding the ledger protectively. "There are outstanding accounts here, which I intend to collect on, now that I have them here."

"Why do you suppose Clara didn't take the journal and collect on those accounts herself?" Beau said. He asked the question softly, his eyebrows raised slightly as if to imply that the answer was obvious. Ida Mae levelled her gaze on Beau, pursing her lips slightly. She wouldn't have her intelligence insulted, nor would she give credence to the question by hazarding a guess. Alex broke the impasse.

"Why?" she said.

"Cashing in those accounts would leave a trail. She's too clever for that," Beau said. "By even keeping the ledger, we will have left a trail. Cashing accounts will leave another. If someone is watching for pursuers and suspects that he's being followed, he will become the pursuer."

"That may have been true in the Wild West," Ida Mae said. "But here in the civilized world, we have laws to protect us, police to enforce the laws, and courts to pass judgements and impose sentences on perpetrators. No, Mr. Starr, I'll keep this ledger and put the settlements I get from it to good use in bringing Clara to justice."

That night, in his room, Ida Mae's words came to Beau: nemo me impunelacessit – no one attacks me with impunity. The quote was from Edgar Allen Poe's short story "The Cask of Amontillado," a story of revenge for a wrong done. It was in one of the many books that his father had obtained for his mother from traders. It was her one indulgence, her one way of clinging to her former culture: reading. She read out loud to him when he was little so that he would learn the white man's language. As he got older, she taught him to read and made him narrate the stories from the many books in her dog-eared and worn collection. Some of the books had blood on the pages and Beau knew they had been taken in raids on white settlements. In that way Beau had learned English, French, Spanish and Latin. She had tutored him in the ways of the whites, their culture, beliefs, manners, totems, and taboos. She knew that the white man's day would come, as inexorably as the winter snows would come to the plains. She had seen it as a young girl in the east, before her parents had decided to embark on their star-crossed pilgrimage to the west. The towering buildings, the cobbled streets, the fire belching factories, and railroads replacing the pristine forests and meadows of a world lost forever. It would be the same in the west, she knew. It was only a matter of time, and she wanted Beau to be prepared for it.

Now, with his mother and father and tribe gone, Beau realized that he was a part of that new world. He had accepted it when the time came but he still longed for the time of innocent youth. It was a time of freedom and promise, of danger and death. But it was his time, a time to do with what he would. A time to do with what he wanted; the consequences not yet written in the stone of the past. A life lived long ago but as real as if it were just now. A memory came to him of his visit to the shaman, his vision quest and the other, different quest that followed.

Boh had an innate fear of the old shaman. Most of the children of the tribe did. He lived alone in a tipi set at the far end of the village and often sang wailing, high pitched songs to the spirits late into the night. Sometimes wolves would answer them, howling in the distance. He was called One Ear, because his right ear had been chewed off in a bear attack when he was a young man. The only time anyone saw him was when he came out to usher a new baby into the world or usher an old or sick person out of it. He burned herbs and intoned strange incantations at those times. At festivals he would lead a wild dance around the fire until, exhausted, he staggered off to his tipi. Rumor had it that he ate copious amounts of the dried can Tus that Mexicans called peyote to induce visions. As a child, Cries and his friends had always shied away from the old man's tipi, fearing that he would put a curse or a spell on them. But Boh was now a man, and he knew that he had to put away childish fears. He sent word that he wished to meet with the old man, and he was told to come to his tipi at dawn the first day after the moon was full.

The village was silent in the early morning hours of the appointed day. Sentries nodded to him as he crept silently across the village grounds. They knew of his appointment; they had all had similar appointments with the old shaman. They knew what Boh was in for.

Boh was early, he didn't want to be late on such an important day. He sat cross-legged at the entrance flap of the tipi and silently prayed, waiting. After a time, a voice came to him from within.

"You are early," the voice said. "That is good." The words seemed to echo in Boh's head, young and strong. Not the voice of the ancient shaman. Boh had the unsettling feeling that the words hadn't been spoken out loud; that they had appeared in his mind.

"Come in," the voice said. Boh stood, crouched, and lifted the flap of hide that was the door covering. He ducked and went in. A beam of light from the rising sun intruded on the interior of the tipi for a moment. In that moment, Boh could see a tangle of buffalo robes, stacks of herbs and piles of indiscriminate items. At the center of it all was a smoldering buffalo chip fire that was surprisingly fragrant. The old shaman, wrinkled and wizened, sat before it. He tossed a handful of herbs onto the fire and gestured for Boh to sit.

"Sage," the old man said. "Fragrant, medicinal, and spiritual. I gather as much of it as I can on my wanderings."

The old man turned and poured a measure of steaming liquid from a dented old pot into a cup and handed it to Boh.

"Drink," he said. "It's 'sang. It will give you strength and help you focus. You've been up all night, worrying about this meeting."

Boh drank deeply. The liquid was warm and musky but strangely soothing. He hadn't eaten and the effect of the tea was immediate. His eyes widened, his heart pumped, and his mind cleared.

"You are the boy who jumped on the back of a buffalo and killed it with your knife," the old man said. "A very brave thing."

Boh shook his head. "I was out of arrows and had dropped my bow. I was desperate, not brave."

The old man smiled. "It is good that you didn't try to claim credit for a foolish act. I tried to kill a bear that way once. I hoped that the tribe would see me as a brave man, maybe even give me a name like "Bear Killer." But, instead, the bear mauled me. I was lucky to escape with my life. I was called "One Ear" after that."

One Ear picked up a pipe, which he stuffed with a mixture of tobacco, herbs, and other substances that Boh didn't recognize. He put a flame to it and drew deeply. Then he handed it to Boh. He took it, put it to his mouth and drew deeply, a mistake. The hot smoke flooded his lungs, and he began to cough violently. The old man laughed.

"Your father coughed like that when he came to me. Most boys do." He took the pipe back and sat it on the ground. Boh began to feel lightheaded. His vision swam and items on the tipi took on iridescent colors. The old man's voice became young again and echoed in his head. Boh noticed that the old shaman's mouth was not moving.

"Fast for four days," the voice said. "Run to the river every morning and swim to the deepest hole. Swim to the bottom and touch it. On the fourth day, grab a handful of gravel from the bottom and come directly to me."

BOH did as he was told. Waking up cold and hungry, he ran to the river and plunged into the cold water. Fighting the current, he swam to the bottom, touched it, swam back to shore, and ran back to the village. On the fourth day he ran directly to the tipi of One Ear. The old man, his eyes milky and staring, smelled of sweat, wood smoke, tobacco, sage, and bear grease. It was a familiar smell, warm and comforting. He hummed a monotonal chant, softly and slowly. The boy sat respectfully, trying to keep his teeth from chattering too loudly. The old man seemed to read his mind. He laughed lightly, enjoying his joke.

"I hear you finished your swim; your teeth told me. How was the water?"

"Warmer than the ice I had to break through to get to it."

"Ah yes, I had forgotten that this was the season of snow. I spend too much time in this tipi, but the dogs and my buffalo robes and my wives keep me warm."

Boh thought how nice it would be to have a robe of his own just now. As it was, he was naked and shivering, waiting for the old man to give him his next instructions. The shaman made him wait a long time. Finally, the old man spoke.

"Show me what you found on the bottom of the river." Boh opened his hand and the old man rummaged through the gravel. He found a large piece of clear crystal which he handed to Boh. "This is your spirit stone. Keep it with you at all times. Refer to it when you have an important decision to make. It will center you and help you to focus on the best course of action. Now," he continued, "You must leave on your vision quest immediately. Choose your best horse. Bring with you only water. Head west, into the mountains until Wahanda gives you a sign to stop. Stay there, pray until you get your vision. It will come. When you return, tell me of your vision and I will interpret it for you." He handed Boh a leather pouch with something dried and woody in it. "Dried cactus, the ancient Nahuatl people called it peyote. Eat it on the fourth day, it will help you with your vision. Go now, without hesitation."

At that the old man stared up at the opening at the top of the tipi and resumed his chant. Boh rose, his teeth still chattering and left the Shaman's tipi. He walked to the horse herd, caught his horse, mounted, and rode west. He rode for many hours, stopping only to water his horse and pray and drink some water. He shivered in the cold air and his empty stomach rumbled, but he understood that privations were a part of the process and he welcomed them. He passed many villages and hunting parties, but he averted his eyes when he encountered anyone, as they did with him. They knew that he was on a vision quest. To interfere with one who is on such a journey is bad medicine.

The air turned even colder as he reached the foothills of the mountains, but still he rode on, even as a moonless night descended upon him. He rode all night, letting his horse choose his path. The scant trail became rocky and steep, and Rabbit's hooves clattered as he struggled to gain purchase on the loose gravel. A wolf howled in the distance and creatures of the night flitted among the sagebrush. Boh was exhausted, his chattering teeth the only thing keeping him from sleep. But he tottered on its edge, drifting in and out of reality. Memories came to him; some pleasant, some not. He remembered the fall that gave him his boy's name and the humiliation that went with it. "Look, he's crying," someone said. They laughed as he tried to wipe away the blood and the tears caused by it. He remembered being thrown by a new pony and his father's disapproving look. But then he remembered the buffalo hunt and his father's prideful announcement of his man's name, Boh.

There were sad times too. The wailing of the women when a brave was brought back from a raid, his body draped over the withers of his pony. He remembered the people dying of fevers caused by the white man's pox. The tears in his mother's eyes when his little sister died. He remembered the fear and anger at the news of white raids against other tribes.

Then he remembered his love for Morning Star, the girl he had fallen helplessly in love with. He remembered her gentle touch, and her sweet breath on his face. Her eyes, bright and hopeful and full of newly discovered love. He remembered her laugh. Finally, he remembered the caress of his mother when he was a child, her hair tied in long blonde braids. He remembered her lessons in the languages and customs of the whites and wondered why she was so insistent on teaching him. They were the enemy. They were foreign. His father and the other braves hated them. It was a puzzlement to him that she would want to cling to her former culture and pass it on to him.

He had many other memories and they ebbed and flowed like the winds and weathers that passed over the plains. He rode on.

Dawn came reluctantly to the mountains and his path grew ever steeper. Finally, just as the sun's rays were bathing the plains behind him in flickering orange light, he reached a flat promontory that overlooked the plains to the east. He found a circle of rocks that others had used in their vision quests. He rearranged the rocks to his liking, lined the pit with tufts of grass and settled in for a period of prayer that he hoped would reward him with his vision.

He prayed through the day and into the night and then into the next day. The rising sun lit the plains below him, catching the scant morning dew on the grass and causing it to sparkle in a million points of light. He

could see antelope grazing languidly on the rich plains grass. His hunger
gnawed at him, as did his thirst. As if to mock him, the small herd drifted
over to a crystal brook to water. He prayed on. By noon the sun, so pleasant
in the morning, began to burn him and small insects wriggled and bit him,
their buzzing echoing in his ears. He prayed on.

As dawn began to approach on the fourth day, he ate the cactus that the
old shaman had given him. The rough, dried substance roiled his empty
stomach and he struggled to keep it down. He felt dizzy and disoriented.
The smells of the receding night filled his head; the metallic fog that lay
over the still dark land, the scent of grass, juniper and pine, the aroma of
a wood cook fire in some distant camp. An owl hooted and the sound
echoed loudly in his head. He heard his horse munching on grass and the
shifting sound of its hooves on the stony ground. He stared toward the
east where a thin line of pink was beginning to appear on the horizon. He
chanted a prayer.

The first rays of the sun burst upon the land. They filled his head with
a thousand fireflies. A dream came upon him, vivid and real. He was running with a pack of wolves, chasing a thundering herd of buffalo. The
ground shook as he ran over it, howling and yipping to his pack. They
howled and yipped back. He sank his teeth into the fetlock of a young calf,
who bawled in terror. He tasted the warm blood, rich and invigorating. He
tried to bring the calf down, but the little beast managed to pull its leg away,
causing Boh to roll in the dust.

As he came up, he found himself flapping wings. They were the wings
of an eagle. They took him up into a cloudless sky, higher and higher. He
could see the buffalo herd below him, running hard toward a cliff. As they
reached it, the animals tumbled off into the void until the last of them
had gone. Of the wolves, there was no sign. As he soared, he saw a plume
of black smoke on the eastern horizon, moving swiftly toward him. Soon
a locomotive came in sight, spewing black smoke laced with red-orange
sparks. As it came, wildfires emanated from it, spreading out like the wake
from a riverboat, consuming everything in its path. A rain came and put

the fire out, but, instead of prairie grass, houses, buildings, and city streets sprang up. Soon the entire plain was covered with them. Of the Indians who had lived there before, there was no sign.

A frightened snort from his horse yanked Boh out of his dream. He looked and saw a white wolf staring at him. He realized that the wolf was real. The horse neighed and stomped but the wolf paid it no mind. It continued to stare at Boh, who stared back. It was not a malevolent stare but one of familiarity and Boh wondered if he had known the spirit of the wolf in some past incarnation. The wolf's eyes seemed to smile at him as if in recognition; then it turned and went away.

Boh untied the hobbles on the horse and calmed it by rubbing its muzzle. He mounted and rode down off the mountain. As he rode, he began to experience a troubling feeling and wondered if he was still partially in his dream state. He began to see wraiths, floating in the hot air ahead of him. They beckoned to him. He saw his mother, his father, and his brother. He saw Morning Star. How was that possible, he wondered? It was well known that only the dead could become wraiths, but when he had left on his vision quest, they had all been alive. He rode on, picking up his pace, troubled by the visions. His pony, Rabbit, also sensed trouble. Boh urged it into a gallop, and they rode hard the rest of the day. By late afternoon he saw a column of smoke on the eastern horizon. As he got closer, he could see vultures circling. He spurred his tired horse and galloped the final miles to his village. What he found there was burned into his consciousness forever.

21

Breakfast in the Brown estate was a quiet affair, with the two children, Jeremy, and Anna, having been sent off to live with a distant cousin who had children of her own about their same age.

"I hope you're prepared to redouble your efforts, Mister Starr," Ida Mae said, cracking a hard-boiled egg with the edge of a silver spoon. "So far, your hunches have been wrong and mine have been right. If I were a younger woman, I would terminate your service and press on with the search myself. As it is, I must watch vicariously as my young and naïve niece accompanies you." She looked over at Alex for a reaction to her insult but got none. Alex smiled and bit a piece of buttered toast. She looked over at Beau and suppressed a playful giggle.

"Don't you dare roll your eyes at me, young lady? I think the two of you are taking this far too cavalierly. You've got your list and you've got your task. I suggest that you finish your breakfasts and see to it."

Beau sat impassively, regarding the two feuding women. It bothered him that one of them seemed to be taking the search far too seriously, and the other far too lightly. It was true that Ida Mae's instincts had brought them to the list of business partners of her late brother. Still, he couldn't shake the feeling that they had made themselves unwitting pawns in a very dangerous game.

The train ride took several hours, and Alex was beginning to resent

Beau for his taciturn nature. The man said little to her other than to lecture her or scold her, and even then, it wasn't so much what he said as it was what he didn't say. Although his face always remained impassive, she could read the slight tensing of his body that indicated to her that he was trying not to say anything. He clearly didn't like the fact that her aunt insisted that she take an active part in the search for her missing stepmother, and he had made that plain from the start. But it was a pain for her to have to suffer through his silence. He was getting paid for his services and she was doing it gratis, and missing school. She would never have agreed to go along with her aunt's wishes if she had the resources to continue school, but, when Clara absconded with what should have been her inheritance, she had had been left with no choice. She held out little hope that she would ever find the woman, and even less hope that they could persuade a judge to rule in their favor. But, in her mind, Alex felt that Ida Mae would owe her for trying and, even though the woman was opposed to Alex's pursuit of a law degree, she would be at least owed a loan for her schooling. Maybe. Besides, she wasn't doing anything anyway.

The names on the list were scattered all over the state, so they decided to begin their search with the address closest to them and then radiate out in an expanding circle. The first man's name was Calvin Oglethorpe, a businessman located in a small town just outside of Syracuse. The man wasn't hard to find. He was, among other things, a real estate developer who had his name all over town in signage, posters, and billboards. His office, located on Main Street, was a two-story building with a peaked roof, six Corinthian columns and a landing. There were two tall, rectangular windows on either side of a wide oak door that was arched at the top. They walked up the steps, found the door open, and walked in.

"Can I help you?" the receptionist inquired with a friendly smile. She was a young girl about Alex's age, neatly attired and well-mannered. Alex smiled back. "I'm looking to buy some property in the area and wondered if Mr. Oglethorpe might be available to discuss the properties he has for sale."

The receptionist turned to a lady standing nearby. "Mary, would you see if Mr. Oglethorpe is busy?"

"Yes Mam," Mary said, turning and walking toward a spacious looking office in the back.

"If you'd like to take a seat, I'll be with you in a little while." The receptionist nodded toward a waiting area where several people sat comfortably, smoking, and reading newspapers.

"Busy man," Alex said.

"We do a good business," the girl said. She put out her hand to Alex. "I'm Jennifer Oglethorpe, Calvin is my father."

"Oh," Alex said. "I planned to work for my father too, until my step mother came along. I'm Alexandra Brown."

"Well, nice to meet you," Jennifer said. She let go of Alex's hand and said, "I'll come get you when he's free. Shouldn't be too long."

"Thanks." Alex said. She and Beau went to the waiting area, each picking up a complimentary copy of the Onondaga Standard. They sat in a quiet corner, out of earshot of the other people waiting for an appointment.

"You shouldn't have given your name," Beau whispered from behind his paper

"I didn't give my real surname, I took my aunt's," she said a little testily.

"The name Alexandra is unusual; something one doesn't forget; and your aunt is part of this too. You shouldn't be leaving so many clues for anyone following us."

Alex gritted her teeth. She could feel the situation coming to a head, but she didn't want it to be here, in public. But she didn't intend to let it go. It would have to wait until later, she reasoned.

Further conversation was forestalled by Jennifer's approach. "My father will see you now," she said. "This way." She gestured toward the office and led them to it.

Calvin Oglethorpe was a man in his early sixties that kept himself reasonably fit and well-dressed. A three-piece mohair suit, starched cotton broadcloth shirt and a silk tie. Gold cufflinks and stickpin. He sported a well-trimmed beard, and his hair was neatly combed back with pomade that smelled of lilacs. He smiled broadly and stood, extending his hand. "Miss Brown and…" He looked at Beau appraisingly.

"My associate, Mr.…" She hesitated for a tick. "…Beaumont," Alex said. "I'm afraid that a young girl, traveling alone needs, shall we say…a companion."

"Ah yes, nice to meet you Mr. Beaumont," Oglethorpe said, extending his hand to Beau. "One can never be too careful." His look of disdain dis appeared when he realized that it was not Beau who was inquiring about property. Indians were by local custom not allowed to buy property. "What agency are you with, Mr. Beaumont?"

"It's a private firm," Beau said, releasing Oglethorpe's hand. He stepped back slightly and crossed his hands in front of him in a classic bodyguard stance.

"I see, Oglethorpe said. He invited the two of them to sit. Alex did. Beau remained standing, staring off into the distance like a soldier on guard duty. Oglethorpe sat. "What can I do for you, young lady?" Oglethorpe asked the question with a slight, flirty wink that said, what would a young, pretty woman be doing looking for property?

"I'm interested in buying some land in the region and would like a list of the properties you have for sale. An estate is what I'm looking for. Two hundred acres, a house, and outbuildings. I raise horses, so extensive grazing land would be important."

"Your husband, I assume, is supportive of your venture?"

"I'm not married," Alex said. "I'm not sure why that would be an issue."

Oglethorpe cleared his throat nervously. "A single woman might have difficulty getting a bank loan. I myself am a progressive thinker but bankers…well. You know what I mean."

He said the last phrase with a little dismissive laugh that only made the insult worse. She started to retort when she felt Beau's hand on her shoulder. She turned and looked at him.

"I'm sure Mr. Oglethorpe meant no harm in his question," Beau said softly. He turned his attention to Mr. Oglethorpe. "Miss Brown is a highly educated woman from a wealthy family. Wealthy enough to afford my services. I'm sure that she would have no difficulty in securing a bank loan, if she needs one at all."

"Yes, yes," Oglethorpe said weakly. "I certainly meant no offense. I hope you will forgive my ill-considered words."

"Thank you," Alex said, smiling slightly. "Now, to business. I would like a list of your most attractive properties. Top five, shall we say? And, as Mr. Beaumont implied, price is no object."

Oglethorpe brightened. "Of course, I'll see to it right away. If you check back in a couple of hours, it will be at the front desk with my daughter."

"Lovely girl," Alex said. She suddenly noticed a framed picture on a shelf behind Oglethorpe's desk. She gestured toward it. "Is that her mother?"

Oglethorpe smiled. He turned to look at the picture. "Yes, as a matter of fact, she was my wife. Marta was the light of my life and gone too soon; we'd been married for thirty years. She did all my books. Now, Mary has taken over that job."

"Sorry for your loss," Alex said. "Was it a lengthy illness?"

Oglethorpe cleared his throat again. "No. Tragically she collapsed in the garden. Aneurism, the doctor said. She died instantly."

Alex blanched. Her own mother had died similarly. "Sorry," she stammered. "I didn't mean to be intrusive. Was it recent, her death?"

"It happened only a few months ago," Oglethorpe said. "I'm still in mourning."

Doesn't look it, Alex thought. She stood, as did Oglethorpe. He extended his hand. "Again, I apologize for my verbal clumsiness. A young, pretty woman is usually not more than that. In your case, I seem to have been mistaken."

"Indeed. One might wonder how many times you have been mistaken in the past."

"Touché," Oglethorpe said. But there was still a slight touch of arrogance in his tone. It reminded Alex of her law professor the first day of graduate classes. He too was nearing the end of middle age and fairly reeked of desperation at having his youth slip away unnoticed. She had registered under the name Alex instead of Alexandra and it came as a visible shock to the professor that one of his students was a woman. He made her life a living hell, picking on her to answer the most complex and arcane questions of jurisprudence while soft-balling questions to her male classmates. But the tactic backfired on him. Alex, forced to up her game, studied for upcoming classes like they were final exams. But still the professor found flaws in her answers, triumphing at her failures until, one day, one of the other students raised his hand. "Excuse me, sir," he said. "But I believe the error is yours." The professor's face reddened, and he was about to speak when the student read a quote from his notes. "You yourself, the other day, gave the same assessment of Minor v. Happersett as she just did." He read the professor's words back verbatim.

The professor angrily dismissed the class, but not before assigning a two-hundred-page reading for the next class.

Her classmates, at first stand-offish and supercilious, came to see the injustice of the professor's actions. They began catching him at his own game and, eventually, made a sport of it. The professor began treating her more deferentially, but the damage had been done. His lectures and inter-pretations were met with snickers and even outright guffaws when some hotshot or another caught the hapless professor in a mistake. The man's name was Gotcham, and soon the phrase "Gotcha, Gotcham" was being bandied about the halls of the University.

Now, standing in front of another supercilious empowered male, Alex could only think to say "Gotcha, Gotcham" to Oglethorpe's "touché. But she didn't. Instead, she smiled, and bid Mr. Oglethorpe a good day, thank-ing him for his time. He stood also and bowed ever so slightly and said, "Good day, Madam." He nodded to Beau. "Mr. Beaumont." Beau nodded back and they left the office.

Alex told Jennifer that they would be back in a couple of hours to pick up a list of real estate properties for sale. She seemed like a nice girl, and she felt bad, making the girl do all that work for nothing. Alex knew that they would be on the next train out of town. They had no intention of stopping by to pick the list of properties.

THE big house loomed large in the late afternoon. The sun hidden behind it left the front in a dusky shadow. Big, old oak trees seemed to be bowing before the darkened building, their branches reaching up in supplication to some man-made idol constructed of their own brethren. The man circled the house at a distance, counterclockwise and slow, like the hand of a giant, earthen clock taking time backwards. As he circled, ever closer, he encountered a line of footprints, one set going toward the house and the same prints going away. They were small, but not from a child. A woman. Then, on his third pass, he saw another print, only one; faint, almost indiscernible. What was remarkable was that the print showed no heel or sole. It was from a moccasin. Who wore moccasins in the east anymore? The man who wore them was good. He left almost no trail at all. If it hadn't been for the woman's prints, he never would have noticed them.

Finally reaching the house, he walked up onto the landing and examined the large, rusty padlock attached to the heavy chain that had been fed through the iron handles on the two oak double doors. It had not been tampered with. He looked at the row of tall glass windows on either side of the entrance. They had also not been touched. He walked down the stairs and circled the house again, but closer this time, looking for any sign of a break in. He walked slowly, examining the overgrown grass, the walls, and the windows. At the back of the house, near the kitchen, he found the grass trampled and skid marks on the wall beneath a window. He deftly jumped up, caught the sill, and pulled himself up. The window had been pushed open and someone, most likely the woman, had squirmed into the store

Room on the inside. He dropped down silently and continued his examination of the house. He encountered a delivery door that had been opened and then shut again. He tried the handle. The door was locked. In front of the door there were the woman's footprints and again, the ubiquitous and faint moccasin prints.

When he had come full circle, he walked up the front steps, and pulled a large set of keys out of his pocket. He tried several until one turned the reluctant mechanism. The shackle toe came clear, and he turned the shack le shank and pulled it out of the two links in the chain that it had held to-gether. The chain rattled loudly as it clanked to the floor. The hinges, now rusty from neglect, gave way reluctantly, groaning like an old man rising from a chair. The room inside was lit by the setting sun, which leaked in through the tall side windows, bathing it in a bloody red hue. He walked in a straight line across the floor until he encountered two sets of footprints in the dust; again, the moccasin prints were faint. He followed them first to the kitchen door where the prints and disrupted shelf told the story of entrance and exit; he then walked back to the front room, mounted the steps, and went to the office door. He used his skeleton keys to unlock it. He opened the door, walked in, and searched the room carefully. The desk had been rifled but nothing was missing. He then deftly cracked the safe. It was an old one, built for private residences, and was very simple. It only took him a few minutes. He immediately saw that John Comerford's leather bound journal was missing. He smiled to himself. The bait had been taken.

22

Eating in the railroad dining car was a challenge. the plates, silverware and glasses rattled and shook as the train made its way over the rough roadway. On bends in the track, the plates tended to slide toward the window or aisle, depending on which side of the train the bend was. Little bumps and jolts made drinking difficult.

"I know you probably would have preferred to eat in a diner at a whistle stop," Alex said between bites. Annoyingly, Beau said nothing. Why do I feel like I have to explain anything to him? She wondered. Yet she continued.

"The meals came with the tickets. It cost a little more for first class, but, well, the other cars are so crowded." Again, Beau said nothing. They had been traveling together now for almost two weeks and his quiet nature was beginning to get on her nerves. He clearly didn't like small talk. She set her cutlery down, patted her mouth with a napkin, and looked out the window and watched the fields of wheat and corn and apple orchards pass by. She saw people working in the fields, driving buggies and wagons, and walking along the dusty dirt roads. She wondered what their lives were like. It was something she liked to do, imagine being in another person's life. An old woman, sitting on a porch, an old dog by her side. Did she have children? Grandchildren? Did she have a husband? Was he still alive? If he was, did she still love him? Had she ever loved him? What had she been like as a child? Alex went into a fantasy where she was that little girl, progressing through her life as fast as a memory. School, college – probably not - marriage, children, grandchildren. Births, lives, and deaths. Happiness. Tragedy. Melancholy. What path had the old woman followed that brought her to that porch, sitting next to that old dog?

"You're s dreamer."

Alex turned, surprised that Beau had spoken and surprised that he was right. "Sorry, I do that sometimes. It used to drive my parents and teachers crazy. "Get your head out of the clouds," they'd say."

Beau laughed lightly and looked at her. It was a strange look, almost as if he were trying to look into her soul. She looked away.

"Why did you do that? Look away?"

"It made me uncomfortable. I've always been embarrassed about getting caught dreaming."

"It's a power. I often wished that I had it myself. There was a dreamer in my tribe. When his ability was discovered, he was sent to the shaman for guidance. I was so jealous. He was my brother."

Alex's interest was piqued. She brought her eyes back to Beau's. "How was his ability discovered? What was the guidance?"

Beau laughed at the questions tumbling out of the girl's mouth. For all the training and tutoring his mother had given him in the ways of the Whites, he still could not quite manage to understand them. Psychic abilities were seen as oddities, and those that possessed them were regarded as strange. If they failed to suppress them, they became outcastes, persons to be ridiculed and bullied.

"Little Otter, my brother, was a finder. If someone lost or misplaced something, they would ask him. He would close his eyes, purse his lips for a moment, and then reveal the whereabouts of the missing item. Once, some horses were stolen from one of the young braves in our tribe. He asked Little Otter to find them. He concentrated for a long time and then he told the brave that they were being held in a box canyon. Then he revealed who had stolen them. When the horses were found exactly where he had said they were, two things happened. Little Otter was sent to the shaman, where he would learn the ways of the shaman and eventually become a shaman himself."

"The second thing?"

"The brave who had stolen the horses was cast out of the tribe. It was the worst punishment that could be meted out. Worse than a beating, worse than torture. Worse than death. A man cast out from his tribe would become a pariah, loathed by all. Doomed to wander the plains alone."

"What ever became of Little Otter, your brother? Did he become a shaman?"

"He was killed in the raid that took my family and friends. I always felt guilty that I hadn't been there, to fight alongside my father and brother and the others. To have died in battle, a warrior. Instead, I was left alone with no family and no tribe."

Alex looked into the sad eyes of Beau and saw him in a new light. His whole life had been cruelly taken from him, his parents, his brother, his friends, and his tribe. Now, instead of following his Indian destiny, he was caught up in the world of the Whites.

Alex and Beau traveled the length of the state, following the leads provided in John Comerford's ledger. They found a dentist who had a gambling problem and whose wife had left him because of it. Then there was a lawyer in Brockport who lived in a small apartment. He was unmarried, alcoholic, and looked as threadbare as his suits. There was a half dozen others who had similar situations. Not prime targets for the likes of Clara. "We have to consider that Clara may have only duped my father and Clifton," Alex said at one point. "She may have gotten enough money from the two of them to retire comfortably with whomever her manager is."

"I've considered that," Beau said. "But chasing after these names is all we have right now."

"It just feels like we're chasing our tails." Alex said. She was getting anxious to get back to her grad work and she figured that she had done enough searching to warrant a loan from her aunt Ida Mae. Why not just let it be?

Especially because Beau seemed to be barely tolerating her at best. He had made it clear that he preferred to work alone, and he criticized just about everything that she did or said. "I feel like I'm in your way all the time anyway," she added.

"Not really," Beau said, surprising her. "Oglethorpe is a racist. He realized I was half Indian and could barely keep himself from throwing me out of his office. Without you, he never would have even let me in, let alone allow me to ask him questions. You're a woman, young, well-off, and easily manipulated. At least in his eyes. We got what we needed, and we weren't overly notice able. Easily forgotten."

Alex looked at him in surprise. She shook her head slightly in disbelief. "What is it that we got?"

"Verification. Another name checked off on the list. And another potential target for Clara.

"We could just wait for her to show up," Alex said.

"How long is the mourning period for a widower?" Beau said.

"For women, it's two years. For men it's six months. Sounds fair, right?"

"How long after your mother's accident did Clara show up?"

Alex gasped, shocked at the question. "Six months," she stammered. "She collapsed while cutting roses for the table. Her rose garden was her pride and joy." she added somewhat wistfully. "The doctor said it was a stroke brought on by the heat of the day."

She looked at Beau with the unspoken question: can someone cause a person to have a stroke and make it look accidental?

Beau understood. He was sorry that he had asked the question, but it had to be asked. "It's possible," he said. "There are many substances that, if administered correctly, can induce a stroke, aneurism, embolism or heart attack."

Alex gasped again, overwhelmed at the thought that her mother – and father – may have been murdered. Why? She wanted to scream. Is greed justification for murder and the ruination of a family? Beau took her hand in his. It was a surprise, but Alex welcomed it. His hand was warm and seemed to emanate strength and comfort. She sobbed silently, squeezing his hand ever so slightly. After a while she recovered and felt something new rising in her breast. It was a white-hot hatred for those that had hurt her family. And a burning desire for revenge.

"Now you understand my quest," Beau said softly

23

THE TRAIN STOPPED with a shrieking whistle and a loud exhalation of steam. Doors clanged open and people milled around at the exits. "Skaneateles!" a conductor bawled. Alex and Beau stepped out onto the platform. It had rained the night before and little puddles steamed here and there on the wooden surface. People squished through them as they greeted passengers, prepared to get on the train, or make their way to the line of waiting coaches. A din of voices filled the air, some rumbling deeply, others rising in tone and still others punctuating the din in a cacophony like a jungle awakened. Alex approached a uniformed railroad employee standing next to the ticket booth.

"Sherwood Inn?" she shouted over the voices of the crowd. "Is it nearby?"

"A short walk down Main Street," the uniformed man shouted back. "Three blocks on your right. Best hotel in town," he added." Alex told him thanks and the two strolled out of the station and onto the sidewalk running along Main Street. The sun was getting hot, and the little puddles from the recent rain gave off steam as they dried up. Pigeons hopped about, snatching at the bits of debris left over from the rain, hoping to find something edible. The strong smell of fresh hay was in the air, along with the shore smells of Skaneateles Lake, the long Finger Lake that ran south from the town. The aroma of dead fish and rotting seaweed, mixed with the fragrance of fresh water was wafted in the air by a light breeze. The hotel was a tall wood frame structure with a peaked roof. It was painted gray with white shutters, windowsills, doors, and trim. It was three stories high and stood above the other buildings on the street like a stately sentinel. There was a columned portico behind a cobblestone driveway with uniformed valets standing by.

"You know anyone following us would expect someone wealthy enough to afford travel expenses and Pinkerton fees to stay in the best hotel in town," Beau said.

"I'll not stay in a rattrap because of your paranoia," Alex snapped back, a little more quickly than she had intended. There was a touch of Ida Mae in her tone.

Beau seemed taken aback for a moment, but then he laughed. "Just because you're paranoid doesn't mean they aren't after you."

Alex laughed lightly, sorry that she had spoken so harshly. She had always been outspoken and knew that it could be off-putting. She vowed to be more careful. Adjusting her attitude accordingly, she stepped next to Beau.

"Shall we?" she said, taking his arm playfully. They walked up the steps and into the foyer of the hotel. A smiling clerk stood behind a large oak registration desk. He was dressed in a dark gray three-piece suit, with a white shirt, silk tie and matching silk cravat. He had iron gray hair combed straight back and wore round, pincenez glasses clamped to a stately, aquiline nose. Below it was a trimmed gray mustache. He could have been the owner.

"Two rooms, adjacent," Alex said in a business-like manner. The man smiled and turned the registration book around for them to sign. As they did, using assumed names, he turned and took two keys down from a key rack. "203 and 204," he said, handing them the keys. "How many days will you be staying?"

"Let's say a week," Alex said, retrieving her wallet from her purse. "We'll pay for the week in advance."

"Wonderful," the man said. "Is your trip business or pleasure, if you don't mind my asking?" He discretely wrote a figure on a slip of paper and slid it toward her. Alex glanced at it and paid.

"A little of both," she said. "I'm hoping to find an old business associate of my father's. My father passed recently and, before he did, he suggested that I look up his old friend. Something to do with a mutual business venture the two had been working on."

"Who is this man if I may ask? I know just about everyone in town?" Alex shot a sidelong glance at Beau, who, she was certain, would disapprove of her open discussion with the man. "His name is Edward Holmes."

A shocked expression crossed the man's face. He stammered slightly. Clearing his throat, he regained his composure. "I take it you don't read the local papers?"

The question was not sarcastic. The man's face said something different, like it pained him to consider it. Like he was trying to decide whether to go further.

Alex pressed him.

"No, I'm from out of town. Enlighten me, please."

Her direct manner seemed to put the man off for a moment and his face hardened. But then, as if having a change of heart, he softened. "Your father and he were friends?"

Alex nodded.

"So was I. Good friends as a matter of fact. More importantly, our wives were friends."

Alex looked at him as if to say go on.

"Edward Holmes was convicted of the murder of his wife. He was tried, convicted, and sentenced to life in prison. He now sits in Auburn, with no chance of appeal or parole. What happened…, well, it couldn't possibly have happened. Not to Edward. He would never have done such a thing to Marjorie. He adored her. But the judge and jury found otherwise. Irrefutable evidence. A miscarriage of justice, I say!"

The last phrase was said with a strong touch of emotion. The man struggled to control himself. He cleared his throat and went on. "Pre-meditated murder, they called it. The prosecutor had a theory that she had caught Edward cheating on her and was threatening divorce. He struck her with a blunt object and then sat down in his study and drank a bottle of whiskey until he was practically comatose. That's how the maid found him the next morning, passed out in his study, his wife dead on the floor and a heavy brass candle holder next to his chair.

"Edward's story was that he had gotten up in the night because he thought he heard a prowler. He walked out into the hallway, and someone grabbed him from behind and put a wet cloth over his mouth. The next thing he knew, the maid was screaming. The jury didn't believe him, but I do. We were friends and I can attest that he was never unfaithful to her. Ever. They didn't even let me testify! The prosecutor said that, because we were friends, my testimony would be suspect! Edward's lawyer agreed!" He stopped for a moment, again composing himself. "His only hope is his adult daughter. She had been in Europe traveling and only found out about the event many months later. She returned and is trying to gather evidence to mount an appeal."

The man seemed ready to cry. His fists clenched and his lips tightened. He had said all he was going to say. Beau touched Alex's elbow. "I'm so sorry to hear that," she said. "He must be a good friend."

"He is, and he's now rotting in a prison."

"Well, maybe his daughter can find something the police couldn't."

"Let's hope," the man said. "Edward's a good man and deserves better than this. His wife was a lovely lady," he added.

"Well, thank you for your time," Alex said. She turned to leave, but the man stopped her.

"There was another man here recently, asking about Edward." Alex looked at him quizzically.

"Big fella. Red hair. He went to the bar."

Alex looked at Beau, who was shaking his head ruefully and smiling slightly. He looked up at the man behind the counter. "In the bar, you said?"

The man shook his head yes.

Alex and Beau had their things sent up to their rooms and walked across the foyer toward the noisy bar.

24

As they walked into the bar, Beau was assailed by a booming and familiar voice. "Beau Starr!" the voice announced. He looked for the source. Not hard to find. The man was sitting at a round table, smoking a cigar and drinking a glass of whiskey. He had a big smile on his face, triumphant at having caught his erstwhile partner off guard.

Mick O'Shaughnessy was a large man, easily six-five and had a girth that hadn't seen the south side of three hundred pounds in decades. But he carried the weight well. He had once been a bare-knuckle boxer and his flattened nose showed it. His hands, gnarled from fights, were huge and made the whiskey glass he was holding look like something a child would use. When he stood to greet Beau, he seemed to grow even larger. Tufts of red hair poked out from under a bowler which looked to be several sizes too big for a normal man. He carried a stout hardwood staff with a thick ball end. He called it his shillelagh. It had several notches on its side that attested to its usefulness in a fight. Beau also knew him to carry a pistol under his coat, a derringer up his sleeve, a leather sap in his back pocket and a dagger in his boot. He chomped on his cigar and extended his paw-like hand. Beau took it and shook it warmly He had worked with the man many times and liked him well.

"Fancy meeting you here," Beau said.

"Same to you," Mick said. His voice was a low rumble, with a thick Irish brogue. "I'm surprised that you're staying in such a high-class place, you usually like dives."

He turned and greeted Alex with a slight bow. He took her hand. "Mick O'Shaughnessy, at your service."

Alex smiled, shook his hand, and said, "Pleased to meet you." Mick bowed more deeply and kissed her hand in a dramatic fashion. He stepped back and motioned to two chairs adjacent to his. They all sat. Alex looked to Beau for explanation. Beau laughed.

"This is my sometimes partner in the agency. We've worked together on several cases and provided security a few dozen times."

"Cigar?" Mick said, pulling a fresh one from an inner pocket. Beau waved it away. Mick gestured toward the bar with his empty glass. The barman nodded and pulled a bottle from behind the bar. "I don't suppose you'd like a glass of firewater."

Beau just laughed and shook his head. "Still the same old Mick," he said. "Whiskey and cigars will be the death of you."

"Yeah, maybe," Mick said. "If a jealous husband doesn't get me first." Mick drew on his cigar and laughed. He took a fresh glass of whiskey from the barman and nodded to Alex. She ordered white wine. Beau ordered a beer.

"So, what brings you to Skaneateles?" Beau said mildly. He could tell that Mick was having a good time with his surprise. It was just like Mick; where Beau liked to keep things on the quiet side, Mick was direct, open, and present wherever he went. It occurred to Beau that Mick and Alex had a lot in common in that respect. He had to admit that she had gotten a lot more out of the receptionist here at the hotel than he could have gotten. Beau waited for an answer.

"I'm on a case," Mick announced matter of factly. "A certain Mr. Edward Holmes. He's in prison for murdering his wife. His daughter thinks he's innocent. Her husband's rich and they're financing my investigation. Cable told me it might be related to yours. Told me you've got a list."

"We do," Beau said. "Business partners of Alex's father. Holmes is on the list."

"I know," Mick said. He smiled and pulled a telegram out of his pocket. He handed it over to Beau without explanation. Beau read it, shook his head, and laughed lightly to himself. Alex looked at him for an explanation.

"It's from our Director, Aloysius Cable. Since our mutual investigations have dovetailed, he's ordered us to work together." Beau looked up from the telegram. "More efficient and, since there's big money at stake, a much bigger payout to the agency," he explained.

"My aunt won't have it," Alex said.

Beau looked down at the telegram and shook his head again. "It says here that your aunt has signed on to the restructuring."

Mick chortled triumphantly and swirled the whiskey in his glass. "It also says that me being the senior agent, I'm to be in charge."

"I won't have it!" Alex said emphatically. "Beau knows what he's doing and, I think he'll agree, I've been quite helpful in a few instances."

"Well, lass," Mick said. "I'd certainly hate to see you leave but leave if you must. But I think your dear aunt might be a bit disappointed. The Director said that your aunt specified that you stay with us to prevent any…what was the word? Chicanery, I think she said." He took the telegram from Beau and handed it to Alex. "It's all there."

Alex took the telegram and glanced at it. It was all true. She realized with a sinking feeling that she'd been given a Hobson's choice: neither response was acceptable to her. But it was clear that O'Shaughnessy didn't really want her tagging along. Well, she thought. That's just fine. If I'm to tag along, then I'll tag along, and Mick O'Shaughnessy can pound salt! It was one of her father's favorite expressions, although she had never figured out what it meant.

Mick watched Alex and knew that she'd come to a decision, the only one she could. It might not be so bad to have a lawyer on the team, he thought. A smart lawyer could gain access to information in ways regular laymen couldn't, as long as they didn't mind bending the law a little. And what lawyer wouldn't?

Beau pulled the list out of his breast pocket, put it on the table and gently shoved it toward Mick. Mick picked it up and glanced at it. "Lotta names," he said with a soft whistle. The ones crossed off have been checked?" Beau nodded.

Mick took a small, battered notebook out of his coat pocket and a short stub of a pencil. He licked the point and began laboriously copying the names. "I'll be needin' me own copy, in case we get separated."

Alex frowned and put her hand out. Mick looked sheepish but handed it over.

"Lawyers write a lot, and we write fast," she said with a disarming smile. "It's one of our skills."

As she spoke, she copied the names and addresses on the list into Mick's notebook.

"We also know a lot about the law, and we know a lot of esoteric legal terms that, when rattled off officiously, have the ring of law about them; whether they actually do or not." She paused for a second and looked meaningfully at Mick.

"Make no mistake, Mr. O'Shaughnessy. I intend to find Clara. She stole my father's legacy and was likely complicit in his murder, as well as my mother's. I don't care about the money, and I don't care about your approval. What I care about is bringing her to justice. If you can help me with that, fine. Otherwise, stay out of my way."

Mick took the notebook and pencil from her, glanced at it, and nodded his thanks.

"We'll finish here with Holmes and then move on," Mick said, pocketing the notebook. He finished his whiskey and stood, hefting his shillelagh in his big red Irish paw. "First, I'd like to get a look at Holmes' office. There might be something there that we can use to establish a connection between him and the other cases. If there is, and we can find this Clara person, Holmes might have a chance at an appeal."

TO Alex's surprise, they drove straight out to the Holmes estate in an open, four-seater buggy, driven by Mick, who took up the entire front seat; the springs bottomed out from his weight. It was broad daylight and the hot noon-day sun glinted off the golden wheat fields that lined the dusty road.

The road was crowded with travelers, some in wagons or buggies, some on horseback, but most on foot. They transported baskets, sacks, barrels, and bales of various items. Some carried infants wrapped in thin blankets while small children danced and skipped along. A motley crew of cur dog's ac companied the procession, sometimes snarling and snapping at each other but all the while wary of the sticks and whips of the travelers. A cacophony of shouts, cracked whips, gleeful children and barking dogs filled the air.

Mick seemed at home, holding the reins of the single horse, snapping them to move it along or pulling at the stick brake and shouting "whoa," as he weaved his way through the crowd. At a large bend in the road, he turned and handed Alex a leather portfolio. She looked inside and found a collection of official looking documents identifying them as officials from a bank, from the county government, granting them permission to be on a property, permission to search, etcetera. They were standard printed forms with spaces where the particulars, names, dates, addresses, were written in smudged and faded ink. Hard to make out. But it was the official stamps and seals that mattered. Something to flash at an illiterate cop, curious official or surprised property owner.

"You're not the only one skilled at, how did you call it, esoteric language?" He laughed and snapped the reigns, causing Alex to wobble a little off balance, holding the sheaf of forgeries.

They turned onto the road leading to the Holmes estate as if they meant to. Mick stopped at the gate, swiftly picked the lock, and opened the creaking, rusty gates. He didn't turn around to see if anyone was watching. Didn't glance furtively over his shoulder. What was it Beau had said? Don't call attention to yourself; you don't want to be noticed. You don't want to be remembered. Same idea, different method. No one noticed or remembered the unremarkable people going up the drive to the Holmes estate.

Mick parked the buggy at the front of the main building, tied the horse to the hitching rail and mounted the steps. He picked the lock, opened the door, and held it for Beau and Alex. They walked in and Mick shut the door behind him. He then pulled a chair up to the door, took a large ceramic vase from beside the entrance, climbed up on the chair and balanced the vase on top of the partially opened door. They would have fair warning if anyone opened the door while they were in the house.

The house itself looked much as her own, Alex thought. And her aunt's. Maybe even the same architect. Tall windows downstairs with heavy felt curtains, ornate tables and chairs, large paintings on the walls, shelves with various expensive looking items. A nice house, Victorian fashion. A wide set of carpeted stairs fanned out onto the main foyer. The three of them walked up the stairs and located what appeared to be Holmes' office. Mick picked the lock, and they went in and began searching it. Beau went through the desk drawers, meticulously extracting the contents of each and then returning them to the exact order they had been in, much as he had searched her father's office. Mick found the liquor cabinet and poured a liberal quantity of amber whiskey into a cut glass tumbler. "Top o' the mornin'" he said in his thick Irish brogue. He lifted the glass in a mock toast and drained it. He set it down on a random table and began riffling through drawers, cabinets, and bookcases. After a while he began shifting paintings on the walls, peering behind each.

"Aha!" he exclaimed as he lifted a large, framed map of the world off its hangers. Behind it, in a recess, was a safe. He set the map down on its edge against a wall and examined the locking mechanism.

"Bring me a glass, lass," he said, looking over at Alex who had just been standing, watching the two detectives search the room.

"I beg your pardon," she said in a huff. "If you want a glass of whiskey, get it yourself."

Mick stopped her with a wave of his hand. "Just a glass. Please." He nodded toward the bar. "A wine glass with a big bell."

Alex swallowed her pride and walked over to the bar. She selected a large glass meant for red wine. She held it up for him to see.

"Yes, that'll do," he said.

She brought it over to him and he put the base of the glass on the metal front of the safe. Then he stuck his right ear in the bell. He put his finger to his mouth, winked, and began turning the big knob, first right, then left. After a while he stepped back with a satisfied smile and pulled the lever. The door opened.

"These old safes only have a few tumblers. Easy to hear if you know how to do it. A strongbox would be harder to break into."

Beau walked over and helped Mick pull the contents of the safe out and set them on a table. There was some jewelry, some cash, a few bonds, and a leather ledger like the one Beau had found in her father's safe. Mick opened it and ran his finger down the entry of names. He looked up at Beau and Alex.

"Look familiar?"

Alex drew a shocked breath. Many of the names were the same as the ones in her father's ledger.

"I'll make a copy," Alex said, looking around the room for a blank piece of paper and pen and ink.

"No need," Mick said. He found a straight edge and tore out the pages. Beau shook his head. "No one will notice a few pages missing," he said. He looked around the room. "Or that anyone has searched the house."

Mick folded the papers and slid them into an inside pocket and laughed. He poured himself another whiskey and filled his flask. He held the glass up appreciatively and looked at the golden amber fluid. "Holmes sure had the good stuff," he said. Then he looked at Beau and nodded slightly. "You're good at what you do," he said with a smile. "You're a better track err than I am, and you have good instincts. When you do a search, you leave the scene looking exactly as you found it. And you do it at night when you can't be spotted. No one would ever know that the place had been searched. Except by someone as good as you, like me, for instance. I would find slight disturbances that no one else would notice. A glass turned the wrong way, a footprint beneath a window, a faint trail in the dust on the floor that could only be seen in the daylight. The faint smell of the kerosene lantern you used." Mick paused and took a sip of whiskey.

"The trouble with your method is that you think it's foolproof, and you become too confident, too secure. A determined adversary would be able to surprise you. For me, I want to be noticed. Not by family, friends, or the casual observer; they would never notice or be alarmed by a few missing pages in a convicted murderers ledger. But by someone interested in not being discovered. Someone covering his tracks - or hers. My sloppiness is purposeful. It's like baiting a trap. And when he comes after me, I'll be expecting him, and I'll be ready."

"I hope you're right," Beau said, a degree of worry creeping into his mind. "You're leaving a trail a child could follow. Whoever is doing this is capable of murder and I don't want to be on his hit list."

A sudden crash from downstairs forestalled their discussion. The three of them rushed to the head of the stairs. There, in front of the open door, a man lay sprawled on the floor, shards of broken vase all around him.

25

Henry Thornton was a curious man, and he took his job seriously, such as it was. He lived alone in a small shack at the edge of the Holmes estate and acted as a jack-of-all-trades for Mr. Holmes. In return, he received a small stipend and was allowed to live in the little shack rent-free. When Holmes was arrested, the estate went into receivership to the bank. The bank president, who was a friend of Holmes, kept Henry on with the title of caretaker. When Henry saw a buggy pull up to the entrance of the big house, he saddled up his sway-backed mule and rode over. He didn't expect to be hit over the head when he walked into the house.

"Oh my god, is he dead?" Alex screamed when she saw the man lying in a pool of blood on the floor at the entrance.

"If he isn't, he will be soon," Mick said, brandishing his shillelagh. He started down the stairs. Beau touched Mick's elbow and pushed past him. "Let's see who he is first," he said.

When they got to him, the man was beginning to stir. He moaned and put his hand to his head, which was bleeding from several cuts. Beau helped him sit up and Alex brought a towel from the kitchen to stop the bleeding. Mick stood over him, holding his shillelagh. "Check him for weapons," he said to Beau. Beau quickly frisked him, looked up at Mick and shook his head no.

Alex went back to the kitchen and brought back another towel, a bowl of water to wash the cuts, and a glass of water, which she handed to the man. He drank it gratefully.

"Who are you?" Alex said when he finished drinking.

"I'm Henry Thornton, the caretaker. Who are you people, and why did you hit me?"

"Agents of the court," Mick said, relaxing a little. "Here to legally search the premises." He looked to Alex who rummaged in her leather briefcase and took out a document. She showed it to Thornton. He looked at it through bleary eyes, nodded, and groaned again. Alex and Beau helped him over to a chair and Mick handed him his flask.

"You took quite a hit, lad, but you'll be alright," Mick said. Thornton drank from the flask and handed it back to Mick, who took a generous swig himself.

"The vase was balanced on the door to warn of intruders while we searched," Alex explained. "You walked right under it." She continued to dab at his cuts with a cloth as she spoke.

"We're here on behalf of Holmes' daughter, who is trying to mount an appeal of Mr. Holmes' conviction. She's convinced that he was set up somehow. We've been hired to find out if that's so."

Thornton laughed. It was a strange chortle, one that said he knew better. He looked to Mick, who immediately got the hint. He pulled his flask out of his pocket and handed it to Thornton. He nodded his thanks and drank deeply. He wiped his mouth on his sleeve and took another drink.

"That's what everybody that knows him thinks," he said "Edward Holmes, the perfect man, the perfect husband. He never would have murdered his wife. They say the court was wrong. But I know different."

"Tell us what you know," Alex said encouragingly. She took out a small notebook, ready to take notes. Thornton looked at Mick again, who again took the hint. He pulled a small leather coin purse out of his pocket and shook out a couple of gold coins into his other hand. He weighed them in his big paw and then gave them to Thornton, who pocketed them.

"His wife was about to divorce him. With the new laws concerning women, she would have won a court case and left him penniless. He must have killed her in an angry rage when she confronted him." "Go on," Alex said, still scribbling in her notebook. "Why was she going to divorce him? What were the grounds?"

Thornton looked again at Mick, who again took out his coin purse and withdrew two more gold coins and handed them to Thornton.

"She caught him red-handed with the housekeeper, from what I was told. Walked right in on him."

"Who was the housekeeper?" Alex said.

Thornton looked at Mick, but this time Mick lifted his shillelagh slightly. "You've gotten enough carrot, laddie. The stick is next."

Thornton looked at the stick and felt his tender head. Four gold coins was way more than he had expected to get anyway. Why push it?

"I don't know anything about her, except that she was referred to as "Lady Jane." Mr. Holmes hired her when his wife took sick. I heard that the doctor didn't expect her to pull through. It was a long illness. But she did, and shortly after that she caught the two of them."

"What do you know of the housekeeper?" Alex asked. "Was she a local woman? What did she look like?"

Thornton shook his head. "She wasn't local. She just showed up in town one day. You couldn't miss her. A real head-turner. Had a bodyguard with her at first. Stayed at the Sherwood Inn for a few nights and then Mr. Holmes hired her. She was young and very beautiful. I used to see her, standing at her window, looking out over the fields. She took a buggy ride every morning along the river road and passed right by my house. Stunning."

"What did the bodyguard look like," Beau asked.

"Don't remember much about him. Big fella in a bowler. Always stayed in the shadows. He left after Lady Jane was hired by Holmes."

"What became of her? Alex asked. "After the murder."

Thornton shook his head again. "The whole staff was let go. I was the only one who stayed on. They all went their separate ways. I don't know what became of Lady Jane."

"One more question," Alex said. "What color was her hair?"

"Black. Her hair was long and black as a raven's."

Thornton left, rubbing his head as he mounted his mule. As the two Pinkertons swept the other rooms of the house, Alex went up to the hall way that led to the bedrooms. Clara had slept with her father, of course, but she kept her original suite of rooms where she spent much of her leisure time. She wondered if Lady Jane had her own suite of rooms. The doors of the bedrooms were unlocked. She looked into each but only found neat, tidy guest rooms, waiting for guests that would never come again. But at the end of the hall there was a much larger room with windows that looked out of two sides of the house. There was the faint smell of perfume that triggered a memory. It was the same distinctive, European perfume that Clara favored. She went in.

Everything was made up, the bed, the nightstand, and the dresser, just like the other rooms. The maid had evidently done it in the course of her regular duties. Alex walked over to the window that faced south and ad mired the view. Orchards, wheat fields and pastures. She looked down casually and noticed that the window was free. Odd. In most houses like this, the windows were painted shut. An open window would invite unwanted guests in the form of birds, raccoons, and insects. Bats even. Alex never opened her own window for that reason. But someone had used a knife or some other implement to break the paint seal. She looked closer and could see the marks of a fingernail file. On impulse, Alex opened the window. It slid up easily in its tracings. A breath of hot summer air assailed her, strong with the smell of manure, another reason to keep windows close to a pasture closed.

As she looked out the window, Alex saw something glint in the weeds just past the path that ran underneath the window. She craned her neck and stuck it a little farther out the open window. There was more glinting. Little points of diamonds reflecting the bright sun. She closed the window, walked out of the room, and went down the back stairs to a door that opened onto the path. She unlocked the door, opened it, and walked down the path to the area where she had seen the points of light. She rummaged around in the weeds and found something surprising.

Beau and Mick were standing next to the buggy when Alex rounded the corner by the front of the house. Mick had lit a cigar and held a tumbler of whiskey in his hand, a satisfied look on his face. A crystal decanter sat on the bench seat of the buggy, significantly less full. Beau stood stoically off to the side, looking up at the front of the house. He turned and smiled when he saw Alex.

"We thought you'd gotten lost," he said in a joking manner. He would never ask her directly what she had been doing. That was not his style.

"Just doing a little looking around," Alex said. She showed the men what she had found. It was a rectangular, light blue glass bottle, the type of bottle you'd find in an apothecary. The name, "Doctor Mulroney's Exemplary Elixir," was embossed on the front, along with the figure of a coiled rattle snake. Beau took it and sniffed it. It had the faint aroma of licorice, mint, and alcohol.

"Snake oil," Mick said unnecessarily. Cure-alls were a common thing, sold in medicine shows, apothecaries and even prescribed by some country doctors. There was no law dictating what could or couldn't be put in them and no law mandating that the contents be disclosed. He gave Alex a look as if to say, so what?

"Clara always had a licorice aroma about her. I never thought much about it until I sniffed at one of the bottles that still had a cork and a little residue. Same smell."

"One of the bottles?" Beau said. He took the bottle and examined it closely.

"There were dozens of them, mostly smashed. In the weeds under her window at the rear of the house."

"Sounds like our Clara, or whatever name she uses, has a little problem," Mick said.

"How so?" Alex said.

"A lot of these cure-alls have opium as an ingredient. Powerful pain killer, but addictive. If there's a big pile of empty bottles under her window, she's got a problem."

Alex nodded but seemed lost in thought for a moment. "Where were Clara, or Lady Jane, getting the bottles?" she said. "If there was a delivery of cases of cure-alls to our house, I would have heard about it. Believe me, the gossip among the staff was considerable. Cases of cure-alls wouldn't have gone un-noticed."

"Maybe she picked them up in town at the apothecary," Mick said. "They usually carry a variety of cure-alls."

Alex shook her head. "The town was full of gossip about Clara and my father already. Her buying cure-alls on a regular basis would have been noticed. She did go on her daily buggy ride, but only out into the country, along the river and then through town without stopping. Other than that, she stayed home."

"Well, nothing much to go on there, Lass," Mick said. "I guess we'd better start thinking about the next name on the list to investigate."

"We should compare the two lists and see how many of the names show up on both ledgers," Alex said. "That might make our task simpler."

"No," Beau said. "He was holding the cure-all bottle and turning it over and over in his hands. "We've been focusing too much on where Clara has been and not enough on where she is going. She gets her medicine somewhere. That's the lead. We'll go to Lockport first."

Mick and Alex each gave him an inquisitive look. Beau turned the bottle upside down and showed them the embossing on the bottom. It read "Lock City Bottling Works."

26

The Lock City Bottling Works had been around since the 1840s, founded by Ira H. Billings on the corner of Market Street and Exchange, in what was then called Lowertown. He hired a gaffer and four glassblowers from Pittsburgh, along with a gatherer and servitor for each shop. He imported four large pots which were filled with silica from Verona, Lime from Williamsville, a measure of crushed glass called cullet and some coloring oxides. The mixture was heated to 2,500 degrees Fahrenheit for thirty to forty hours and then pressed into bottle molds. He made bottles for mineral water, medicines, perfumes, and beer. He did a good business and soon expanded his operation to four more pots, another furnace and more blowers, gatherers, and servitors. Other laborers, usually boys, were hired to run the bottles to an annealing oven for cooling, then on to packaging and shipping.

Billings shipped his bottles up and down the Erie Canal, and points north and south on the newly constructed railroads. He had an estate built overlooking the canal west of the city, married and had a son named Hiram who took over the business when Ira retired. Hiram expanded the business even further. He hired more blowers, gatherers and servitors and workers until his factory employed almost one hundred employees, one of the biggest employers in the city. Times were good in Lockport and the city grew. But a devastating economic downturn shrank demand for glassware, and

Hiram was forced to downsize. Then the high heat of the furnaces caught fire to the wooden building and the factory was destroyed. Hiram lost everything. He took out a large loan and rebuilt the factory on the upper side of the city and, although he brought production back to the previous level, he found himself upside down on his loans. He was made an offer by a consortium of businessmen who bought him out and took over production of the factory. They diversified, making vials, patent medicines, sodas, perfumes, lamp globes and fruit jars. One of their customers was a patent medicine company called Doctor Mulroney's Exemplary Elixir.

Alex, Beau, and Mick departed the train at the Lockport station and considered their next move.

"Let's find a hotel and get our rooms," Alex said. I hear the Park Place is the best hotel in town."

"As long as you're paying," Mick said. "And it has a bar."

"Sure, why not," Beau said. "Maybe we could hire a brass band to announce our arrival while we're at it."

"Ha!" Mick exclaimed, lighting his cigar stub, and taking a sip from his flask as he spoke. "Why not? If someone is following us, it might flush him out." He held his shillelagh up. "Another notch if the bugger's not careful about it!"

Beau shook his head and looked at Alex. But he didn't say anything.

Alex had a porter bring her things up to her room and flopped on the bed in exasperation. What had started out as a simple arrangement had become immeasurably complicated? She had gotten used to Beau and his ways only to find that the agent in charge, Mick, had a completely different style of investigation. Which one was right, she wondered? Beau moved in the shadows while Mick moved in the light. She herself preferred a direct approach to things, the law on her side. Beau acted as if the law didn't exist; he operated like a thief in the night, slipping into buildings, picking locks, and stealing documents. But at least he seemed to recognize that he was breaking the law. Mick, on the other hand, boldly blustered into buildings, openly defiant of the law. It didn't apply to him, he seemed to say. Catch me if you can.

Alex preferred neither approach. The law was the law, and a person knowledgeable in its elements could gain access to whatever was needed legally. Bluff, bluster, and shady methods had no place. The law was sacrosanct. Inviolate. To her, not following the law to the letter would invite a repudiation of whatever evidence had been found. She had never been a cheater, yet she found herself with two men who seemed to believe in the dictum: "the end justifies the means."

Mick was at the bar when Alex entered the hotel restaurant an hour later. He was enrobed in a cloud of cigar smoke and was talking loudly with the bartender. Alex noticed Beau, sitting at a table in the back. He nodded to her, and she walked over, ignoring the loud Irishman at the bar. Beau gestured toward an empty chair at the table. She took it.

"Mick thinks that we should lay low and be watchful," he said as she sat. "He wants me…us, to watch his back in case he flushes out someone purr suing us. Risky, but its Mick's way. And his call."

Alex nodded. She could see that Beau was uncomfortable with the situation and began to understand Beau's attitude toward her early on in their quest. Mick was obviously experienced and, one might guess, successful, but his head-on, aggressive style was beginning to make her nervous. If he made a misstep, the quest to find Clara and serve her papers would be at risk. Clara might abandon her scam and disappear forever. Or, worse yet, the mysterious bodyguard might terminate their mission himself. Suspect end murders were mounting up and Alex didn't want to be added to the list. Beau seemed to read her mind.

"Be very watchful and very discrete," he said. There was a note of nervousness in his voice and it surprised Alex. Beau had seemed fearless up to this point, devoid of emotion of any kind. As she thought about it, she suddenly realized that his concern was not for himself. It was for her. His face suddenly registered her unasked question of why?

"These are very dangerous people that we're up against," he said. "People who will stop at nothing to get what they want. What I can't figure is what that is."

"Money," Alex said.

Beau shook his head. "They've got plenty of money from the scams that we know about, and probably a lot more from ones we haven't yet discovered. Whoever they are, whoever she is, there's something more than just money involved. And that's what worries me."

Alex looked at him questioningly. "What is it, if it isn't money?"

"Think about it," Beau said. "Aside from the men who look like they might be future targets, the men on the list that were scammed were wealthy men. But the other men that we checked were not just average businessmen, making a decent living. They were ruined businessmen."

"Revenge?"

The pattern is obvious if you look past the money. All the men we've checked have either been murdered or ruined. And the families of the murdered men have been left penniless. Like yours."

"But why?"

Beau raised his eyebrows and shrugged. "To what lengths will a person go to get revenge for a wrong done?" He thought of his own quest and how it had brought him here. He could understand a scam for money, even committing murder for it. But a well-thought out and executed campaign of revenge would imply a very serious wrongdoing. Also, the team involved seemed to be growing. There was Clara, of course, and the two farm hands that had brought Clifton to the doctor. Then there was the mysterious Mr. Douglass, who had bought the Clifton Estate, taken out a large loan and then disappeared. Add in the bodyguard, who was beginning to worry Beau. Were there others? It was hard to tell. In Beau's opinion, it would be wise to lay low, until they could determine the size of the scam team. But that just wasn't Mick's style.

MICK walked up the steps to the office door of the Lock City Bottling Works, the tip if his shillelagh banging on the brick. He opened the door, walked in, and looked around. "Who's the pooh-bah?" he boomed. The factory noise and heat seemed to absorb his question. He banged his shillelagh on a large drum that was sitting next to the door. Boys hurried to and fro, oblivious to the big man with the hardwood stick. Mick banged the drum again. A man sitting behind a large worn looking desk looked up from a pile of order forms. He stood and wiped his hands on his apron and walked up to the big Irishman.

"Can I help you?" the man shouted above the din. He wore pincenez glasses that were smudged. He adjusted them and waited impatiently for an answer.

Mick produced a leather wallet and opened it to reveal a gold badge and ID card. He waved it briefly at the man and put it away. "Officer Mick O'Shaughnessy," he said. "Department of Agriculture."

"What can I do for you, officer?" the man said. He didn't seem impressed with the badge.

Mick held out the empty cure-all bottle and said, "You make these bottles. I'm investigating several deaths believed to have been caused by ingesting too much of Doctor Mulroney's snake oil. I need to know who your customer is and his location."

The man's eyes widened in surprise for just a mere moment, then he caught himself. But Mick caught it because he was looking for it. The man cleared his throat, his eyes darting briefly toward the door to an inner office.

"I'm afraid I can't divulge that type of information," he said firmly. "Company policy."

Mick made a show of rummaging around in his battered leather brief case. "I thought that might be the case," he said absently, still looking. "I obtained a warrant from the Department. It allows me to search your records."

The man cleared his throat again and turned toward the inner office door. "Just a moment," he said over his shoulder. He rapped on the door and a voice told him to come in. He opened the door, went in, and shut the door behind him. A moment later the door opened, and the man emerged, an officious smile on his face. "Mr. Billings will see you now," he said, holding the door open. Mick walked over to it and entered. Mr. Billings was obviously the owner of the factory. The office was more like a gentleman's drawing room than a working office. There was no secretary, no filing cabinets and no piles of order forms and bills piled up on his ornate oak desk. There was a bar with decanters of different spirits and a shelf with cut glass tumblers and wine glasses. One wall held a dozen or so specimens of ornate glass creations made at the factory. He noticed a back door, slightly ajar and there were two smoldering cigars in a large ashtray. A guest or client would have left by the front door, and a regular employee wouldn't be lingering by the door. A trusted lieutenant, advisor, or friend.

"Mr. O'Shaughnessy," Mr. Billings said, standing. He was tall with a shock of dark hair going grey at the sides. He wore a three three-piece suit tailored to his well-kept body and looked to be in his late fifties. His intelligent eyes flashed as he greeted Mick. He extended his hand in greeting. Mick took it.

"I've been given to understand that you're seeking a certain buyer of mine on behalf of the government. Something to do with some deaths caused by a cure-all."

"Yes," Mick said, withdrawing the wallet with the badge from his pocket. "Department of Agriculture."

Billings waved the wallet away with an easy hand gesture. "No need," he said. "I've never trusted cure-alls myself. You never know what's in them. May I see the bottle?"

Mick took the bottle out of his pocket and handed it to Billings, who turned it over in his hand, examining the embossing. He looked at the bottom. "Definitely one of ours," he said, handing the bottle back. "An apothecary in Albion has a contract with us. Several different bottles for various medicines, including Doctor Mulroney's Exemplary Elixir." He went back around his desk, got out a piece of paper, dipped his pen in a pot of ink, and wrote down the address of the Apothecary. He rolled a blotter over the wet ink, waved the paper in the air to further dry it, and handed it to Mick.

Mick took it, glanced at it briefly and put it in his pocket. "Thank you," he said and left.

As they waited for Mick, Beau and Alex took a table in the hotel restaurant. The waiter brought menus and water. Alex looked at the menu and ordered a chicken dish. It was lunchtime, after all. Beau ordered nothing. Alex had noticed that he rarely ate much, preferring to eat jerky, pemmican, and a mix of nuts and dried fruits that he kept in a small rawhide satchel that he called his possibles bag. Alex drank coffee and Beau sprinkled some dried herbs into his water.

"What is that?" Alex asked impulsively. She hated when she did that, blurt out what was on her mind. He must think me such a naïve little girl, she thought. "Sorry," she said. "I was just curious."

"Not at all," Beau said. "It's 'sang – ginseng, a powdered root that's good for energy, endurance, and mental clarity. Would you like to try some?" Without waiting for an answer, he sprinkled some in her water. She looked at it, picked up the glass and sniffed. Then she took a sip. It tasted a little bit like carrot, but more earthy and bitter.

"Don't think about it, just drink it down," Beau said with a sly smile. She did, banishing a slight gag reflex. It wouldn't do to choke on it in front of Beau.

Beau nodded his approval. "A little bitter, isn't it? But I've come to like the taste for the result it brings."

"What should I feel?

"Nothing; it's subtle. You'll just realize that you have a little more energy; you'll feel as if you're a little more on top of things."

Alex nodded and resisted the urge to ask for another glass of water to wash away the taste. Strange man, she thought. He had a lot of strange habits and mannerisms, but she found that he was growing on her, his unique ness was somehow attractive.

Beau looked at Alex, trying to make a brave face with the bitter taste still in her mouth. He raised a finger to summon the waiter and asked for more water.

"Right away sir," the waiter said. He brought a pitcher and filled both of their glasses.

"I think I put a little too much powder in your glass," Beau said as Alex gratefully drank her water. "For the first time, that is."

Alex laughed. "I feel its power already!" she fake-flexed her arm and gave Beau a steely look. "Want to arm wrestle?"

Beau held his hands up in surrender. "You've already beaten me intellectually; I would lose all pride if you beat me physically."

Alex impulsively gritted her teeth and punched one of Beau's upraised hands. It made a loud slapping sound. Beau pulled his hand back as if in pain. He shook it as if to restore feeling in it. "That's quite a punch," he said. Then he laughed. It came out strange at first, it had been so long since he had laughed. Then it consumed him. He laughed so hard he almost cried. He noticed, through teary eyes, that Alex was doing the same. She was convulsing with laughter, tears rolling down her cheeks. They laughed together for a long time, bringing shocked looks from other diners. After a while, the waiter brought Alex's food. He smiled.

"Sorry about the outburst," Alex said. "It's just that we…"

"I understand," the waiter said. "How long have you two been married?"

Beau's eyes widened and he choked on his water, almost spitting it out. Alex got a playful twinkle in her eye.

"Two weeks," she said. "We're on our honeymoon."

"Well, I hope you enjoy your stay. "How do you like your accommodations?"

"Beautiful," Alex said. She entertained the thought of saying that the bed springs were a little loud but banished it. Beau was suffering enough. "The hotel has been completely refurbished," the waiter said. "Top to bottom, thanks to Mr. Billings. It was run down and squalid, because of the depression. But he bought it and had it re-done. He's done the same all over town. Lockport owes a lot to him and his bottling works."

Alex's ears perked up. The bottling works was where Mick had gone. "He owns the bottling works?"

"Bought that too and refurbished it. It's the city's biggest employer. Used to be in his family originally, but somehow, they lost it. It happened before my time here. He lives in a big estate west of town. Beautiful wife. They're furbished the Opera House, which was also run down. She has a big hand in it. It brings in big acts from all over the state now."

Just then a booming Irish brogue could be heard at the bar, calling for a whiskey. The waiter gave them a baleful look. "Sounds like I'm needed at the bar," he said. "Nice talking with you. And congratulations, by the way." Alex smirked.

"I owe you one," Beau said. He dropped another measure of powder into his glass and drank it.

27

T HE DUCHESS WOKE Ida Mae at precisely six o'clock, as she always did. It might have seemed uncanny, except that she had been doing it for at least a decade. Precisely at six o'clock. You could set your watch.

"Why don't you ever let me sleep in a little," Ida Mae said to her favorite cat as she threw back the covers and sat up. "It wouldn't hurt, once in a while."

She swung her feet around and scooched forward, letting her feet land on her slippers. She shoved her feet into them and stood, slipping into her enormous velvet robe, and tying it at the front. She ruffled her hair, blinked her eyes, and headed toward the door. "I suppose Hazel has our breakfast waiting," she said, referencing her long-time housekeeper. "She doesn't like to be kept waiting." She padded down the corridor and then down the stairs, the Duchess following.

"Good morning, Mam," Hazel said brightly as they entered the kitchen. "Duchess."

Two places had been set, as usual, and the food was on plates under silver food covers. Ida Mae's place had silver tableware set on a lace napkin. There were crystal glasses containing water and orange juice and a China cup next to a China teapot.

"What do we have this morning?" Ida Mae said, lifting the lid over her plate. A pleasant gush of steam escaped, fragrant and inviting.

"Poached eggs on toast, a slice of Virginia ham, and Potatoes O'Brien for you; poached salmon for the Duchess," Hazel said. At that, she lifted the Duchess's food cover. The cat purred contentedly and began wolfing down the savory fish.

"I like cats much more than I like most humans," Ida Mae said, pouring herself some tea. "They can be trusted to be exactly what they are; nothing more, nothing less."

"Yes, Mam," Hazel said, stepping back from the table, but remaining in case she was needed further. She had heard it all before. Many times, truth be told. She had worked for the Browns for many years and had seen them through a good deal of changes in their lives. She helped raise their children, saw them through sicknesses, cooked their food, cleaned their house, and did their laundry. Now she was helping Nurse Jacob Brown through his sickness. He had been crushed by a stack of hay bales that had accidentally fallen from an upper platform in one of the barns. He suffered broken bones and crushed ribs, but the worst part of the accident was a head injury that left him comatose. He required constant care and Hazel made sure that his sheets and bedclothes were changed daily. There were always fresh flowers in the room and the blinds were kept open to admit plenty of sunshine. It was the least she could do for the man who had saved her life.

The accident had happened on a Saturday afternoon. Jacob was working in the barn, tossing bales of new, heavy hay up to a worker who was stacking them on the second floor. Hazel had brought Jacob and the workers their lunch and was setting it up on a table just below the open second floor platform. As the worker piled more bales on the stack, it became uneven; unsustainable. As he hefted another bale on the stack, the stack tipped. He shouted a warning, but it was too late. Hazel had just enough time to look up and see a mountain of hay bales coming down toward her. Jacob rushed forward and pushed her out of the way. But as he did, he fell. He was buried alive under a mountain of hay.

Farm workers frantically tore at the pile of bales, throwing them off to the side as they struggled to free their boss. They finally reached him, pushed away at the last of the bales and lifted him out. He was still breathing, but he was badly injured. But worse, he had sustained a head wound that caused his brain to swell. The doctors were powerless. Jacob Brown slipped into a coma from which he would never emerge. Hazel's reaction was one of unparalleled grief. The man's injury was due to her own carelessness. She should have set the table up in a different, safer spot. She was consumed with guilt. It was then that she decided to dedicate herself to tending Jacob for as long as he was still alive.

As the days turned to months, she washed him, changed him, and fed him. She rubbed salve into his bed sores and washed and cut and combed his hair. She shaved him as clean as any barber. She kissed him and read stories to him and put fresh flowers in his room. And she came to love him.

Ida Mae kept her on, of course; who else could she get to tend to the man so cheaply. She suspected that Hazel and Jacob had had an affair; why else would anyone take such tender care of a man who was nothing more than a vegetable?

Her reaction to his accident had been predictable, "The fool brought it on himself," she told people at the time, and long afterward if the subject came up. "Play acting at being a farmer when we had hired people to do those jobs. He should have been pursuing his business interests instead of cavorting around in a barn! I wouldn't be surprised that he shoveled manure too! He certainly had a funky smell about him when he came in. Wouldn't let him touch me 'till he'd a bath and a change of clothes, not that he ever did anyway. The romance left our marriage years ago. But, to top it all off, the man didn't even have the good sense to die, and so I'm stuck with a vegetable that needs daily tending!"

As time went on, Hazel spent more and more time with Jacob and less and less time on her other duties, a fact which irritated Ida Mae to no end. It all came to a head that afternoon when Ida Mae burst into Jacob's room, angry that her cats hadn't been fed recently. She saw Hazel kissing Jacob's forehead as she gently wept.

"I might have known," Ida Mae exclaimed. "Under my own roof!"

Hazel sat up swiftly, smoothing her dress and wiping her tears away with a quick swipe of her hand.

"There's nothing going on," Hazel said defensively. "How...how can there be? I was just feeling sad for Mr. Brown's condition. Sometimes I wish that he would just go ahead and...well..."

"Die?" Ida Mae said, vitriol creeping into her voice. "And then what would you do? The only reason I keep you on is for you to tend Jacob; or what's left of him. But now you've gone too far. You've neglected your other duties to a fault! My cats need your attention more than he does! I suggest you start spending your efforts on your real duties rather than wasting your time here!"

"Yes Mam," was all Hazel could think to say. She bowed her head contritely. "I'll try to do better."

"See that you do," Ida Mae said, turning toward the door. "Your job is hanging by a thread."

Hazel felt a cold chill up her spine, sucked out by the closing door. She turned back to Jacob and said, "I'm sorry."

The next day Hazel walked into Jacob's room to find his lifeless eyes staring up at the ceiling, his mouth gaping open as if trying to get one last breath.

28

ALBION IS ONE of the many stops along the Erie Canal. East to west, the canal runs from Albany to Buffalo, a town every fifteen miles, a day's travel in a canal boat. As the song goes, "I've got a mule and her name is Sal, fifteen miles on the Erie Canal."

"Clinton's Big Ditch," it was called when Governor DeWitt Clinton pushed for its completion. When it opened in 1825, it served as the first transportation system linking the east coast with the western states. It immediately brought prosperity to the state and to the little towns that sprang up along it. Albion was one of those little towns. Its businesses all faced the canal and so people walking down Main Street entered those businesses from the rear. The Albion Apothecary was one of those businesses.

Beau sat on a bench outside the pharmacy while Alex went in. Mick had established himself at a bar across the street, watching to see if they had been followed. A bell suspended over the door dinged as Alex opened it. She was immediately assailed by the smell of a dozen different medicines, perfumes, and unguents. She sneezed. The bell and the sneeze brought a man from a back room.

"God bless," he said pleasantly. He was a frail looking man, slightly stooped from years of bending over the vials and beakers of his lab. His eyes were red and glassy, and his nose twitched like a rabbit's under a thin brown mustache. "Can I help you, Miss?"

Alex didn't answer immediately. She stood with her hands clasped behind her back and scanned the shelves that lined the walls. They were filled with bottles, vials, and jars. After a time, she found one shelf filled with light blue bottles labelled Doctor Mulroney's Exemplary Elixir. She walked over to the shelf and selected one of the bottles. She took it to the counter.

"Ah, Doc Mulroney's," the man said, wheezing slightly. "One of our best sellers. Do you have an empty to exchange?"

"I'm afraid not," Alex said. "Is it required?"

"No, but you get a ten-cent discount if you have one."

"I'm buying this for my mother. She's getting older and has a lot of aches and pains. My aunt recommended it."

"A lot of people swear by it," the man said, putting the bottle in a sack. "I've never tried it myself."

"You make it, and you haven't tried it?" Alex said. "What's in it?"

"I don't know, I just sell it. It comes off the shelf as fast as I can stock it."

Alex paid the man and he thanked her. "Who does make it?" she asked as she put her wallet away and closed her purse. It was a casual question.

"I don't know that either," the man said. "I get deliveries every week or so, no set time or date. They drop off a number of cases and pick up the returned bottles and the new bottles, which are shipped here from the bottling works in Lockport."

"Strange that they wouldn't have the bottles shipped direct."

The man shrugged. "They come in on a canal boat. Less breakage. The lab must be somewhere far enough away from the canal and railroads that they have to ship the last leg by wagon."

"I see," Alex said, turning to leave. She wanted to ask more questions, but Beau's influence stopped her. Keep it casual, she thought, so that he doesn't remember you. She walked out the door and turned down the street on which their hotel, the Lockstone, was situated. When she arrived Mick was at the bar, loudly discussing sports with the bartender and anyone else who would listen. He noticed her and, after a discrete amount of time, followed her to a table in a dark corner where Beau was sitting. She told them her news.

"We'll have to watch for the delivery and follow them when they leave," Mick said. "Clara had to get her supply somewhere and this is our best lead."

Beau and Alex agreed. "We'll have to take turns and watch day and night," Alex said. "Our rooms face the apothecary, so the only real challenge will be staying awake."

Mick laughed. "The bar faces the apothecary as well. I'll bite the bullet and watch from there."

"We'll have to be ready to move on a moment's notice when we see them," Beau said. "I'll keep a horse saddled in front of the bar. No one will notice that."

"You'll leave a trail of breadcrumbs for us?" Alex said, an impish smile on her face.

Beau ignored the comment. "You two will follow me in a wagon. I'll have it ready at the livery stable." He looked at Alex with just a hint of a smile. "I'm sure that, between the two of you, you can track me."

Beau went to the livery stable; Mick went to the bar to watch the apothecary and Alex went to the Western Union office to cable Ida Mae. When she got there, there was a cable waiting for her. It read: "Your uncle has died. Come home immediately. Ida Mae."

AT just that moment, two men were sitting in a drawing room, thirty miles away, drinking brandy and smoking cigars. It was a typical business meeting in all respects, except that this meeting had grim overtones.

"I'm hearing things," one man said to the other. "Someone has been ask in questions. Investigating. I want you to find who it is and neutralize him. We can't afford to let him get ahead of us, there's too much at stake."

The other man smiled, but it was a smile devoid of mirth. He shift end slightly in his seat, leaning back and regarding the first man through half-lidded eyes.

"Find him?" he said, his voice a half whisper, the smile broadening slightly. "I won't need to find him. He will come to me. I've already set things in motion."

"I hope so," the first man said. "You botched the Holmes thing and now I hear that his daughter is in town, trying to gather evidence to mount an appeal."

"Botched? It was your fault that the man's wife didn't die," the second man said, menace in his voice. "The dose wasn't strong enough. And then the dose I gave Holmes didn't kill him either, and now he rots in prison and the will I placed in his safe will remain there for who knows how long."

"The doses would have worked if administered correctly," the first man said. "Too strong a dose would have drawn attention to the injection site, as it did with Comerford and Clifton."

"If you want a perfect administration of the solution, maybe you should have done it yourself," the second man said. "But that would require you to take an active part in something you're too squeamish and weak to do. You would have to get your well-manicured hands dirty."

The first man's eyes flashed angrily. "We both have our roles to play," he said tersely. "I have to maintain appearances, you know that." He paused for a moment and looked at his cigar as if seeking its council on what he was about to say next.

"I've been thinking," he said in a softer tone. "I think that, after this last one, we should go dark for a while. There's too many loose ends and these questions I'm hearing about are worrisome."

The second man smiled. It was the type of smile that made the first man cringe. It was a smile laden with evil intent.

"I'll take care of the loose ends," he said. "As I have been all along." He finished his drink and stood.

"Just make sure that you don't become one of the loose ends yourself." He turned and walked out the door.

The first man stood and went to the bar. He poured himself another brandy and drank it off in one gulp. Meetings with his brother always put him on edge.

WHEN she got back from the telegraph office, Alex explained her situation to Beau and Mick. They both agreed that she should leave immediately but stay in touch. "Daily cables on our status and progress," Beau suggested. "Say, nine in the morning?"

Alex nodded her agreement and realized that the two of them were probably happy to see her go. Professional investigators prefer to do their work their own way. Still, she felt like an athlete that was being taken out of the game prematurely. Benched, at the height of the game. She said her goodbyes and prepared to catch the next departing train.

29

Alex sat in the rumbling train, looking out the window and playing her game of fantasizing people's lives. She saw a couple in a buckboard wagon loaded with fresh produce. She imagined them picking the tomatoes, onions, radishes, and other items early in the morning, wiping the dirt off and placing them in baskets, the morning sun dappling the field. Insects buzzing, birds chirping. Did their children help them? Did they have children? As her mind wandered, she found herself thinking of Beau. He had grown up in an Indian village. What was that like, she wondered? She tried to imagine waking up in a tipi, wrapped in a Buffalo robe. Was it smelly? Were there bugs on it? Where did you go to the bathroom? How did you wash up? Did you put on fresh clothes?

She suddenly realized that she knew nothing of the natural world. She woke every day in a bed with a fine mattress, clean sheets, and a comforter. She rose to wash in a basin of fresh, warm water, put there by servants. She combed her hair in a mirror with an ivory comb, donned fresh, clean, tailored clothes and went downstairs to a dining room where a table was set with plates of eggs, bacon, fresh bread and butter and pitchers of milk and juice. There were pots of tea and coffee. She then went to her father's library where she read and studied.

She had seen the country of course. Picnics by the river, buggy rides, and horseback rides across the fields. She loved riding and had equestrian lessons on the family estate. But she had never camped out, started a fire, or cooked over it. She had never hunted or even fired a gun. The word "civilized" sprang to mind, the result of hard-working engineers, altering what had evolved perfectly. Tools. Tools to hunt with, tools to farm with, tools to build with. Ever changing, ever improving until an artificial world had been imposed on nature. An artificial world with borders to be fought over and resources to be gouged from the earth and fought over. Territories claimed and reclaimed. Tools of war to slaughter enemies ever more efficiently. Alex thought of the inventions of the past century that helped man in his never-ending quest to dominate the natural world. She wondered what the next century would bring. She shuddered at the thought.

Alex arrived at the Geneseo train station in the early afternoon. She had wired ahead, and a carriage was waiting. She didn't recognize the driver who took her bag and held the door for her. Another new hire, she thought ruefully. She wondered how long he would last under Ida Mae's withering supervision.

The day was rainy and there was a chill in the air. Alex was glad of the enclosed cabinet as she listened to the patter of rain on the roof, it mixed with the sucking clop of the horses' hooves on the muddy road and the squish of the wheels. She thought of the coachman, sitting up front in the open, his hat and his cape poor protection against the elements. Funny, she thought, she had never considered such things before she met Beau; she had grown up thinking that a coachman riding in the rain was simply the natural way of things. She again thought of Beau's early life and wondered what he thought of the civilized world. He seemed to fit in just fine; his mother had trained him well. But she also noticed that he didn't accept all the trappings of civilization. He wore un-soled moccasins of dark brown leather, and his clothes were simple and loose fitting. He didn't drink much, smoke or chew. His table manners were impeccable, but he ate little and never reached for a second roll or biscuit. When he spoke, he spoke softly and in measured phrases, his voice never rising. He remained stoically indifferent in every situation, his emotions were never revealed by his words, voice, facial expressions, or body language. She found herself attracted by him in a way she had never felt before. The men she had known were invariably loud, self-serving, and opinionated. Beau seemed to be the antithesis of that, and she found him refreshing. As the carriage bumped jostled along, she suddenly realized that she missed him.

When Alex arrived at the house she was met at the door by Hazel, the housekeeper. Strangely she was dressed in black, the color of mourning. She had obviously been crying. Her eyes were bloodshot and red around the edges. Her face was gaunt, her cheeks hollow and her mouth set in a bitter smile. She held her arms wide as Alex walked up the steps.

"So good of you to come dear," she said. She gave Alex a perfunctory hug. She let go of Alex, turned, and gestured toward the door. "I'm sure you'd like to pay your respects," she said as she opened the door for Alex.

Alex walked in and headed to the parlor. There were the usual bouquets of flowers and cards and people paying their last respects for a man who had been dead to them for a long time. There was a medicinal smell to the room that was not well hidden by the fragrance of the flowers. Alex hated the smell of funerals, and she hated funerals in general. The macabre display of a dead body, with people praying and wishing the family well and saying what a shame it was that another person's life had come to an end. She found it ironic that her uncle's life had come to an end a long time ago, yet here now were people he had once known, offering up platitudes of respect, friendship, and sorrow.

Hazel acted more like the bereaved wife than her aunt, who was nowhere to be seen. As if in answer to Alex's unasked question, Hazel took her aside.

"She's in her salon," she said, a bitter tone to her voice. "Happy that he's finally dead, I'm sure." She hesitated for a moment, then leaned in uncomfortably close to Alex. "She did it, you know," she whispered. "Smothered him with a pillow! That's how I found him; mouth open as if gasping for air. Can't be proved, but I know it!"

She looked around furtively, as if she'd spoken too loudly, which she had. People shuffled around uncomfortably, trying to look anywhere but toward Hazel. Alex guessed that she probably had mentioned her accusation to others. A look around the room confirmed her guess.

"She fired me, you know," Hazel said, now in full voice. "Said I was no longer needed! After all I've done for that poor man! Fired! Pack up and leave, she told me! Well, I'll be damned if I leave before everything is taken care of, I can tell you that!"

Alex was puzzled at Hazel's choice of words, but she attributed it to the ravings of a very distraught woman. Her exaggerated hysteria made Alex think there was much more to the situation than met the eye.

Alex made the rounds, said all the right things, and then made her excuse to leave. She wondered what state her aunt was in, to have not been present at the wake. The whole household seemed to be in some sort of turmoil, and she was glad that her cousin had decided not to make the trip with her little brother and sister. Too long a trip, too much school lost.

Ida Mae was sitting in her salon. She had a cat in her lap and a frown on her face.

"I see you finally made it," she said, the annoyance in her voice evident. "Such an important event!"

"I came as soon as I got your cable," Alex shot back. She had traveled all day and been torn away from her quest to find Clara. She was in no mood for Ida Mae's accusatory tone. "I've done everything you've asked of me and more!" she blurted. "I don't appreciate…"

Ida Mae stopped her with a wave of her hand. She stroked her cat a few times, deep in thought.

"I've been under a lot of stress during the last few days. That woman, Hazel! I had threatened to fire her the day before Jacob died. She suspects me, but I suspect her! I think she killed him out of spite for me. I did fire her immediately after he died. No need for her services anymore. But she refuses to leave, and she acts like she's the bereaved widow. And the rumors she's been spreading! Can you imagine how they make me feel?"

Well, did you? Alex wanted to say. Let's clear the air, Auntie. Everyone knows you wanted him dead and now he is. How convenient! But Alex knew better than to raise such a question. She said nothing and waited for her aunt to continue.

Ida Mae stroked her cat a few more times, calming herself. She cleared her throat slightly and continued.

"Be that as it may, I've come to a certain conclusion about your mission to find Clara. You've certainly proved yourself worthy. Those two agents can continue the search without you. I think it's time you finished your graduate work, much as I think it's a waste of time and money. But you do deserve a reward for your hard work. Now that Jacob's dead I won't have the bank looking over my shoulder as to how I can spend Jacob's money, so I'm willing to finance your schooling. How does that sound?"

Alex was shocked. She had just been offered everything she wanted. Her hard work looking for Clara had paid off. Now she was free to go back to school and finish her studies. But an emotion tugged at her. She didn't like the idea of leaving a job unfinished, plus, she would never see Beau again. That idea bothered her more than she would have thought. She looked down for a moment, thinking. Then she came to a decision. She looked up at her aunt.

"I've decided that I'd like to stay on the case," she said. "We've discovered a lot of promising leads and I feel like we're getting close. Besides, my father's legacy belongs to me and my brother and sister. If we can get it, I can put myself through law school and my brother and sister will have an endowment for when they grow up. Not to mention that we'd have a house to live in. Our own house. You of course would get the share that was in the original will."

"The money means nothing to me," Ida Mae said. "I'll have more than enough once Jacob's will is read. But I see that you are determined, although one must wonder at your real motivation. You wouldn't be getting involved romantically with that uncivilized... detective, now, would you?"

"Preposterous!" Alex said, a little too emphatically. She stuttered slightly. "He's not my type. But more importantly, I'm not his. I'm not too sure that anyone is."

"Well, speaking of your friend, Mr. Starr, there is one little thing I would like you to do for me before the will is read, and I would like him to be here to assist you."

Alex looked at her aunt questioningly.

Her voice was calm, measured, and insistent, "I suspect that Hazel may have had an affair with Jacob before his accident. She may have gotten him to alter the will. That would explain her having smothered him, as I suspect. If so, I would be pauperized. Left without a penny, except for the small amount I've been able to save. I want you to bring Mr. Starr here to help you investigate Hazel Smith. Find out everything you can to challenge the will, should it turn out to have been altered."

She poured more tea, added sugar, and stirred the cup thoughtfully, clacking her spoon.

"Cable Mr. Starr immediately," Ida Mae continued. "I'll arrange a room for him, and another one for you, in the hotel. If you're here, Hazel might get wind of your investigation."

THE funeral was a somber affair, with everyone saying the right things and acting the right way. Gentlemen and ladies, the highest social strata of the city. Ida Mae stood by the door and greeted the well-wishers as they came in. Hazel, still dressed in black, stood by the coffin gently crying, dabbing at her cheeks with a lace handkerchief and looking sadly at the departed.

Alex stood off to the side mostly, keeping to herself. Most of these people didn't know her and were more interested in each other. Always networking, Alex thought. That's the way business is done. But then, after having been introduced to a few of the businessmen, Alex got a shock. Two of the men corresponded to names on her father's Ledger. One of them, a man named Stark, seemed interested in her in a slightly lascivious way. As she shook hands with him, she noticed his eyes glancing down at her chest. He held her handshake a little too long.

"Are you married Mr. Stark?" Alex said, pulling her hand away and clearing her throat slightly.

"I was," he said stepping back a little in regarding her body once again. "Sadly, my wife passed away a few months ago."

"How sad," Alex said. "Sorry for your loss. Was she ill?"

"No, a tragic accident", Stark said. "She collapsed while walking on a path that runs along a little brook behind my estate."

"How awful," Alex said." Did she die quickly?"

"Aneurism, the doctor said. She never felt a thing."

Alex suppressed a shocked gasp. She wondered if he noticed, but then saw that he was glancing at her chest again. He presented her with his card.

"I'm told you're studying to be a lawyer. When you get your shingle come see me. I might have some work for you."

Alex took the card and thanked him. Just then the minister arrived, and the festivities got underway in earnest. Prayers were intoned, a eulogy was read, and people felt led to make complementary comments about the deceased. The coffin was closed and six men, business associates of Jacob's, took it to a waiting hearse. Alex rode to the burial in a carriage with Ida Mae. It was a gloomy, rainy day befitting a funeral. The two of them were escorted to the waiting grave by helpers with black umbrellas. Hazel arrived moments later, riding in another carriage.

"The nerve of that woman," Ida Mae hissed. "Jacob's favorite Landau Carriage! How presumptuous! She's acting like she's the mistress of the house! Look at her!"

Alex did, and saw a woman so consumed with grief that she had to be helped to the gravesite, a helper at each elbow.

The minister emerged from his own carriage, made a few perfunctory remarks, and said a prayer as the coffin was lowered into the grave. A man with a beautiful Irish tenor sang "Amazing Grace."

One of the helpers approached Hazel with a small silver trowel filled with a measure of dirt. She shook her head and pointed to Ida Mae. The man walked over, mumbled an apology, and handed Ida Mae the trowel. Without stepping closer, she threw the dirt in the general direction of the grave. A gust of wind caught most of it and it blew into the minister's face.

He brushed himself off, muttering something unintelligible. Then, he composed himself and smiled indulgently at Ida Mae as if it were his fault. He hadn't been paid yet.

30

As Alex waited at the train station early the next day, she tried to suppress the butterflies in her stomach. Foolish little girl, she thought. She had once had a crush on a professor while doing her undergraduate work; flutters and a red face every time she saw him. He was young, handsome, and affable. Of course, she was young and pretty and the only girl in the class, so their eyes often met. One day, acting on her feelings, she stayed after class with a trumped-up question on a piece of legislation the class had been examining. He listened to her question with interest, told her it was a good question and suggested that she come over to his house that evening to discuss it further. Her heart leapt. For a moment.

"My wife is a little younger than me, and I'm sure she would enjoy your company," he said, gathering his papers into a leather briefcase and looking absently at the wall clock. "We moved here just before the semester started, and she's a little bit bored, I'm afraid. She always complains that she has no friends here."

Alex's spirits crashed mightily, like a train going off a trestle into a deep canyon. Fumbling with her words she begged off the evening meeting. She vowed to never again let her feelings get the better of her. Now, as she stood on the train platform, she felt those feelings rising again. She took a deep breath and imagined Beau getting off the train with his usual taciturn expression and scolding look. He would say something like, "You were being too obvious. When you're waiting for someone, stand back in the shadows and wait for the person to emerge from the train. Let him find you. That's how we do it."

But when the doors of the train opened, Beau stepped out, noticed her, and walked directly over to her wearing a friendly smile.

"And I thought the honeymoon was over," he said. "I guess you just can't get rid of me after all."

He took her arm, and they walked toward the exit. It felt good walking next to him arm in arm, but she tried to remind herself that he was a hired private detective. Nothing more, nothing less. But she couldn't ignore the feeling in her breast. She felt happy. She realized that it had been a long time since she had felt that way. She smiled as they entered the hotel lobby. The clerk looked surprised when Alex asked for the keys to two adjacent rooms.

That night, at dinner in the hotel dining room, Alex and Beau discussed the case regarding Hazel. Alex was convinced that it would be fruitless to try and prove that she had had an affair with Jacob. After all, with no hard evidence, anything they found would only be hearsay. She had read of many such cases failing in court, and with better evidence than they would be able to find. But Beau didn't agree.

"I've worked on a lot of cases like this," he said. "A jealous husband is convinced his wife is cheating on him. A businessman thinks his partner is conspiring against him with a rival. A father thinks his son is secretly dating a girl from the other side of the tracks. Many times, the suspicions end up being unfounded. But the client still pays happily."

"Happily?" Alex said.

Beau smiled. "It brings them peace of mind. We only have rumor, conjecture and innuendo about an affair. There would be no proof. Circumstantial evidence at best. And, as to the will, if it was your uncle's desire to change it, so be it. But, when the will is read, we may find that it hasn't been changed at all. In that case, Hazel will go her merry way and Ida Mae will have peace of mind."

"Then why did you come here to take a case that has no substance?"

Beau gave her a funny look but didn't say anything.

The two of them spent the next day nosing around the city, looking for clues. Alex searched for information on Hazel, and Beau investigated Jacob. Much later, they met to discuss what they'd found.

"Hazel's completely clean," Alex said, starting the conversation. "Middle class, decent education, married young; three kids. The kids grew and moved away; her husband died. To make ends meet, she applied for a housekeeper position through an agency. Ida Mae was the one who hired her. She did her job competently; I found no hint of an affair. He saved her life the day of his accident and she watched over him after that, out of a sense of guilt-driven duty, I think. If he was smothered, it wasn't by her. And I doubt that she convinced Jacob to change his will before the accident, but we'll see about that. Nothing to go on legally if it has been altered, despite Ida Mae's wishes."

"Same with your uncle," Beau said. "No gambling debts, no frolicking in the brothels. Drank, but no more than most men. Certainly not a problem. I did find out one thing, though. I was in the library, checking the trade directory listing for your uncle's business. I found that he was an investor in an acquisition company. It's the kind of company that specializes in the aggressive takeover of small, privately owned companies; you know, squeeze them until they sell or fold. Like J.D. Rockefeller. Cutthroat competition, no quarter asked, none given. People are ruined by the stroke of a pen."

"My uncle was involved in that sort of thing?"

"It was business. An investment company," he said. "He may not have known what the company was doing. These types of businesses are managed by CEOs who do the dirty work. The investors only look at the numbers."

"What has this got to do with the case?" Alex asked.

"Because of the names," Beau said. He withdrew a folded piece of paper from his pocket and handed it to Alex. She opened it and looked at it. It was a page ripped out of a trade directory. It read: "Northeastern Acquisitions."

It listed the CEO and board members. Below that there was a list of major stockholders in the company. She saw her uncle's name, her father's name and many of the names listed in her father's ledger.

"We need to find the CEO of that company and speak with him," Alex said.

"That's what I was thinking," Beau said. "Northeastern Acquisitions is based in Buffalo, New York. I think we should go there. Ida Mae won't miss us, and the will won't be read for a week."

31

THEY SAT NEXT to each other in a comfortable booth in the train, watching the scenery flow by. It was a warm morning, and the windows were open, letting in the smell of the countryside. Hay, manure, earth, and the occasional waft of smoke from the engine. The car rocked gently and, on inside turns, Alex was pushed toward Beau, their shoulders touching. It was a strange sensation, sitting next to so beautiful a girl, Beau thought, although he was convinced that she wasn't aware of her beauty. She was being playful, leaning into him when the car rocked one way and grabbing his arm for support when it rocked the other way. Was she flirting with him, he wondered? He knew that clients sometimes came on to agents. Lonely women attracted to an agent hired as a bodyguard or to investigate a cheating husband. But Alex was a young girl, didn't appear lonely, and probably had a boyfriend waiting for her back at college. But her hand was on the armrest, and it was everything he could do to keep from laying his hand gently on hers.

"What do you do for fun, Mr. Starr," Alex suddenly asked him. He was taken aback by the question.

"I mean, when you're not working, that is," she added. "Unless work is fun."

"I'm usually working, so I don't have time for hobbies, if that's what you mean," Beau said. He thought about her question and realized that he had no real desire to do anything but pursue the man who had killed his family. Working for the Pinkerton agency gave him opportunity to travel the state, searching for him. That and doing the jobs that Cable assigned him took all his time.

"Let me re-phrase that question," Alex said, a sarcastic smirk on her face. "What did you do for fun before you got immersed in your job?"

Beau chuckled. The girl is not to be denied, he thought.

"I used to like to hunt," he said.

"Oh, pheasant, ducks, rabbits, that sort of thing? With a shotgun, I assume."

Beau laughed again. "Yes, I hunted those animals when I was a boy, but not with a shotgun. With a bow. But the most thrilling hunt was for buffalo. There's nothing more exhilarating than riding your fastest horse at full speed, entering a stampeding buffalo herd with your brothers beside you. One misstep and you're dead. You ride alongside a charging buffalo that weighs twice as much as your horse and you let go your arrows, one after another in quick succession." Beau stopped for a moment and looked at Alex. "A buffalo is a hard animal to kill."

Alex regarded him, her eyes wide. It was hard to imagine the taciturn Pinkerton agent astride an Indian pony shooting arrows into a buffalo. A thought occurred to her, "How did you steer your horse while you were shooting your bow?"

"With my knees. And my mind."

Alex furrowed her brow. "Your mind?"

"The horse and buffalo are everything to the Arapaho people. They define us. We learn to ride before we learn to walk. There's a certain connection between a man and his horse that I can't explain. The horse reads your mind and you read his. Without thinking. You are as one."

"My aunt has horses," Alex said. "We could go riding someday. Ida Mae had the horses from my father's estate brought to her stable. They're beautiful animals and I'm certain that they could use the exercise."

Beau told her that he would enjoy that, but he knew that he never would.

Thinking of the hunt had caused him to remember his family, and his loss. His mind became freshly focused on finding the man who had killed his family.

THE train station was bustling when they got off at their stop. It was closing time for most businesses and people were hurrying to catch the last train home. They made their way through the crowd and headed down Main Street. The day was warm, and the city smells of horse manure, uncollected garbage and the sweat of laborers was strong. There was a faint smell of fish from a fish market down one of the side streets. They had to walk several blocks to reach their hotel and, by the time they got there, both were sweating. A red-capped doorman held the oak and brass door open for them. Alex noticed a little brass plaque to the left of the door that read, "Restricted." She glanced at Beau, and he nodded, indicating that he'd seen it too. They walked up to the registration counter.

"Two adjacent rooms reserved for Alexandra Brown," she said. She had wired the money for the room to the hotel before they left. She didn't know it was restricted.

The receptionist looked uncomfortable. He glanced down at the reservation book, cleared his throat, and said, "Just a moment." He walked toward a door behind the desk, opened it, and walked in, closing it behind him. Shortly after, an officious looking man stepped out and walked toward them.

"I'm sorry, Mrs. Brown but..." he looked at Beau meaningfully. "Our company policy states that..."

"Yes," Alex said tersely. "You're restricted. A horrible policy. I can assure you that, if I'd known, I would never have booked rooms with you. I'll take my business elsewhere. I'd like a full refund, please."

"I'm sorry, but our policy doesn't allow refunds on short notice. May I suggest that you take the rooms, but have your companion seek lodging elsewhere?" There was just a hint of a smirk on the man's face as he said it.

"No, you may not!" Alex said hotly. "Mr. Starr is my bodyguard, provided by the Pinkerton agency. "They don't restrict," she added, a look of disdain on her face.

"Well, then it appears that we are at an impasse," the man said, his little mustache twitching slightly. Suddenly Beau stepped forward, grabbed the man's bowtie, and twisted, choking him. Beau held the twist until the man's face turned red. His eyes bulged and he made little squeaking sounds as he stood on tiptoe, trying to relieve the pressure.

"Aloysius Cable is my boss. He is the regional director of the Pinkerton agency; he has a team of lawyers under retainer who will sue your weaselly little ass until you're bankrupt and, on the street, if I'm not allowed to do my job." He let go of the little man go. The man slumped back against the wall, clutching his throat, and wheezing loudly.

"Full refund," Beau said firmly. "Plus, a ten percent gratuity for the trouble you caused my client."

The man opened the cash drawer, counted out the refund, plus ten percent and slid it across the table to Alex. She took the money, opened her purse, and put it in her wallet. She gave the man one more disdainful look, turned on her heel, and walked toward the door. Beau continued to stand in front of the desk, regarding the man coolly. Waiting.

The man cleared his throat, straightened his tie, and said, "I'm sorry. It's the company's policy, not mine."

Beau nodded once, turned, and followed Alex out the door.

"He told you that it's the company's policy, not his, right?" Alex said as they walked down Main Street toward another hotel.

"How'd you know?" Beau said with a short laugh. "But he did apologize, although a little breathlessly."

The next hotel, a block or two away from the first, wasn't restricted. The desk clerk registered them for two adjacent rooms on the second floor. As Alex was getting settled in her room, Beau made a quick but thorough assessment of the hotel. He checked the stairways, hallways and doors and windows. He preferred the second or third floors in hotels; ground level windows were easy to break into. The rooms all had fire escapes, but they were the kind where a metal ladder had to be dropped down. It couldn't be reached from the ground. Reasonably satisfied, he escorted Alex to dinner in the hotel restaurant.

"You grabbed that man's neck faster than a snake," she said between sips of wine. "I thought you were going to kill him."

"He thought so too," Beau said. "A near death experience can be a real incentive to provide a refund."

Alex laughed. Beau was beginning to show a very dry sense of humor. "A ten percent gratuity? You've got a lot of…"

"Balls?"

Alex almost spit out her wine. "Cad," she said when she had recovered. They both laughed.

"I violated one of my rules though," he said, getting serious. "That clerk will definitely remember us both. Also, you registered the rooms under your aunt's name. Anyone following us won't have a hard time finding us."

"If someone is," Alex said. "A big if. He would have had to have figured out the trail we're on. How could anyone possibly? We've spoken to no one, not even Ida Mae knows where we are."

"You're probably right," Beau said. "But I can't trust "probably." Tonight, make sure that your door is firmly locked. Knock three times on the wall if anyone comes to your door but me. In the morning, wait for me to come and get you."

"What if you don't come? Alex said playfully."

Beau gave her a serious look. "Go out through your window and down the fire escape and run like hell."

That night, lying in bed, Alex thought about Beau. She thought about rapping on the wall three times. What would he do? Take her in his arms and kiss her passionately? Or scowl at her like a big brother scowled at a little sister's silly pranks? Probably the latter, she thought. She abandoned the idea.

As she began drifting off to sleep, she thought about Beau's description of the buffalo hunt. How would it feel to be riding free, bareback on a fast horse, chasing a herd of buffalo? She slipped into a dream. In it, she was riding in a thundering herd of buffalo, bareback on a pony. The horse felt good between her legs, responsive and vibrant. As he surged forward, she was bucked up and down, almost erotically. She saw Beau, firing arrows into a charging buffalo, his bare back and chest glimmering with sweat and oil. Suddenly, she fell from the horse into the herd, but instead of being crushed, she was enveloped in the soft fur of the animals. She found herself in a tipi, covered in buffalo furs and, instead of the horse, she found Beau between her legs. She gripped his muscled back and responded to his actions. Their bodies merged into one and she suddenly felt complete. She woke and looked around the room in surprise, a little embarrassed at her dream. But she wanted to be back in those buffalo furs with Beau. She closed her eyes and drifted back into a deep, satisfied slumber

Alex awoke to a soft a soft knocking at her door. She dressed and opened it. Beau was standing patiently across the hall. She felt her cheeks flush as she remembered her dream. He can read a horse's mind, she thought. Can he read mine? He smiled. Sweetly?

"Have you been waiting long?" she said, embarrassed at the hour. The sun was fully up, and the street was alive with the sounds of a new day well on its way.

Beau shrugged. "I've been up awhile. I don't sleep well on flat wooden floors."

"You sleep on the floor?" she said. You should have come over to my bed, she thought, and felt her face redden even further.

THEY had a light breakfast and then set out to find the offices of Northeastern Acquisitions. They had only an address, 305 Clinton Street. After wandering around, looking for the street while trying not to appear be to be looking, they found it. They walked down it, checking the numbers on the old, wood-frame buildings built a half century ago when the city was young. But 305 Clinton was a brand-new structure, with its bright orange bricks standing in contrast to the other buildings. They walked up the steps and opened the door. They found themselves in a tidy waiting room, with several leather chairs and a receptionist behind a maple desk. She was young, bright, and happy looking. Glad to have someone to greet.

"Can I help you?" she said, her undivided attention focused on the new-comers.

"These are the offices of Northeastern Acquisitions?" Alex said, approaching the desk with a smile.

"Oh, no" the girl said. "This is Bennet and Bridges Architecture. We're a new company in town."

Alex looked at the slip of paper in her hand with the address of North-eastern Acquisitions written on it. "This is 305 Clinton?" She knew it was, the address had been on a bronze plaque next to the door.

"Yes, it is," the girl said. "But, like I said, this is Bennet and Bridges Ar-chitecture."

Just then a door opened and a man in rolled up shirtsleeves walked out. "Monica, could you draft a letter to…" He suddenly noticed Alex and Beau. "I'm sorry," he said. "Is Monica taking care of you?"

"Yes," Alex said. "It appears we've come to the wrong address. We're looking for Northeastern Acquisitions."

"That company no longer exists, I'm afraid," he said. "You're not from around here?"

"No," Alex said. The man glanced at Monica for a moment. She was a new hire from out of town and likely didn't know what had happened to the former company either.

"The building that was here before ours was a wood-frame structure, one of the earliest buildings in town, I'm told. There was a fire. Six people perished. The building was a total loss. We bought the frontage and had this building built." He hesitated for a moment. "I'm sorry. I hope none of the dead were kin?"

"No," Alex said. "We were just inquiring about, well, I guess it doesn't matter now."

"No, I guess it doesn't," the man said. "Can I help you with anything further?" He shot a quick glance at the wall clock. He was a busy man, and time waits for no one.

Alex and Beau turned to leave. Then Beau turned back. Not all the way, just far enough to address Monica's boss.

"Was arson suspected at all?" he said. He said it softly, as an unimportant afterthought.

"Why, yes it was," the man said. "Routine. For insurance purposes. The police found no evidence of arson and the company that owned it collected. The same company also sold the land to us. "Lake Ontario Securities," it's called. "CEO's name is Douglass. Based in Niagara Falls, although I suspect it's only a P.O. Box. We did all our business with them by mail."

Beau nodded as if it meant nothing to him. He thanked the man with a tilt of his head, turned, and followed Alex out the door.

"Looks like another dead end," Alex said as they walked down the street toward the train station. "An anonymous company with a P.O. box. Probably not even listed in the trade directory."

"Right," Beau said. "But we did get the name of the company, and the CEO. Douglass was the name of the man who bought the Clifton estate and then defaulted on a loan, remember?"

Alex nodded. The coincidences were starting to mount up, she thought, and Clara seemed to be the one constant that tied them all together. But how to find her? The closer they seemed to get, the more elusive she became.

"I'd like to see the police report on the case," Beau said. "Arson for insurance usually happens at night. No one in the building, no witnesses to see the arsonist. Usually attributed to lightning. But this one happened during the day, and people were killed. The police are usually highly motivated in such a case. If they catch the arsonist, they charge him with homicide."

Alex suddenly stopped. A small smile on her face. They were standing in front of a printing shop. She grabbed Beau by the arm and walked up to the door. The bell above the door rang as she pushed it open. A man, dressed in shirtsleeves and wearing an ink-stained apron, looked up from a pile of printed handbills he was examining. "Can I help you?" he said. Alex said yes and asked him for pen and paper. She printed out what she wanted and paid him in advance. He told her that her order would be ready in an hour. An hour and fifteen minutes later they were standing in front of the sergeant's desk in the police station. Alex flashed her newly printed card.

"Eva Reynolds, Erie Mutual Insurance," she said in a bored, semi-official voice that said: this is just a routine assignment. Beau stood behind her, looking the part of a Pinkerton bodyguard/assistant. The sergeant squinted briefly at the card and then glanced at Beau. He had assessed the situation. This wasn't the first time an insurance adjustor had come to the station.

"What can I do for you?" he said.

"I'm investigating an insurance claim bought my company in a bundle from another company that is going out of business. It concerns a fire that destroyed a building located at…" she looked down at a piece of paper she held in her left hand. "305 Clinton Street."

A cloud passed over the sergeant's face. "Destroyed a building and took six lives," he said. There was a slight tone of bitter anger to his voice that said that the fire was personal.

"Yes, a tragedy," Alex said. "I'm so sorry. It must have hit the town hard."

The sergeant's angry face softened. "The owners were out of towners, but the secretaries and receptionist were local."

"I understand," Alex said softly. She waited.

"You need to see the police report on the fire," the sergeant said.

"Yes, and the investigating officer, if possible."

Another cloud passed over the sergeant's face. "I'm afraid that's not possible. He's no longer with us. But his former partner might be able to help you." He turned to a young cop who was filing some papers behind him. He had been eavesdropping intently.

"Bobby, see if Lieutenant Drake is available, would you?" the sergeant said. He turned back to Alex and Beau.

"You can sit if you like," he said, gesturing towards a line of chairs against the far wall.

Alex thanked him and she and Beau sat down. Beau stared straight ahead, while Alex busied herself with her briefcase. After about ten minutes the young cop called Bobby appeared in the doorway.

"Lieutenant Drake will see you now." He held the door open and gestured with his head for Beau and Alex to follow.

He led them down a narrow hallway with offices on either side. He arrived at Lieutenant Drake's office and knocked lightly on the door.

"Come in," a tired sounding voice said from within. Bobby opened the door and held it for them. They walked in.

The room reeked of stale coffee and cigarettes. Typical cop office, Beau thought. He'd been in enough of them. The way Alex wrinkled her nose and winced told him this was her first visit to one.

"Please, come in," Lieutenant Drake said, rising from behind his cluttered desk to formally greet them. His face told Beau that he hoped that this visit would be short.

Alex showed Drake her card. He glanced at it and invited them to sit. There were two worn chairs facing his desk. They all sat.

"If I could just see the police report on the Clinton Street fire, I'll take a few notes and be on my way," Alex said. Beau, still playing the bodyguard stared at the wall impassively.

Drake had the report on his desk. He handed it across to Alex, who took it and prepared to take notes in a small notebook. She glanced at the title and the investigating officer's name, Lieutenant Henry Winters.

"How long ago did Lieutenant Winters retire?" she said absently, scribbling notes with a pencil.

"He didn't retire," Drake said. "He died."

Alex stopped writing and looked up from her notebook. "I'm sorry, was it sudden?"

"Very," Drake said. "Self-inflicted gunshot wound to the head."

Oh," Alex said. "That's tragic. Again, I'm sorry."

"The whole thing's tragic," Drake said. "Six people killed, a good officer takes his own life out of grief, a town in mourning. It's tragic and the case stinks to high heaven."

"How so," Alex said. Drake seemed ready to unburden himself of his own grief.

"Henry was a good man," Drake said. "Straight arrow, excellent officer. He was our homicide detective and he had to investigate the deaths. One of them was his own sister! An innocent secretary! It tore him apart."

"I can understand that," Alex said. "Must have been hard for him."

"You can't imagine. He went at the case with a vengeance. He wanted nothing more than to catch whoever started the fire."

"The report says that it was accidental, arson wasn't involved."

Drake scoffed and lit a cigarette with a sulfur match. The acrid stink of it was strong.

"We all knew it was arson. Happens all the time. A lightning strike in the middle of the night, total loss, and the owners collect on the insurance. But this was different. The fire started just after lunch when everyone had returned for the afternoon. The offices were on the third floor and the fire exit doors were locked. The fire shot up the building like a chimney. They never had a chance!"

Drake took a long pull on his cigarette and continued.

"A few days later, Henry came into the office smiling. "I found some evidence," he told me. "I think I can prove it was arson, and I think I can find the perpetrator!" He didn't say what it was. He was like that. Played his cards close to his chest." He stopped for a moment and shook his head, a sad look on his face. "His housekeeper found him the next day, slumped in his chair, gunshot wound to the head. They found the report, that report," he gestured toward the police report Alex was holding. "Neatly typed and signed. No reason he would write the report the way he did! No reason he would kill himself! But, as you know, police work is rules driven. Case closed."

"Could someone have forced him to fill out the report and sign it and then kill him?"

Drake again scoffed and shook his head. "If you'd known Henry you would know that no one could ever force him to do such a thing. Others might have done it for a bribe, but not Henry."

"I see," Alex said. "The insurance company sent no adjustor?"

"They did, but the man left after Henry's body was found, and after he read the report. Probably a big payout to the company that owned the building," he added.

"No doubt," Alex said. She made a few more notes in her notebook, closed it, put it into her briefcase and stood.

"Thank you so much for your time," she said. She handed the police report back to him. "And I'm sorry for your loss," she added.

Drake smiled, stood, and wished them a good day.

"Did you smell it?" Beau said as they walked down the street.

Alex laughed. "The stale coffee, the cigarette smoke, or the B.O.?"

"No, the fear. Drake is afraid of something."

"You can smell fear?" Alex said.

Beau nodded. It's a peculiar smell, like a sixth sense. Animals can smell it in their prey as they get close. Dogs can smell it in a human. Humans can smell it too if you train yourself."

"What do you suppose he's afraid of?" Alex said, wondering if she could train herself to smell fear.

"I don't know," Beau said. "But Winter's death sounds suspicious. He was on to something and then killed himself after typing the report and signing it? I sure would like to talk with the adjustor that dropped the insurance claim."

Alex smiled and pulled her notebook out, opened it and showed Beau her notes from the police report. The insurance company that was mentioned in the report was Hallstrom and Runkle Insurance, 215 Eighth Street, Niagara Falls, N.Y." It also listed the insurance adjustor's name, Delbert Coughlan.

Another train ride, another hotel, and, the next morning, another reception room. This one was clean, almost antiseptic. A far cry from the reeking police station. The receptionist was young, friendly, and officious. Beau showed his Pinkerton identification card, his thumb over his name.

"To see Mr. Coughlin," he said. The receptionist seemed a little shocked.

She took the card and went to the door of an inner office. She knocked lightly, opened the door, and went in. A few moments later she came back out, handed Beau his card and said, "Mr. Runkle will see you." She gestured toward the door, which she had left open.

Edward Runkle was a silver-haired man in his late 50s. Tall, reasonably fit for an insurance man, he wore a pin-stripe three-piece suit, a trim gray mustache and round, steel glasses, which he took off and put in his breast pocket as they entered the office. As he stood, he said, "Thank you Miss Olson," with a smile. She turned slightly and smiled back.

"This is Samantha Kramer," Beau said, nodding toward Alex, who held her hands together and looked down shyly. "Our company has been hired by her to investigate the death of her uncle, Roy Kramer, in a fire in Buffalo, New York. Your firm held the insurance on the building and one of your adjustors, a Mr. Coughlin, investigated the case, along with a police lieutenant named Henry Winters. I'd like to speak with Mr. Coughlin."

"I'm afraid that's impossible," Runkle said. He gestured for the two of them to sit and he sat down himself. He pulled his glasses from his pocket, breathed on the lenses, and polished them with a cloth.

"The case is an old one, but I remember it well. It was a big payout. I wanted to fight it on the grounds of arson, but several things happened that changed my mind. Coughlin came back from Buffalo with a copy of Winter's police report that said the fire was accidental; also, the news that Winter's had taken his own life. Coughlin told me that he felt the report was contrived and that he and Winters had discovered some evidence of arson and perhaps the identity of the arsonist. He hoped to connect him with Lake Ontario Securities. But then…" he trailed off for a moment. Beau gave him a quizzical look.

"He disappeared," Runkle said, his voice cracking a little. "His wife came into the office the next day. She was hysterical. She told me that Delbert had gone on his usual evening walk along the river and that he had not come home. Police searched the area but found nothing. We searched his office and his wife let us search their home, hoping to find the evidence he and

Winters had discovered. There was nothing in his office or in his home. He must have kept the information in his head. What evidence he had died with him."

"He died?" Alex said. "You said he disappeared."

"A week after he disappeared his body was found by some fishermen in the lower Niagara. It was in bad shape. Evidently, he threw himself into the current above the falls."

"THE death toll is starting to mount," Alex said with a shudder. They were riding on the evening train to Geneseo with nothing to show from their trip except six people killed in a fire, and two apparent suicides: one by a self-inflicted gunshot and another by a man hurling himself over Niagara Falls.

"Not exactly nothing," Beau said. "I think, after the will is read, we should hook up with Mick and see what he's found."

"When last we left him, he was looking for the bottom of his glass."

32

Mick O'Shaughnessy was sitting at the bar, regaling his new-found friends with his exploits as a Pinkerton. His stories were well-told, exciting, and heavily embellished. Truth be told, many of them were outright fabrications. But the stories kept his little audience enthralled – and buying. He had been keeping a watchful eye on the apothecary across the street for several days, sometimes from his hotel window, but mostly from his seat at the bar. He was waiting for a delivery of Doctor Mulroney's Excellent Elixir.

As he boomed out one of his stories, he saw a wagon pull up in front of the apothecary. It was one of those tall, enclosed wagons favored by Gypsies and medicine shows. Two young men jumped down from the driver's bench, rolled up a canvas at the back of the wagon, and began carrying crates into the pharmacy and then, after a time, bringing other crates out. Mick took out his pocket watch and timed the trips. They averaged two minutes each.

Mick excused himself with a "have to see a man about a horse," and slipped over toward the wagon. He stood in the shadow of a building until the young men hefted another two crates from the wagon and went inside. Quickly walking over to the wagon, he lifted the canvas on the side of the wagon and looked at the painted sign. It read, "Doctor Mulroney's Exemplary Elixir." He took a quick look at the crates. They were filled with light blue glass bottles filled with an amber fluid. He walked toward the front of the wagon, bent down as if he was tying his shoe, and tied a short piece of thin rope around the wheel. He then headed to the livery stable.

The horse Mick rented was old, swaybacked, and unused to the weight of someone his size. It plodded on slowly, with Mick forced to put his heels to it at frequent intervals. He rode heavily, swaying from side to side, smoking his cigar and taking frequent nips from his flask. The afternoon was hot, and insects buzzed heavily around his head, attracted to the sweet smell of alcohol that he breathed out. He puffed harder on his cigar, hoping to discourage the insects, but it didn't work. He was sweating profusely and breathing hard by the time the wagon he was following stopped for the night. He backtracked a little and dismounted among a copse of trees on a small rise. He could see a fire crackling in the distance and could smell food cooking. His stomach rumbled as he realized that the only thing he had had to eat all day had been in liquid form. He made a cold camp and drank off the last of the contents of his flask. He hobbled his weary horse, gave it water and some feed, and rolled himself up in his wool coat.

Mick woke to the chattering sound of a blue jay. He had a headache, and his mouth was parched. He realized that he had not thought to bring any water or food. He groaned and thought about what he would give for a cup of coffee. He unhobbled his horse, saddled it, and heaved himself up and into the saddle. He kicked the horse on the flanks and headed to where the two young men had made camp.

The fire was cold, and he realized that the young men had gotten up at the crack of dawn and moved on. Judging by the sun, it was mid-morning, and they had a good lead on him. People, wagons, and horses were already on the move on the dusty road, but the rope he had put on the wheel identified the wagon track from all the others. He followed it eastward for a while and then, inexplicably, the wagon turned south. After a few miles, it turned west. Mick realized that the two young men were taking a circuitous route to their destination to throw off anyone who might be following. Strange behavior for a simple delivery wagon, he thought.

33

Aloysius Cable lumbered up the backstairs to his office. They seemed to get steeper and taller every day and, halfway up, he was short of breath and wheezing. He'd had a late lunch, and a few too many whiskeys and he was a little light-headed. And that's why he made the mistakes he did. The first one was that, when he noticed a thin line of yellow glowing from under the bottom of his office door, he assumed that his secretary had lit a lantern before she left for the day. The second mistake was that he didn't draw his revolver as a precaution. He clambered loudly up the last few steps, stood panting on the landing for a few moments, grasped the doorknob, turned it, and pushed the door open.

"Hello Aloysius," a soft voice said. It came from a man sitting comfortably in a leather chair on the other side of the room. He was holding a double-barreled shotgun in his lap, pointed directly at Aloysius' chest. But that wasn't what sent a cold, sobering shiver up his spine. It was the man himself; a man he hadn't seen in several years.

"Sit down," the man said. He nodded toward a chair identical to the one he was sitting in. His voice was soft and even, but devoid of emotion. His sharp, bottle-green eyes stared at him like a snake regarding its prey.

Aloysius sat down in his chair. He thought about the loaded pistol in his pocket but knew that he could never get to it in time. He smiled and leaned back slightly in the chair.

"To what do I owe this pleasure, Quint?" he said. He tried but failed to keep a quaver out of his voice, another mistake.

Quint smiled at the quaver. Along with the whiskey, he could smell fear.

"As I remember, you had me dishonorably discharged," Quint said. No tone of accusation or bitterness in his voice. Just business. "After all I did for you. After all the risks I took. Cut loose."

"Your methods were…unsound," Aloysius said. "You were warned, but you persisted. My command was on the line," he added.

Quint smiled again. "Unsound," he said with a slight chuckle. "Those methods served us well in the west, as I recall."

"There was no law in the west. We were at war. But even then, you went too far. The atrocities I had to cover up! You were no better than the savages we were fighting."

"Plenty of our friends lost their hair to those savages. You remember the Fetterman massacre. There wasn't enough left of those lads to scrape into a pail. And the Little Bighorn! I have no sympathy for those people."

"You proved that! That's why you were cashiered. It took a lot to be kicked out of the army in those days."

"The only difference between you and me is that I got caught."

Aloysius shook his head. "For you, it wasn't duty or even revenge, it was pleasure. You liked the killing. And the taking of scalps."

"The scalps I took were equal measure for the ones taken from our compatriots; from the families we found, skewered like fish. Gutted. You saw it."

"I never took scalps, I found no pleasure in it, as you did. And then you turned it into a business. You took captives and sold them into slavery, and not just from the savages."

"Only after I was released from the army. A man has to make a living."

Aloysius looked at his old compatriot and shook his head sadly. He knew how this was going to play out.

"This doesn't have to happen," he said. "If it's money you want…"

"Money? I can get all the money I want, anytime. No, I want something more important."

"What is it you want from me?"

Quint chuckled again. That strange, hollow chuckle that sent shivers up Aloysius' spine. He knew there was no way out, but still he had to try. He had to play his part, like some kind of macabre play, the ending already written.

"A simple consideration," Quint said. "A courtesy, if you will, between two men engaged in the same line of work. My client would like to see the Comerford file. The agent in charge. The particulars. The actions taken. The findings. Give it to me and I'll be on my way."

It was Aloysius' turn to laugh. "If that's all you wanted, you wouldn't be sitting here with a shotgun pointed at me. You would have made an appointment and we would have discussed your request."

"And you would have told me no, as you will now. But I thought, considering our past relationship, I would give you a chance."

"Give up two of my most trusted agents? You knew I would never do that."

And that's when Aloysius made his last mistake. Quint raised an eyebrow at the revelation that there was more than one agent on his trail. He just had to figure out who the second one was. That shouldn't be too hard, he thought as he pulled the triggers on the shotgun.

34

ALEX WAS NERVOUS as they arrived at the Brown estate in the late afternoon. She knew that her aunt, convinced of an affair between her late husband and housekeeper, would be expecting verification of her theory. When told otherwise, Alex fully expected to receive a scathing lecture on her incompetence. Ida Mae didn't like to lose. A valet held the door open for them, and another valet escorted them up the steps. When the big oak and brass door was opened, they were greeted by a loud shouting argument between two female voices. Alex recognized them both, it was Ida Mae and the housekeeper, Hazel. Both stopped when they noticed Alex and Beau in the doorway.

"Oh, goodness," Ida Mae exclaimed. "Now see what you've done!" She shot a hot look at Hazel, then looked back toward her visitors.

"I'm so sorry about this brouhaha," she said in a steady and controlled voice. "Please come in." She turned back to Hazel.

"If it wouldn't be too much trouble, perhaps you could arrange some refreshment for our...my guests."

Hazel stood defiantly; her arms crossed. She had been officially fired and had no intention of doing her former boss' bidding. But she did remain silent. Her argument with Ida Mae had no place in gentle company.

Ida Mae glared at her. Hazel glared back. Alex broke the tension.

"Perhaps we can all sit for a moment. We have news. I'll get some wine."

Ida Mae and Hazel sat, facing each other in two of the room's many overstuffed chairs. Beau walked over to the window and looked out disinterestedly. Alex went to the bar, selected a bottle of claret and three glasses. She opened the bottle and poured a generous measure into each glass. She handed them around and sat, roughly between the two feuding old women. "Cheers," she said brightly, holding her glass up in a toast. The two women sat sourly, but each lifted her glass and tilted it slightly toward Alex. Each took a sip.

"Some new information has come to light that might interest you," Alex said, looking first at Ida Mae, and then at Hazel.

"As you probably know, Hazel, Beau and I were tasked with an investigation into your relationship with Jacob Brown. Ida Mae was concerned that you and Mr. Brown had been having an affair and that you had convinced him to change his will. I investigated you, Hazel, and Mr. Starr investigated Mr. Brown. There was a suspicion that Mr. Brown may have been blackmailed into changing his will. Outstanding gambling debts, drunkenness, cavorting in bawdy houses, those sorts of things. Things that you may have used to convince him to make changes.

Hazel glared hotly at Ida Mae but said nothing. Ida Mae sipped her wine self-righteously, certain that her suspicions would soon be confirmed. An altered will could then be contested in court.

Alex cleared her throat and said, "Neither of us found anything about an affair, dalliances, gambling debts or blackmail."

Hazel broke down in tears while Ida Mae gasped, a shocked look on her face.

Hazel looked up and dabbed her eyes. She looked directly at Ida Mae. "I'm sorry," she said. "I never meant for it to happen, but, taking care of him every day, and feeling guilty over the accident, I found that I had developed feelings for him. We never had an affair. I hardly knew him before the accident."

Ida Mae fanned herself with an ornate hand-fan and stroked her cat thoughtfully. "Be that as it may, the fact remains that someone smothered

Jacob with a pillow." She looked at Hazel and said, "I know that you have accused me, but I say that it was you!"

Hazel started to rise, flabbergasted at the bald-faced lie. Beau stepped up to the group

"Neither one of you could have killed Jacob Brown," Beau said. "His brain was dead, but his body was alive. Neither one of you could have held him down long enough to smother him, and there would have been signs of a struggle. Hazel found him unresponsive, as if he died in his sleep."

"Then how...?" Hazel began.

"He was murdered by someone else. I don't know why. But I bet, if his body was exhumed, you'd find twin needle marks on his body, and necrosis all around them."

The two old ladies looked at him blankly.

"Think about it. How did John Comerford die? We found the same thing with another man, William Clifton. Heart attack brought on by a snakebite."

"Coincidence?" Ida Mae said, clearly not convinced. "There are snakes about in the fields. Rattlers, copperheads, others. But no snake could have gotten into Jacobs' room, let alone his bed."

"I lived in a region that had nineteen different types of rattlesnakes. I knew of a lot of people who got bit, usually through carelessness. But none of them died. Rattlers usually don't inject venom when they're warding off what they see as a predator. It's called a dry bite. When Clara brought John Comerford in, the doctor said he was non-responsive. His leg was badly swollen, and necrosis had set in. I think he was murdered by someone who injected him with a massive amount of snake venom. I think the same thing was done to the others, including Jacob."

Ida Mae looked shocked. "You're saying that someone slipped into this house, while I was sleeping, and injected Jacob with snake venom?"

"It's not that hard to do if a person knows how to do it. Locks, security, watchmen, and codes mean little to an experienced man. He can come and go like a ghost, with no one the wiser."

All three women shuddered at the thought.

Beau walked back over to the window and stared out. He didn't want to tell them who he thought the murderer was.

THE next day was the reading of the will. An official from the bank, a man named Caleb Newsome, had been designated as the executor. He arrived at the Brown estate at precisely ten o'clock. A small group gathered in Jacob Brown's office, where the safe containing the will was located. The sheriff arrived shortly thereafter, acting as a witness. There was Ida Mae, Hazel, Alex, and Beau, who had been invited by Alex and approved by Ida Mae. The discussion of an intruder the night before had thrown a scare into her, and she liked the idea of having a private bodyguard around.

Without undue ceremony, Mr. Newsome, a dour, short man with a receding hairline and expanding girth, took a slip of paper from his pocket, and approached the safe. He squinted at the paper through steel framed spectacles and turned the knob to the appropriate numbers. There was an audible metallic click as the lock was released. He twisted the lever and pulled the safe's thick door open. He extracted a bound document, squinted at it, and showed it to the sheriff. The sheriff looked at it and then at the small gathering.

"The seal is unbroken," he said.

Newsome held the document up for everyone to inspect. He then pulled the covering apart, rending the wax seal. He pulled the will out. It was written on one piece of standard legal paper. He held the sheet up to his face and read it.

"I, Jacob Brown, being of sound mind and body, hereby bequeath my holdings and properties to the Ontario Securities Company."

Ida Mae gasped, and Hazel fainted. Beau, standing next to her, caught her, and eased her into a chair.

"Impossible!" Ida Mae shrieked. "It's a forgery!"

Caleb Newsome examined the document and then showed it to the sheriff.

"It's signed by Jacob Brown and notarized."

Beau looked at Alex, whose eyes widened at the information. Both knew that the Ontario Securities Company was the company that had profited by the insurance on the fire at the offices of the Northeastern Acquisitions Company. The same company that sold the city lot to the architecture firm. Everyone remained in stunned silence for a while. Caleb Newsom glanced nervously at the sheriff, who simply shrugged. Finally, Alex spoke.

"How does the money, stocks, bonds and deeds get transferred to the Ontario Securities Company?" she asked the executor.

He furrowed his brow, pursed his lips, and thought for a moment.

"We will send a note to the company's address informing them that an endowment has been bequeathed to them. They will then send us a confirmation letter and request that the pertinent documents, the deed for the estate, stocks, bonds, and other holdings, be sent to them. We'll have to locate the address of the office first, of course."

Beau shook his head. "The company's address is a Post Office box in Niagara Falls. They'll send you instructions to liquidate all the holdings included in the endowment and deposit the money in a numbered account. They do have a representative, a certain Mr. Douglass, but I'm sure the name is a pseudonym."

"They'll sell the estate?" Ida Mae said, clearly troubled. "Where will I live?"

"They'll not only sell the estate," Alex said. "They auction off everything on it and in it. As they did with Father's."

Ida Mae looked at the sheriff imploringly. "There must be something that can be done. Something to stop or delay the process."

The sheriff sadly shook his head. He had been a friend of Jacob's and hated this kind of duty. "Only a judge, having been shown sufficient evidence of a forgery, could issue a stay. I'm afraid I don't see any evidence that this will has been forged. I'm sorry."

He then got a very contrite look on his face. He cleared his throat.

"I'm afraid you'll have to vacate the premises, Ida Mae. Only your personal belongings." He looked over at the executor. "Can we give her ten days?"

"I think ten would be fair. It will take a few days for the letter to get to the Ontario Securities Company, and another few for them to respond. It'll take me a few days to draw up the papers," he added, casting a hopeful look toward Ida Mae.

The sheriff turned his attention to Hazel, again a sad look on his face. "I'm afraid the household staff, grounds men and field workers will also be terminated. I'll appoint a caretaker in the meantime. The animals will have to be impounded and moved to a stable. But that will take some time also."

Ida Mae, Hazel, and Alex shared looks of sadness and concern.

The executor and the sheriff bid the group farewell, gathered their documents, and left.

"Perhaps we could go to the Post Office in Niagara Falls," Alex said. "You know, stake it out and see who collects the company's mail."

Beau shook his head. "We don't have the company's P.O. Box number, and the executor wouldn't be able to tell us. We don't know what Douglass looks like and, in any case, he might have someone check it for him. We could be sitting there for days."

"What do you suggest we do?" Alex said. She too was starting to sound desperate.

"I think we need find out what Mick O'Shaughnessy has been up to."

35

MICK O'SHAUGHNESSY WAS miserable. It was raining, his back and butt hurt from riding the sway-backed rental horse, he had no food and had run out of whiskey. But he trudged on, following the wagon loaded with empty cure-all bottles as it clanked its way west.

Strange, he thought. The wagon had started out heading east, then it had turned south and then again, after many miles, it had turned west. Evasive action. But why? Wagons loaded with goods traversed the state every day, with no one paying them much mind, if any mind at all.

He made cold camps at night, sleeping wrapped in his wool coat and listening to the horse chomping on grass. "At least you've got something to eat," Mick said to the horse, who ignored him. It occurred to Mick that humans might be the least evolved animal. Horses could always find grazing, and it was free, at least to the horse. Wild animals hunted or were hunted, living on what nature provided. Domestic animals were fed and sheltered until they were used for work, slaughtered for food. Or shorn of their fur, blithely ignorant of their condition. Humans could think about their situations. Worry about them. Overthink them. Be disappointed in outcomes. They could regret decisions made in the past. Animals only lived in the moment. For them, there was no past or future; only the now.

The third day dawned cold and rainy. A typical central New York summer, Mick though wryly. He broke his wet little camp, rued his lack of food, whiskey, and dryness, saddled his horse, unhobbled it and mounted. He followed the wagon's trail rather than the wagon itself, not wanting to be seen. His clever trick of tying the rope to the wheel served him well; there was no mistaking the wagon's trail.

Somewhere around noon he came to a crossroads. The wagon went straight but a sign pointed north to the little burg of Medina. The lure of food, drink and dry clothes proved too much. He turned north, reasoning that he could easily pick up the trail the next morning.

It was late afternoon when he reached the little farming village. He found a general store where he bought some dry clothes, a big piece of cheese, a sausage, a loaf of bread and a bottle of whiskey. He dropped the horse off at the livery stable, rented a room in the town's only hotel, stripped off his sodden clothes and flopped on the bed with his food and whiskey.

He awoke the next day late in the morning with a pounding headache. He looked over and noticed that he had drank the whole bottle of whiskey. Crumbs and chunks of sausage and cheese lay all around him. Groaning, he dressed in his dry clothes and went downstairs to the hotel dining room where he ordered coffee, toast, and eggs.

Feeling much better after the food and several cups of steaming black coffee Mick paid his bill and walked over to the telegraph office.

"Heading west from Medina," the message read. "Wagon heading toward Niagara County. Am following." He got a different horse from the livery stable – the first one was worn out. He bought another bottle of whiskey, some food, a canvas tarp, and fresh cigars from the general store, and set out south toward the crossroads he had left the day before. When he got there, he got an unpleasant surprise. The rain had washed the tracks out of the road. Mick took the western road, traveling blind and hoping to pick up some trace of the wagon.

As he traveled, Mick thought of Beau. He would have been better suited for this kind of pursuit; Beau grew up on the plains and would have been better prepared. He would have not gotten soaking wet and hungry and then been forced by circumstances to leave the trail. Beau would have stayed on the trail, eating a little jerky and camping under a tarp that he would have wisely brought along in the first place. As it was, he was back in Geneseo, investigating an alleged affair with that cute little law student. Mick was angry with himself for letting Beau go off on a mission that he was much better suited for; after all, Cable had put him in charge of the case. But, at the time, Mick thought that sitting in a bar and watching for a delivery had seemed uncomplicated and easy. Plus, he knew that Beau was eager to rejoin Alex, even though he tried hard to hide it. So, while he sat a horse and scanned the road for signs of the elusive delivery wagon, Beau was happily snooping around Geneseo with Alex.

Mick traveled west for the rest of the day, hoping to find a sign of the wagon. The weather had cleared, the road had dried and, just outside of Middleport, he picked up the track of the wagon again. "I'd rather be lucky than good any day," he said to the horse with a smile. He lit a cigar, took a drink from his newly filled flask, and rode on.

He followed the wagon tracks to another crossroad. Surprisingly, instead of taking the back road, the wagon turned directly toward the city. "Ah," Mick said to the horse. "We have a final destination. Now we'll find where the bugger's home base is. He looked at the name of the city on the sign and turned his horse down the road toward it. I'll have to send Beau and Alex another telegram, he thought.

He never made it to the Telegraph office; it being late in the day, the office was closed. Instead, he went directly to the nearest bar he could find. He had seen the wagon trail and followed it to where it turned off on a lane leading toward an estate set high upon a hill. He would have to wait until well after dark to investigate. Until then, well, there was the bar.

A few hours later, sometime after sunset, a boy approached him with a note. He looked at it, tossed the boy a coin and finished his whiskey. He walked out the back door and into an ally, where, the note had promised, there would be a man with news from Aloysius Cable. Instead, he found five men with clubs, knives, and the look of ill intent on their faces.

"Only five of you?" Mick said, brandishing his shillelagh.

He dispatched the first man with an overhead strike to the top of his head. There was a loud crack as the man's skull shattered. His body sank to the wet ground like a sack of rivets. A swipe to the right took care of a second man and a swipe to the left took care of a third. A fourth man advanced with a knife. Mick brought his shillelagh down on his forearm, breaking the man's wrist. A forceful swipe up broke his jaw, and another swipe down crushed his skull. The fifth man, the last man standing, hesitated, and looked like he was ready to turn and run.

"Not likely, mate," Mick said. His blood was up, and he didn't intend to have one of his attackers at large. He hit the man first on one side of his head and, as the man fell, hit him again on the other side. The man collapsed on the ground next to his dead compatriots.

"That's five more notches on me trusty shillelagh," he said as he turned to head back into the bar. But as he turned, he was confronted by a sixth man who plunged a long knife deep into Mick's belly and yanked upward, lifting Mick onto his toes. The last thing Mick saw was the man's face, contorted into a cruel grin. He breathed into Mick's face as he worked the knife.

"I knew that five wouldn't be enough," he said in a hollow whisper.

36

Two days later, Alex and Beau arrived in Albion. They went directly to the telegraph office to see if there was a cable from Mick. The last communication they had gotten was, "in pursuit, heading west." There was no subsequent message.

"Yes, there is a message for you, Mr. Starr," the telegrapher said. He handed him the telegraph. "Heading west from Medina," the message read. "Wagon heading toward Niagara County. Am following."

"There's also a package, the telegrapher said. The man took a small item, about the size of a shoebox, from behind the counter. It was wrapped in brown paper and tied with twine. He gave it to Beau, who signed for it. It was addressed to Beau Starr. There was no postmark or return address on it.

"It was here when I came into work this morning," the man said. "There was a note with it. I have it right here," he picked up a slip of paper from his desk and handed it to Beau. It read, "A small gift for Mr. Starr from Mick O'Shaughnessy."

Beau showed the note to Alex. He took the package and walked over to a counter on the opposite side of the room. Alex followed; a questioning look on her face.

"A gift from Mick," Beau said pensively. He took the lid off, looked at the contents, and gasped. He staggered backwards, clearly shocked.

Alex craned her neck to look into the box.

"Don't look!" Beau exclaimed. But it was too late.

Alex looked into the box and saw an animal pelt of some sort, red, like a fox. She pondered it for a moment, then she realized what it was. She screamed in horror, put her hands to her face, and sank to her knees, sobbing.

Beau grabbed her by the arm and put his other hand around her waist and guided her out of the room. He took her around the side of the building where she sobbed into his chest. He put his arms around her comfortingly. Inside, the curious telegrapher walked over to the shelf, looked in the box and vomited.

Later, after she had sobbed herself out, Alex drank some water that Beau had brought her.

"I've never seen anything so barbaric," she said, her voice shaking.

"I have," Beau said. "The man who did this did it to my whole family. I've been looking for him ever since. But now it looks like he's found me."

"Why would he send you that... that thing?" Alex said, still horrified at the aspect of the contents of the box and what it meant for their compatriot, Mick O'Shaughnessy.

"He wants me to know that he knows who I am, and that he knew who Mick was. And that he knows what we are up to."

"Did Mick tell him about you? Do you think he... tortured Mick into telling him?"

Beau shook his head. "I knew Mick well enough to know he would sooner die than give up another agent. It's a code of honor with us."

"Well, it's clear that he wants to scare us off. It's worked on me. There's no amount of money worth confronting a man capable of such a hideous crime.

I'm just as capable, Beau wanted to say. He thought about his campaign of revenge against Quint's gang and wondered again if he was more like Quint that he cared to admit. He didn't speak for a moment. He was thinking.

"The scalp isn't a warning," he said finally.

Alex gave him a questioning look.

"It's bait. He wants me to come to him."

"You can't possibly be thinking of confronting a man like that!"

"It's all I've thought about for these last years. I'm going, that's for sure, and you're coming with me!"

"No, I'm not!"

"Yes, you are. You have to."

"Why?"

"Because if you don't, and I can't find him right away, you'll be the next bait."

37

Back in the hotel room, Beau seemed strangely happy, Alex thought. She was scared to death. She had never seen a scalp before, and the fact that it was from a man she had known was even more disturbing. But Beau went about the task of outfitting them for their journey with a sense of enjoyment that puzzled her. She finally confronted him about it.

"Yes, I feel happy," he said. "I'm nearing the end of my quest. The fates are pulling me forward toward my destiny. I have been adrift for so long. Forever. And now I feel as if I've reached the final shore."

"The Odyssey?" Alex said, surprised that he knew the tale.

"Something like that," Beau said. "Every journey, every quest, has its beginning, its middle and its end. Like a chess game, only this game is final. Winner take all."

"And if you lose, I will be the take all," Alex said. She felt as if she were chips in a poker game. Something to be won or lost, regardless of the outcome for her. Beau seemed to read her mind.

"Quint and I have been like ghosts dancing in the dark," he said. "He has been hunting me as I've been hunting him. He knows that a reconning is coming. He heard what happened to his compadres."

"What happened to his compadres?" Alex asked, alarmed at the implication.

Beau realized that he had said too much, and he chided himself for it.

It wasn't that he was ashamed of what he had done, or that he was worried that Alex would think less of him. It was out of concern that Alex was being drawn into a dark world where evil was a prominent inhabitant. Her sheltered, pampered life would never be the same, and he felt responsible for the change. He wished now that he had never taken the job; another agent could have done it and Clara would have gotten away scott-free, with no one the wiser. But he knew that he could no more change the past than he could stop the sun from rising. He looked at Alex, who was waiting for an answer, and probably dreading it. He realized that she was going through the same emotions that he had experienced the day he had discovered his ruined village: shock, disbelief, agony, grief and then, finally, acceptance and a determination fueled by an anger that would never go away. He knew that killing Quint would never bring his family and Mick back and it would never bring back the carefree lightheartedness of his youth. Yet it had to be done and Alex would have to be a part of it. There was no other way.

His lips were tight, and his face became a mask as he looked at Alex intently.

"They were evil, and they had to be stopped. The details are unimportant. Lives were saved. We can't bring your parents and Mick back, but we can stop him from killing others. And now that he knows who we are, we can stop him from killing us, for killing us is what he intends to do."

Alex shuddered. She felt as though she was caught between two inexorable forces with no escape. Like a small boat caught between two ships, she would be crushed no matter which way it went. She looked at Beau and wondered if she was starting to see a side of him that she didn't know existed.

Beau walked Alex to a park and got her to sit on a bench. She was shaken by what she had seen in the box and couldn't get the image out of her head. He walked over to a nearby vendor and got her something to drink. Her hands shook uncontrollably as she accepted the bottle. It was sarsaparilla and she was only able to get a few sips down before she gave it back to Beau. He sat down next to her, took her shaking hand, and spoke to her in calming tones.

"I'm sorry that you saw what you saw," he said. "A memory of something like that stays with you forever. It will haunt your dreams. But you must try to put it out of your head. You must try to focus on the new task ahead."

She shivered and wiped her eyes with a hankie. She took another sip of the sarsaparilla and looked into Beau's eyes. She saw a great sadness there. He had told Jeremy and Anna that his village had been destroyed in a raid while he was away on a vision quest. What had he found when he got there? She realized with a start that the raiders probably hadn't buried the bodies but simply left them where they lay. What sort of visions haunted his dreams, she wondered?

Beau looked away. What Alex had seen was but a small fraction of what greeted him when he returned to his village. The memory of it returned, drifting into his consciousness like a mist rising from a dank swamp, swirling around him, engulfing him with its sights, its sounds, and its smells.

The village was utterly destroyed. Amidst the smoldering tipis lay the bodies of his family and friends, some horribly mutilated and all scalped. He found his mother and his father and brother. He found her. He fell to his knees and cried to the heavens. He took out his knife and, consumed by guilt and grief, prepared to join them. But then his grief was replaced by an emotion more powerful than he had ever felt. It was rage. Rage at the men who had done this. If he was going to die, it had to be in battle against them. Their tracks were new and would be easy to follow. He would take as many of them with him as he could. But as he stood to mount his waiting horse, he realized that he first had to take care of the bodies. He knew that he would not be coming back, and he didn't want them left to the coyotes and vultures.

He went to each one individually, said a brief prayer and tossed a bit of dirt into the wind. As he did, the pattern of the attack became apparent. They had come in the night, silencing the guards and dogs with knives. They then entered the tipis, dragging the slumbering occupants out by their heels where they then set upon them with pistols and knives. The villagers fought bravely and killed several of the attackers. There were three dead men next to his father. Next to his mother, there was a man with a knife in his throat. The strange thing was that the dead attackers had also been scalped.

It took several hours to tidy the bodies and bury them. The dead attackers he dragged off to a gully where he dumped them unceremoniously, spitting on each of them as he heaved them over the side.

When he returned to the village, he was surprised to find an old man sitting astride a sway-backed burrow. He wore a raggedy serape, a broken sombrero, a long white beard, and a sad smile.

"I am Pascal DeLeón," he said in a rheumy voice that bordered on a whisper. "And I thank you."

"For what?"

"For doing my job." The old man swept his hand over the remains of the village. "Scalp hunters did this, as they did to my village. They are Comancheros. They raid from Comanche territory in the Ilano Estacado and then return there. They are friends of the Comanche and trade between them and Mexico. When they get enough scalps, they will take them to Ciudad Juarez. There, they will be paid a bounty for each scalp by a Hacendado who lives in a closely guarded Hacienda at the edge of the city. They are led by one of the worst creatures to be called human. His name is Quint and few who have seen him have lived to talk about it. Some say he is a ghost who only appears at the moment of death. Others say that he is the devil incarnate, traveling the land to mete out punishment to all he encounters. But I know him to be a vicious killer who enjoys killing more than life itself. He murdered my family while I was away. I tracked them, hoping for a chance to kill as many as I could but, as you can see, I am a powerless old man whose purpose is to follow the band and clean up the corpses they leave behind. And that is why I thank you."

"These are my family and my people," Boh said. "It is for me to bury them, not some strange old man."

"How is it that you survived the raid?"

"I was on a vision quest."

"Did you have the dream?"

Boh nodded.

"Tell me about it."

He did.

"The buffalo are disappearing," the old man said. "Farther east, they are all gone. Harvested for their hides. The wolf is your spirit animal, and the eagle is your spirit bird. The locomotive signifies the arrival of the white horde that will cover the land with its buildings, roads, and fences. The way of the Arapaho will be no more."

"How do you know these things?"

"I was a shaman to my people before the scalp hunters did to them what they did to your people. I was away, seeking my own power – as you were. I wear the guilt of not being killed with them."

"I see," Boh said. "Can you tell me what my purpose is now?"

The old man laughed. But it was a sad laugh. "Only your power can tell you that."

"What is my power?"

"You must pray for it. Have you consulted your spirit stone?"

"Of course, but it has told me nothing."

"Look at it again," the old man said. But put the image of your village out of your head. Look past your grief to find your purpose.

Boh took out his crystal and looked intently at it. It seemed to almost glow in his hand. He wondered if he was still feeling the effects of the cactus he had eaten. Then it came to him: It wouldn't do to track them from the rear and then attack them; they would be prepared for such a pursuit. Instead, he would go to Juarez and be waiting for them there. Boh was determined to set off on a new quest, one that would bring retribution to the men who had butchered his family. When he looked up, the old man was gone.

In the ruins of his tipi, he found his bow and a quiver of arrows secreted under a pile of old furs. He realized that his mother must have hidden them for him as the raid started. He also found a leather sack with some pemmican and dried buffalo jerky. There was also a small, embroidered leather purse containing a small quantity of gold coins. His mother's legacy. He knew then that his mother, rather than save herself by running off while his father fought, had sacrificed herself so that he would have food and weapons. She had then run out into the compound and died fighting.

Continuing his search, he found her little pile of books. It was her library, compiled over the years and from which she had taught him everything that he knew. He looked through the collection and selected one book, which he put in his bedroll. It was a bible. In it, he hoped to find clues as to the strange beliefs of the Whites. He said one last prayer over the graves, mounted up and rode off.

Boh traveled south for many days, across some of the harshest land on the continent. Along the way he picked up scraps of information about the notorious scalp hunters he was pursuing. In every village he heard stories of the gang that appeared in the night, slaughtering entire villages and scalping everyone, only to disappear like ghosts. News of Boh's quest spread among the tribes, and he too seemed to pass into legend. It was said that he had big medicine. He was allowed to pass through dangerous territories unmolested. As he traveled, he avoided the Comancheria, where the last of great horsemen of the southern plains still roamed, friends of the scalp hunters.

As he approached the farthest white settlements, he began to shed his Arapaho identity like a snake sheds its old skin. He cut his braids and trimmed his hair. He traded his buffalo fur for a broken hat, ripped pants, and a ragged shirt at the homestead of terrified German immigrants.

He rode into Durango several days later. A couple of drunken cowboys made fun of his appearance and made rude comments, but he paid them no mind. He booked a room in a seedy little hotel and signed the register as Beau Starr, his new white man's name. Beau was the anglicized form of his Arapaho name and Starr he took from his one love, Morning Star. Visions of her came to him often, haunting both his dreams and his waking hours. He had a bath and went to a general store where he bought two sets of pants and shirts, a sturdy coat, and a new hat. He went to a barber and got a haircut. Shorn and dressed in white man's clothes, he wondered what his friends would have thought of him. Feeling extremely uncomfortable, he went to the hotel dining room and ordered dinner. He took pains to use the table manners his mother had instructed him in, once again thanking her memory for the training that he had once thought so pointless.

He went to his room and tried to sleep in the bed, but it was uncomfortable. He tossed and turned for hours on the soft, feathery mattress. Finally, he got out of bed and curled up on the floor.

In the morning he went to the livery stable, got his pony and led him out of the station and into the bustling, dusty street. He went a tack shop where he bought a used, single-tree saddle, a horse blanket, a metal bit, leather reins and a set of saddle bags. Those items he carried to an empty corral. He led Rabbit into the corral and snubbed him to a post. Rabbit didn't like it, but Beau calmed him by talking to him in Arapaho. He threw the blanket over his back, which he was used to. Then came the saddle. Rabbit nickered, snorted, and stomped. He splayed his legs and leaned back. His ears swiveled back and forth rapidly, and his eyes bulged wide. His tail flagged. Beau patted Rabbit's withers and got him to lower his head. He spoke to him softly. Rabbit responded by calming somewhat, but he was still clearly unhappy with the saddle and new bit. Beau continued to talk as he untied him. He went to Rabbit's side and vaulted up into the saddle. Rabbit was used to Beau and accepted him. He put Rabbit into a gentle gait, circling the corral. After a while, he put him into a canter and then into a gallop. Soon Rabbit forgot about the saddle and became his usual self, enjoying the ride. Not so for Beau, who was unused to the saddle himself. The new clothes were stiff and constraining. This is going to take some time, he thought wryly. But he gradually got used to the new gear and rode Rabbit out of the corral and into the countryside. He once again felt the freedom of the open plains. Riding free, as his father's ancestors had for countless generations, living off the land. No, living with the land. Following the buffalo, killing, and using what they needed; no more. Nothing wasted.

He thought ruefully about the white hordes that had come to the land. A new tribe. But they were different, they didn't follow the customs of the land. They built houses and plowed the earth. And when they were raided men in blue coats would march out seeking vengeance. They didn't discriminate between the tribes that had raided and those who had not. All were guilty in their eyes, and all were killed for the crimes of a few. Worse, the whites brought horrible diseases that wiped out whole tribes, leaving behind a few survivors who had no way to function as effective hunting bands. Finally, the whites sent men among the buffalo herds to slaughter them. They took the hides and the tongues and left the rest to rot in the sun. Beau wondered how soon another, even more vicious tribe would come and take the land from the whites. But he knew that, until that time, the whites would rule the land. And he had no choice but to join them.

Beau camped out on the open plains that night. He shot a rabbit with his bow and cooked it over an open fire. He slept under a blanket of stars. It was more comfortable on the ground than on the feather bed or the hard floor of the hotel. He realized that he was trading one lifestyle for another. It was not something of his choosing, it was something thrust upon him, whether by the spirits or the fates or just happenstance, it was happening. His mother had foreseen the inevitable change and had prepared him for it.

He crossed the border into Mexico several days later and entered Ciudad Juarez on a dry dirt road choked with dust from the many travelers, moving into and out of the city. He passed hundreds of campesinos, carrying their loads of corn and vegetables in woven baskets balanced on their heads or packed onto small burros. They paid him no mind. The day was hot and dust devils swirled on the road, dancing among the heat waves emanating from the sunbaked earth. The air was thick with the earthy smell of sweat, animals, and manure. Beau took his hat off and wiped his sweaty forehead with a dirty bandana. He wrung the sweat out of it and wrapped it around his neck. He tied it with a loose single knot and put his hat back on.

The city was a cacophony of shouting voices, barking dogs, cackling chickens, and laughing children. Smoke rose from a dozen charcoal fires next to brightly colored kiosks where travelers could buy street food. Music from several mariachi bands blended in atonal harmony. A woman sang an aria on a small stage near the gushing central fountain. She was tall, dark-haired, and beautiful and a crowd of half-drunk campesinos stood and listened, drinking mezcal from earthen jugs. Beau dismounted and tied Rabbit to a post next to a water trough in front of a dusty cafe. He drank deeply with a loud sucking sound that reminded Beau of walking across a muddy field, the thick slurry gripping his feet as he struggled to pull each foot free. He walked through the arched doorway of the cafe, ducking to not bump his head.

Inside, the room was dark, noisy, and smoky. He walked up to a plank bar and ordered some tamales and a cervesa, which tasted impossibly refreshing. He drank it and ordered another.

A fat old woman in a dirty, torn apron brought a steaming pile of tamales to him on a wooden plate and held out her hand for payment. "Cuanto cuesta?" he said. She told him and he paid. He walked over to an empty table and sat in a rickety chair with a ladder back. He ate tamales and drank the second beer. He looked out an open window with a clear view of the square. It was a good vantage point. He watched the people moving to and fro on the plaza, with special interest on those entering the city from the north. He watched for a long time. Finally, the fat old woman in the dirty apron approached him. She spoke in broken English.

"Will there be anything else?"

Beau looked around the café, which had become quite crowded. She needed the table.

"Donde es un hotel?" he said. She nodded towards the fountain.

"Al otro lado de la plaza," she said. He thanked her and she told him to go with God.

Beau left the café, unhitched Rabbit, and led him to a stable. He paid the stable hand for a week's stay with grooming and feed. He paid an additional fee to store his saddle and blanket. He took his saddle bags and the wrapped bundle that contained his bow and quiver of arrows. He walked across the dusty, noisy plaza to the hotel and booked a room with a window facing the plaza. He paid for a week and walked up the creaking stairs, found his room, unlocked the door, and entered.

Inside he found a single bed, a wooden table with a wash basin and pitcher of water and a sitting chair. He placed his saddle bags and bundle on the bed, walked over to the window and drew back the curtain. As he had hoped, the window looked over the plaza and the main road into town. He moved the chair to a position next to the window, sat down and memorized the layout of the plaza, kiosks, stores, stables, and buildings. Then he slept.

For the next three days Beau watched the plaza and the road. He saw vendors, dignitaries, casual visitors, vaqueros, and hundreds of campesinos carrying their produce. But the ones he was interested in were the Comancheros; motley groups of traders who went into the Comancheria to trade with the Comanches. They were hard-bitten bands comprised of Mexican bandits, American outlaws, half-breeds, and renegade Indians. They came in small groups, trailing horses and captives and towing wagons loaded with buffalo hides and items taken by the Comanches in their raids. Beau noticed that these groups headed straight for a hacienda at the edge of town where they entered through a large oak door, guarded by armed mercenaries. When they came out, they headed for the bars in town where they spent all their money on tequila and women. Days later, hungover, and broke, they loaded their wagons with trade goods, mounted up and rode north.

On the fourth day, sitting in the café, he saw them for the first time. The men and horses matched the descriptions given to him by the people he had encountered on his journey. They looked like all the other Comanchero groups that seemed to use Ciudad Juarez as a headquarters. Scruffy, unshaven, red eyed and wearing arrogant sneers as they pushed their way through the throngs of people in the bustling city. They led a two-wheeled wooden cart towed by a brace of sturdy plow horses. Behind it, on ropes, staggered several bedraggled captives, on their faces, looks of resignation.

Beau noticed the leader, the man called Quint. He was exactly as an old woman had described him: large, barrel-chested with black hair and a white scar running down the side of his face. He rode a black horse and had a long string of scalps hanging from the pommel of his saddle. The group headed straight for the hacienda at the edge of town where guards opened the large doors and waved them in. The doors closed behind them, and the guards took up their positions again.

After an hour or so, the Comancheros emerged on foot, carrying bottles of mezcal and staggering, already drunk. They headed for the line of bars and taverns on the eastern side of the plaza. People in the plaza gave them a wide berth as they proceeded. They entered the bars like ants filing into their anthills, swallowed up by the dark holes of the doorways. Beau went into the hotel and slept; it would be several days before the Comancheros ran through their money and headed out again.

Beau woke before dawn, fully dressed, as usual, and went to the window. The plaza was empty and dark and silent except for a few dogs who scampered across the dusty ground looking for scraps. There were a few lights on in the bars, the candles flickering eerily as if holding some dark vigil for those yet to be dead. It had been four days now and Beau expected the Comancheros to be nearing the end of their debauch. He checked his kit, put on his hat, and slipped out of the room.

The café was dark, but the door was unlocked, and Beau walked in. A light was on in the kitchen, and he could hear the old woman slapping tortillas. He stepped up to the doorway. The old woman looked up at him without stopping her task. "Desayuno?" she said.

"Si."

"Huevos con salsa y frijoles?"

"Si, por favor. Y café."

It was a ritual that had been repeated for the last several days. He knew that the Comancheros, when they left, would leave early, heading toward the relative safety of the Comancheria from where they would begin their raids again. He took up his usual position by the window and casually scanned the plaza. The old woman brought him his breakfast and he thanked her and paid her. As he ate, a thin ribbon of red light appeared on the eastern horizon. A rooster crowed, then another. The dark from just a few minutes ago gave way to a gray gloom A few vendors drifted onto the plaza, bearing the tents and supplies for their kiosks. The sun came fully up and promised to bring another hot day. As the plaza came alive, Beau noticed several of the scalp hunters walking unsteadily toward the hacienda. Shortly after, several more emerged from the strip of bars, heading in the same direction. Beau finished his breakfast, went to the hotel, got his kit, and walked over to the livery stable. Rabbit nickered when he saw Beau. He had been well fed and groomed.

"You're not going to have him shod? The stablemaster said as Beau saddled the pony. He was a friendly old man who insisted on speaking in broken English, even though he knew that Beau spoke Spanish. It was a matter of pride with him. He had taken good care of Rabbit, so Beau answered.

"I don't like shoeing my horses, it's not natural."

The stablemaster nodded. "Indians don't shoe their horses. This one acts like it has some Indian in it." He looked at Beau as if appraising him, his eyes traveling up and down his face. The ruddy skin, the high cheekbones; but then the aquiline nose and the blue eyes. The man seemed to suddenly realize what he'd been doing and looked away. He said sorry.

"You've got a keen eye," Beau said with a laugh. He tightened the latigo on the saddle and slipped the end in the keeper. "I don't like saddles much either," he said as he leaped up into the saddle without putting his foot in the stirrup.

"I see you don't like boots much either," the old man said, regarding Beau's moccasins.

Beau laughed. "You don't miss much, Viejo."

"Good luck with your quest, whatever it is. I can tell that it is a just one. Vaya con Dios."

"Gracias, but God will not be with me on this quest."

"When one fights evil any means to an end is justified and therefore, como se dice, bendecido."

"Blessed," Beau said. "Maybe not by your God, but it will be by mine."

The old man nodded that he understood and wished him good luck anyway.

As Beau rode out of town, the old woman from the café stepped out of the doorway and gestured to him. He rode over to her, and she handed a bundle up to him. She told him that it was something to sustain him on his journey and that she hoped that he would find that which he was seeking. She said that she could see that he was a very young man with a great weight on his conscience. She hoped that he could lift that weight but that the past is the past and nothing can change it.

Beau thanked her and nodded reverently when she made the sign of the cross. She also said vaya con Dios. He thanked her for the food and the good wishes and took the northern road out of town, following the Comancheros at a discrete distance.

A few hours later he saw that the Comancheros had turned off from the main road and followed a scant trail, overgrown and rarely used. It ran east toward the Llano Estacado, the vast dry plain that was the home of the Comanche. He followed the tracks up an arroyo with steep, rocky cliffs on both sides. He proceeded slowly, the arroyo was a perfect place for an ambush, and he was a little surprised that no one had been left behind to see if they were being followed. But then, what kind of a fool would ride blindly into Comanche territory in pursuit of a group of vicious Comancheros?

After a few miles the arroyo spread out onto a treeless, grassy plain. You could see for miles in the shimmering heat. Beau dismounted and walked his horse to present less of a silhouette. He made a wide loop around the trail, stopping every so often to scan the plain with a spyglass he had bought in the general store. Nothing. He rode on in the open country, keeping well to the south of the trail. Finally, while scanning the plain, he saw a glint of metal reflected off the afternoon sun. He looked closer and saw a small column of dust, kicked up by the wagon and the riders. Knowing that they would be stopping soon for the night, Beau swung even farther southward until he was shielded by a group of low lying, rocky hills. He rode up and into them, dismounted, hobbled his pony, and crept up to a ridgeline that overlooked the trail. From his vantage point, hidden among some rocks, he could see the Comancheros making camp. They started a large fire and seemed oblivious to any danger. But then they were the friends of the Comanches and under their protection. In the distance he could hear them arguing about something, their voices slurred by mezcal. Beau went back to where he had left his pony and began making preparations.

Beau unsaddled Rabbit and put the saddle, saddle bags and his bedroll in a neat pile. He took off his hat, shirt and pants and took his leather breechclout out from his saddle bags. He regretted having cut off his braids but made do with some bear grease to smooth his hair with a part down the middle. He tied a red bandana around his head and then took out some war paint from the saddle bags. He carefully painted Rabbit and then himself. He became his former self again, Boh'oohoox – the mountain lion. Taking his bow out from its wrappings, he strung it, tested its tension, and then checked his quiver. He had thought about using pistols, but they only had six shots apiece. His quiver was full of arrows, and he could fire them faster than he could fire pistols. As a kid, he'd been in contests where the goal was to fire all the arrows in your quiver before the first one hit the target.

When he was ready, he sat and began to pray as he had on his vision quest. It was going to be eight to one and he didn't expect to live. He was close enough to hear the drunken Comancheros arguing in their camp.

"If you didn't want to come along, you shouldn't have," one of them shouted. "We don't need a fat-assed beaner like you anyway, Gordo."

"You shut your mouth, or I'll shut it for you," the man called Gordo shouted back in thickly accented English. Two loud clicks could be heard as the man cocked his pistols.

"Put your pistols down, Gordo!" another voice commanded. His voice was high pitched and squeaky, and it cracked often when he spoke. "And you shut up, Mushroom!"

Several of the men could be heard laughing. To Beau, it sounded like the name Mushroom was some sort of insult. The Comancheros went on with their drunken argument, oblivious to Beau's presence.

"Only thing I'm sayin' is, we already made our decision," the man with the squeaky voice continued. "If'n y'all want to second-guess that, well, it's just too late. Ana-way, chasin' that son of a bitch could only end two ways, either we never find him or, if we do, we're sorry we did."

There was a murmur of agreement from some, although Gordo grunted his displeasure. "You are many in number, yet you fear one man. Of him I have no fear. A man is a man, nothing more."

Beau, sitting cross-legged, began praying out loud, slowly transforming his prayer into his death song. It rose in pitch and timbre, rising into the night sky. The stars, representing all the great warriors of the past, looked down upon him.

He unhobbled Rabbit, mounted and galloped hard toward the camp, shouting his Arapaho war cry. The men in the camp were caught by surprise. They had heard the death song, but only thought it to be some lone Comanche, ready to join his ancestors. But when they heard Beau's Arapaho war cry, they began staggering to their feet, looks of panic on their faces. They fumbled for their rifles and pistols. But before they could form a defensive line Beau was upon them, firing arrows into their midst. One man fell, screaming. Then another. A couple of men managed to get shots off, but Rabbit was too swift. Beau circled the encampment again and again, firing all the while. More men fell, skewered by the lethal arrows that came relentlessly, like a rain shower of death. The last man standing broke and ran for his horse, but, as he mounted, he caught an arrow in the back of his neck. He fell awkwardly, landing on a jumble of rocks.

Beau circled the encampment twice more, looking for targets. He found none. He stopped his pony, dismounted, and ran to each body looking for signs of life. When he got to the fallen rider, he found the man still alive, a pistol next to his outstretched hand. He kicked it away.

"No need," the man said. "I'm paralyzed. My neck's broken." He coughed and turned his eyes on Beau. "Who are you?" he managed weakly.

"My name is unimportant. You won't need to remember it. But think on this in your last mortal moments. I am justice. I am the avenger for those you tortured and killed. Among them were my parents, my brother, my cousins, uncles, aunts, and friends. My world. It was taken by you and now I'm taking yours."

The man laughed, a sneer on his face. The action caused a coughing fit that brought up blood. "You killed me and all the others, but that won't bring your family back. They died because they were sheep, and we sheered them."

Beau grabbed the man by the face roughly and twisted, causing the man to scream in pain. "Where is your leader? Where is Quint?"

"Quint? Why that son of a bitch stole our money and lit out. You'll never find him. And if you do, you'll be sorry that you did."

"Where did he go?" Beau twisted again.

"Agggh!" the man screamed. It was an angry scream, full of hate and vitriol. More choking and blood.

"Tell me!"

The man tried to spit. Beau twisted again.

"All right, all right. Let go!"

Beau did.

"Alright. Quint sometimes talked about a brother that he had somewhere in New York State. Said he was rich and owed him. Said he'd go there someday to collect. That's all I know."

Beau nodded. He stood.

"Wait!" the man said, a touch of panic to his voice. "Don't leave me here like this. The coyotes will come and eat me alive!"

"I've seen what coyotes do to the dead," Beau said.

"Please! I was only the interpreter and scout. It was the others done your family. Do me quick like, so's I don't have to suffer."

Beau reached down into the man's coat and pulled out a leather sheaf. He opened it. It was full of highly sharpened knives of different sizes and lengths. "You think I didn't find out things about your band in my travels? You're Leggatt, a white captured in a raid and raised by the Comanche.

Each man in your group had a specialty. Yours was knives, and you liked to torture people before you scalped them alive. I saw your work firsthand."

Leggatt groaned as Beau walked away, then he started crying and blubbering curses. As Beau got farther away, Leggatt began begging. Beau stopped and examined the sheath of knives. There were two excellent throwing knives inside. He took one, turned and threw it hard at Leggatt. Leggatt went silent. Better than you deserve, Beau thought as he went back to retrieve the knife. He realized that the man had most likely visited great pain on some of his friends and family. Still, he couldn't bear to leave a man like that, alone and paralyzed on the prairie, food for coyotes and vultures.

BEAU rode back to Ciudad Juarez. He'd washed off his warpaint, donned his pants, shirt and hat and saddled his pony. As he entered the city, he encountered Pascal DeLeón, sitting on his burrow, watching him approach.

"Your being alive tells me that the scalp hunters are dead," he said.

Beau nodded. "All but one. Quint ran off with their money and headed north. I will go there and find him."

"Be careful that he doesn't find you first," the old man said. He sat his burro, pondering for a moment. Then he said, "If you are heading north, why did you come back to Juarez?"

"The Hacendado is the one who pays bounties for scalps. I plan on preventing him from doing that anymore."

"How do you plan on getting past the guards?"

Beau showed him.

The old man nodded. "When you leave, make sure you ride fast. He has many friends in Juarez."

Beau thanked him and rode off.

TWO men were talking, well dressed, and groomed. Brandy and cigars. A fireplace. They were talking business in Castilian Spanish. As Beau entered the room the two men turned in surprise.

"Which of you is the Hacendado?" Beau said, using Castilian Spanish himself.

"Who are you?" one of the men demanded. "How did you get in here?" He shouted towards the door. "Enrique!" But the guard couldn't answer.

"You're the Hacendado," Beau said flatly. "The one who pays for the scalps."

The man didn't answer. "Enrique!" he shouted again. He looked menacingly at Beau. He started to stand, and Beau could see a pistol in a shoulder holster inside his jacket. The man raised his hand as if to go for it. The other man began standing also. Beau forestalled their actions with two quick throws of the two knives he'd taken off Leggatt. The Hacendado fell forward onto the floor and the other man fell backwards into his chair. Beau walked up to them, checked their pulses, and retrieved his knives, wiping the blades on the Hacendado's silk shirt.

Beau took two kerosene lanterns, unscrewed the tops, and sprinkled the kerosene around the room. He struck a match with his thumb and tossed it. The kerosene caught, flared up, and began spreading around the room. He left the room, stepped over the dead guard whose name had been Enrique, and walked back down the hall. He walked out the front door, nodded to the guard, untied his pony, and walked it to the main gate. He pounded his fist on the door and one of the guards who stood outside opened it. He mounted, tipped his hat to the guards, and rode off. As he left town, he could see the hacienda behind him, engulfed in flames.

38

THAT NIGHT, BACK in the hotel, Beau told Alex of his plan, "We won't use trains, hotels, or restaurants for the trip. Quint will be looking for us at those places. He obviously ambushed Mick. He will likely be looking to ambush us. He knows who we are, but he doesn't know what we look like. You're a young, precocious ingenue and I'm a hired Pinkerton agent. That's who he'll be looking for. We'll be something entirely different."

The next morning, the first stop was the general store. Beau outfitted himself in the clothes of a local farmer. Tan pants, a little too short, a checkered shirt, a khaki coat, and a slouch hat. Alex got high button shoes, a frilly dark skirt with petticoats, a puffy white top, and a vest. To top it off, she got a white bonnet that she absolutely loathed.

"Obedient little housewife? I won't do it!"

"Trust me," Beau said. "We need to play the part. It's the only way to get close unnoticed."

Beau left Alex to get dressed while he attended to other business. "Meet me out back when you're done," he said. She finished dressing, put her old clothes in a carpet bag and went out back where she waited on a bench, uncomfortable in her new clothes, and her new role.

A little while later, Beau showed up, driving a buckboard wagon and a big grin. He stopped, set the brake, and got down.

"Milady," he said, gesturing toward a rough plank seat set on rusty springs. He helped her up into the seat with exaggerated gentility. She sat, folded her hands on her lap, and stared straight ahead. Beau flicked the reins and the horse snorted and began clip-clopping forward. Soon they were in the indiscriminate crush of travelers on the dusty road.

It was a warm day, and Alex felt confined and hot in her new outfit. She held a handkerchief to her nose and mouth against the dust, pollen, and stench of manure in the fields. The rough plank seat was uncomfortable and her back and bottom were already starting to ache. Worse, Beau seemed to be enjoying her discomfiture immensely as he maneuvered the wagon down the rutted, bouncy road. She glared at him from time to time, between sneezes.

Soon they found themselves on a two-track lane in the countryside. Few people were on the road and the dust had subsided. The sun peeked through the shady trees lining the lane. Quaint farms, orchards and wheat fields could be seen in the distance. They stopped for lunch at a meadow.

Alex climbed down from the wagon, stretched, and adjusted her uncomfortable clothes. Beau unhitched the horse, hobbled it, and turned it loose to graze and drink from the brook. He got a blanket from the bed of the wagon and spread it on the grass. Then he got a lidded basket, set it on the blanket, and took out a loaf of bread, a large piece of cheese wrapped in cheesecloth and a sausage.

"Lunch," he said with a smile. He took a large container out of the basket, uncapped it, and took a long drink. He handed it to Alex.

"Porter," he said. "It's a dark ale preferred by teamsters, farmers and, you guessed it, porters.

"You're in a mighty fine mood," Alex said as she accepted the ale. She was terrified at the prospect of hunting down a man depraved enough to take another man's scalp and send it in the mail. But Beau's good spirits were reassuring and even a little contagious. She relaxed a little and took a tentative sip of the porter. It was sweet, thick, and delicious. She took a longer sip and wiped her mouth on the back of her sleeve.

"Is that how it's done?"

Beau laughed lustily and took the ale from Alex. "Now you're getting the hang of it." He took another long drink and wiped his mouth on the back of his own sleeve.

Alex sat down and looked at the food. "No silverware? Napkins? Plates?"

Beau laughed again and pulled out his belt knife. He cut off a slice of bread, a piece of cheese and some sausage, put it on a piece of cloth and handed it to her. "This is how it's done. He cut off a piece of sausage, bit into it and chewed contentedly.

Alex shook her head and laughed. "You're on a mission to face one of the most dangerous men on the planet, and you act like a kid on a picnic."

"We are on a picnic," he said. "Right now, at least. When we get closer, the danger will increase, and we'll need to be especially watchful. But for now, we might as well enjoy the picnic."

Alex broke off a piece of cheese, bit into it and started chewing. She had to admit that it was delicious. She looked around at the meadow, with its burbling brook and shady trees and decided to enjoy the moment.

They traveled for the rest of the day, heading west. Toward evening, storm clouds appeared in the western sky. "It looks like we're going to get some weather," Beau said. "We should probably make camp early."

Alex nodded, aware that there were no hotels nearby. After a time, Beau pulled off the road onto another meadow, unhitched and hobbled the horse and took a large roll of canvas from the wagon. It was rolled around some long wooden poles.

"A tent?" Alex exclaimed. "We're sleeping in a tent?"

"No," Beau said. "You're sleeping in a tent. I'll sleep under the wagon."

He set the tent up, started a fire and then walked off toward a wooded area.

"Keep the fire going," he said over his shoulder. "I'll be back in a little while."

Alex tended the fire, moved her bedroll and belongings into the tent and then sat waiting.

A little while later, Beau came walking up to the campsite with two rabbits. Without saying much, he sliced the rabbit's skin with his belt knife and pulled the pelt off in one fluid motion. He did the same with the second rabbit, skewered both with sturdy sharp sticks and placed them on small branches he had cut to a "Y" and stuck into the ground on either side of the fire. He sprinkled them with a little salt from a pouch and adjusted their position. He put several ears of corn, still in their husks, at the edge of the fire. He sat down to tend the food and took a long drink of porter.

"So, this is camping," Alex said, accepting the container of porter. Night had fallen and cicadas were buzzing in the trees. A light breeze had sprung up, causing the fire to flare and spit with the fat from the rabbits. The wood smoke and aroma of cooking food was enticing. Alex realized that she was quite hungry, not having eaten since their lunch.

"This is nothing, compared to the feast we had after a Buffalo hunt," Beau said. "Everyone dancing and singing, the hearts, tongues and livers sizzling over fires. We were up to our elbows in blood, skinning the big beasts." He looked over at Alex, who had a shocked look on her face.

"Sorry," he said. "I got a little carried away there."

"Not at all," Alex said. "It sounds wonderful. A different world from the one I live in."

Beau smiled and took one of the rabbits off the fire. He handed it to Alex. "Careful, it's hot." He took an ear of corn out of the fire and peeled back the husk. He sprinkled some salt on it and handed it to her. "Hold it by the husk."

Alex took it and blew on it slightly. It smelled wonderful and she took a tentative bite. The kernels burst in her mouth and some juice ran down her chin. Beau handed her a cloth.

"Not a lace napkin, but it'll do," he said. He began biting into his rabbit judiciously, careful not to break the fragile bones. Alex did the same.

"This is amazing," she said. "I've had hassenpfeffer but never rabbit cooked over an open wood fire. Delicious."

"It is good, but nothing compares to buffalo tongue. It's a flavor you never forget."

"You eat tongue?" she said. She wondered if he was pulling her leg and gave him a dismissive smile. Sure you do, it said.

Beau wiped his mouth daintily on a cloth. "We ate tongue raw, and roasted steaks of hump, shoulder, and tenderloin. The rest was either boiled or cut into strips for smoking. Nothing was wasted. We used the bones for tools and the hides for clothing and furs. The moccasins I wear are made from cured Buffalo hide."

Alex glanced at his moccasins and shook her head. What would Ida Mae think about her feasting on freshly killed game at a campsite with a man raised by plains Indians.

They finished their meal and tossed the remains off into the darkness. The wind had picked up even more and they could feel the first stinging droplets of rain. Alex crawled into the tent and looked out expectantly at Beau.

"Good night," he said with a smile as he unrolled his blanket and crawled under the wagon. Alex shrugged and pulled the tent flaps closed.

During the night, the rain came down in sheets. Lightning and thunder rent the skies. Alex, awakened by the chaos, looked out at Beau, sleeping under the wagon. He was clearly awake and clearly soaked. She opened the flaps on the tent and beckoned to him. He approached the tent, wrapped in a wet blanket and shivering.

"Are you too proud and stupid to come in out of the rain?" she said.

Beau crawled in and discarded the blanket. He stripped off his soaking shirt and accepted a dry blanket. "Thanks," he said, his teeth chattering.

"After living in the wild for so many years, I can't believe you would let yourself get in such a state."

Beau laughed, glad to be out of the downpour. "No, I would be in a tipi, warmed by a few willing squaws."

Alex laughed and then kissed him hard on the mouth. Enjoy the picnic, she thought.

Alex woke alone, feeling a healthy glow. It had been years since she had been with a man. But then it had been nothing more than drunken fumblings with a sometimes boyfriend in college. Memories long forgotten. Beau had proved to be virile yet tender, and she longed for him to return to the tent. Almost as she thought about it, the tent flap opened, and Beau came in smelling of wood smoke and carrying a blue porcelain pot of steaming coffee, two porcelain mugs, and two sticks wrapped with golden baked dough.

"Sabrechets," he said. "Napoleon's cavalry, when on the move, would ride into an infantry camp and have the cook mold dough on their sabers. They'd stay on their horses and cook the dough over an open fire."

He poured coffee into the mugs and Alex peeled a piece of dough off the stick and ate it.

"Delicious," she said. She sipped the hot coffee and ate more dough. She hadn't realized what an appetite she had worked up.

After they ate, Beau looked at her with a sly smile.

"The roads are too muddy for travel just now. We should wait for them to clear."

Alex smiled back and gently pulled him to her.

After, they lay in each other's arms, each thinking their own thoughts. Alex broke the silence.

"Have you been with many women?" She asked. She had suddenly become concerned about prostitutes, and the diseases they carried. Beau liked to stay in ratty old hotels, and those hotels were known to be frequented by prostitutes. Who knew if Beau didn't avail himself of their pleasures. He certainly seemed experienced.

A said look came over his face. "Only one," he said. "Her name was Morning Star. I took her last name when I entered the world of the whites. She was killed by the man I pursue."

He said no more, and Alex was sorry she had spoken. It occurred to her that there was much more to Beau Starr than she knew. She wondered if he would ever tell her. She wondered if she would want to know.

By midmorning the rain stopped, the sky cleared, and they were on the road again. The road was muddy, and the horse's hooves made sucking sounds as the wagon squished along. At one point the road ran beside some railroad tracks. As a train steamed by, Alex imagined herself sitting in one of the seats, looking out at the countryside and at the people going about their business. Farmers in the fields, people walking the roads, people driving wagons, and people riding horses. She suddenly realized that she had sat in that seat and had watched a couple in a buckboard wagon. Now she was in that wagon, and her business was to find and confront a man who was evil incarnate. She shivered at the thought.

"What do you suppose is the connection between Quint, Clara, and the cure-all?" Alex said a little later. They were passing a large cornfield. Crows and pheasants scurried about. The sun dappled the lane through the shady trees. There was a constant buzz of insects enlivened by the recent rain.

"Hard to figure it," Beau said. "But Mick got close. Maybe he even found the connection."

"Close enough to get him killed," Alex said with a shudder. She was tempted to suggest they give up the quest. She laughed to herself at the thought. Just live the life they were pretending to live. A farmer and his wife, tending a little farm. Selling apples, and vegetables at the local farmer's market. Again, Beau seemed to read her mind.

"Somehow, he knows everything about me," Beau said. "How he found out I don't know." He hesitated for a moment and then looked directly at Alex. "He knows everything about you. If we run, he'll find us. He won't rest 'till he does. Quint is the type of man who lives by the feud. It's not about money, it's not about pride; It's not even about vengeance. It's about some kind of twisted moral code."

"Moral code?"

"Not moral in the sense that we know the concept. Moral in his own sense. A code he lives by. Sick and insane as it is."

Alex shuddered again. She felt trapped, caught up in something that would not let her go. Something clinging. Something drawing her toward a fate unknown. Like a river, sweeping someone toward a waterfall. Sharp rocks at the bottom? Of course, she thought ruefully.

They traveled all afternoon, always heading west. The mud in the road dried and became hard. The wagon bounced and jostled, reminding Alex how uncomfortable the seat was.

"How much farther?" Alex asked, grimacing in her discomfort.

"The last telegram I got was from Medina," Beau said. "I thought we'd start there. He said that he took a night off. He must have put his horse up in a livery stable. I'll look at his horse's prints and be able track him."

Alex looked at him questioningly. "It's been days since he's traveled. It rained in the meantime. People have traveled the roads. How can you possibly track him?"

"Mick was a big man," Beau said. "He would sit his horse heavily. The horse will have left a deep print. Horseshoes are individually made, each by the local blacksmith. No two horseshoes are the same. They're like snow-flakes. Once I see the horseshoes that are on the horses in the livery stable, I'll be able to find Mick's on the road."

Amazing, Alex thought. She had heard about Indians being good track-ers, but she thought it was just stories and legends.

"Everything leaves a trail," Beau explained. "The obvious things are prints in mud or in the loose dirt. But a person or animal moving through a field or in a forest leaves a trail. Like a boat leaves a wake, something mov-ing disturbs the grass, the dirt, the leaves, and branches. It is said among my people that a good tracker can follow the path of a hawk flying over a flat rock."

Just then Alex heard the scree of a hawk and looked up. There, circling high above, was a red-tailed hawk looking for prey.

"Do you see it? It's trail?"

Alex watched the hawk for a while then turned and shook her head no.

Beau looked at her and laughed. "Neither do I," he said.

Alex punched him playfully on the shoulder. "Very funny," she said.

That evening they camped at another meadow by the brook that the road followed. Beau made camp while Alex gathered firewood. Beau lit the fire and then went off to the brook. He arranged some rocks in an inverted u shape. He then did something even more curious. He stripped off all his clothes and dove into the brook with them, washing as he swam in a deep pool. After a while, he stepped out of the brook, walked up to the campsite, and hung the dripping clothes on some branches. He then sat down next to the fire, completely naked and acting like it was the most natural thing in the world to do.

"You should wash too," he said. "You've been in those clothes for a while. They put a lot of starch in new clothes and the water will take the stiffness out of them."

Alex thought about it for a minute, and then thought why not? She walked down to the brook stripped off her clothes and plunged into the same pool Beau had swum in. A little embarrassed at her nakedness, Alex turned her back to the campsite; she didn't hear Beau approach from behind. He wrapped his arms around her and kissed her on the neck. Alex kissed him back and soon they were thrashing in the cold clear water, oblivious to anything but each other.

Later, dried and dressed, Beau made preparations for dinner. He walked off into the woods and, an hour later, returned with his satchel bulging. He pulled a Dutch oven from the bed of the wagon and set it in the coals of the fire. As he pulled items from the satchel, he talked.

He took some green shoots from the bag. They had long white tips. "These are ramps," he said. "Wild onions." He cut them up with his belt knife and tossed them into the pot, where he had some clear brook water boiling. Then he took some light brown objects from the bag. They had short, stout stems and oblong caps. "These are morels, wild mushrooms that have an earthy taste." As he cut them up and tossed them into the pot, they released a heady aroma that mixed with the fragrance of the cooking onions. Next came purslane, chickweed and various herbs and plants that Alex had never heard of and would never remember.

Beau put the lid on the Dutch oven and scooped some coals onto the top with a couple of pieces of bark. He then took a canvas bag down his fish trap and, with much splashing, threw several silvery fish into the bag.

Alex laughed as she watched, and soon Beau was fully soaked again. But he came up from the water with a bulging bag and a broad grin on his face.

"I've lost my touch," he said, laughing. "A few got away."

He swiftly gutted the fish with his knife, put the fish on skewers as he had done with the rabbits the night before, and placed them on forked sticks over the fire. He pulled out another skin of thick brown ale, took a long drink, and handed it over to Alex. She took it and took a lusty drink herself.

"I've never seen fish caught that way," Alex said. "Come to think of it, I've actually never seen fish caught before at all." She laughed and took another long draft of ale.

They laughed and talked about nothing as the food cooked. Alex felt relaxed and safe with Beau, but she worried about what the next few days would bring. The thought loomed in her mind like a gathering storm cloud.

Beau read the worry on her face. "I know you're worried, but you're safe with me. Quint doesn't know what I look like, and he doesn't know what you look like. He'll be expecting us to come west on trains, stopping at every town and city and asking questions. He probably paid some conductor or ticket master or porter to watch for two people traveling west, asking questions about a big red-haired Irishman. He knows your profile, if not your face. A young, rich, spoiled ingénue would never be caught dead riding in a buckboard and camping in the wild."

At spoiled, Alex slapped him on the arm playfully. "We'll see about spoiled later," she said.

They ate their dinner by the fire. Alex had attended many gourmet dinners in her young life but had never had food so rich and succulent. They drank more Porter and then, when they had finished, Beau pulled a white root from his pocket. He cut a piece off with his knife and handed it to Alex.

"Ginseng root," he said. "It's what the powder I put in my water comes from." He cut a piece off for himself and chewed it with gusto.

Beau gave the root a funny look, sniffed at it, and wrinkled her nose.

"It's a little bitter, but it's good. It'll give you energy."

Alex gave Beau a sly look and bit into the root. "You'd better eat more," she said. "You're going to need it."

They made love long into the night. Not furtive and rushed like the night before, but tenderly, lovingly, and passionately. It was well toward morning when they finally fell asleep in each other's arms.

Beau woke well before dawn, as was his habit. Some internal alarm woke him. He didn't carry a watch but if he checked one, he knew that he woke at precisely the same time every day. Without fail. The tent was pitch-black, but he could almost see Alex lying there, smiling contentedly. He undid the tent flap, carefully peered out at the darkened campsite, and slipped out. It was a cloudy night and a slight fog had enrobed the land. The metallic smell of the fog mixed with other morning smells. Juniper, pine, humus from the forest floor, faint wood smoke from the dying embers of the campfire and a slight fishy smell from the brook. The water sliding over rocks and pebbles and some rustlings of small animals made the only sounds.

He moved silently, like a ghost. His old shaman had taught him how to walk using loose ankles, and toes in semi-circles to detect obstacles and avoid tripping or cracking twigs and branches. He did the same with his hands and arms. He listened, he smelled, he used his peripheral vision. But most importantly, he used his sense to feel the rhythms of the forest, and to detect the presence of other beings. There were the usual night animals, squirrels, mice, owls, snakes, deer, and insects. He could sense a panther nearby and a weasel on the prowl. He sensed no humans. Good, he thought. He knew that Quint had skills comparable to his own and, as they got closer, the danger would become more extreme. He hadn't told Alex that, of course. He didn't want to frighten her. But he worried that his false confidence and bravado might leave her complacent and incautious. He needed her to be watchful too.

Beau made his way up to a small rise overlooking the campsite. There was a jumble of rocks and brush. He wanted to make sure no one could come up on him from behind. He crawled backwards into a little niche and settled down to wait. If someone was coming, they would come just as the dawn was beginning to break. Quint might not need the light but if he had others with him, he would want to make sure their approach was noiseless.

As he waited Beau thought about Alex. He was feeling things he hadn't felt since he was young, before the raid. Was she feeling those things too? Or was he just a temporary dalliance? He wondered if she had an erstwhile boyfriend back at college. He wasn't worried about getting his heart broken, his heart had shattered irretrievably the day he found his family and her. Her face came to him again, smiling. He felt the breath sucked out of his lungs. Again. Control yourself, he chided himself. Bury those emotions, as he had buried her. Yet Alex had reawakened those emotions. Beau was afraid of nothing; he was living on borrowed time. Yet he began to feel a fear building in him. Not a fear of anything horrible, just the opposite. He realized that he was afraid of being happy.

As dawn began to break, Beau dragged his thoughts away from Alex and keened his senses. There was the usual fluttering and scuffling as night animals went to their burrows and nests and the day animals began moving. A crow cawed, the announcement of dawn. There was movement in the woods, a twig snapped, leaves shuffled. There were four or five of them, Beau sensed. They were moving downstream directly toward the campsite. Then they stopped. He could see their leader now breathing in, testing the air. Then there was a loud snuffle. Wood smoke! Deer hated wood smoke. It meant that men were around. The leader turned, flashed his white tail, and scampered off into the woods. The others bounded after him.

When dawn had fully broken, and the fog had lifted, Beau could see clearly up and down the bank of the brook. Relieved that there was no imminent danger, he stood up, brushed himself off, and went down to build the fire, boil some coffee, and make some breakfast. Alex was sitting up, the tent flaps open.

"Where did you go? I woke and missed you."

Beau smiled and dropped down to his haunches. "Just checking the area," he said. "You can never be too cautious."

A worried look came across Alex's face. "You told me that Quint wouldn't think that we would be traveling this way. You said he would be looking for us in train stations."

"Right, and I stand by that. It's just an old habit of mine to get up before dawn and check around the campsite. Don't worry, you were safe."

"After what he did to Mick, after what I saw in that box, a terrible fear has grown in me," Alex said. She started shuddering and hugged her shoulders with her arms. "I don't like it when you're away from me."

She stopped and made herself control her emotions. She forced a little laugh. "I guess I miss more than you just being around. That ginseng was amazing, by the way. I've never had such energy.

"I noticed," Beau said. He turned and began working on the fire. Alex went down to the brook to freshen up.

As they rode west Alex and Beau talked again about the case.

"There must be some sort of connection that we just haven't seen," Alex said. "We're missing a clue. Why would Doctor Mulroney have men travel to Albion to pick up bottles that had been shipped there on the canal? I understand bringing new supplies and taking back empty return bottles. But I can't put a finger on why the new ones are shipped there. And what's the connection between Clara and the cure all? She seems to have had an unlimited supply, but it was only sold in the apothecary in Albion or from the medicine show itself. She had to have a secret source."

"I'm more surprised at the killings," Beau said. "Not the ones that were set up to look like accidents for insurance purposes. I'm talking about the outright murders. The accidental deaths, though questionable to us, were closed cases; signed off on by the authorities. If we found Clara, it would still be a questionable case in a court of law. Mick must have gotten close, but why murder him? It would have been his word against Clara's."

"Because Quint is a sociopathic killer," Alex said, the fear rising again in her breast.

"True, but one with a strange, twisted moral code. Somehow Mick violated that code. He found out something that was not supposed to be found out. He found the location of Doctor Mulroney's home base. Mick's death is the key to this whole puzzle."

"But if he got too close, what will happen to us when we get too close?"

"Quint will die."

39

"Get many travelers through here?" Beau asked the man who was re-shoeing his horse. He looked around the stable, drinking in the familiar smells of horse, leather, hay, and manure. It reminded him of his time working as a stable hand when he first came north in search of Quint. He wondered again if he should have continued moving from town to town, finding work in stables along the way. Working as a Pinkerton brought him more money and greater movement, but it was high-profile work that often took him away from his search. But then again, he had finally stumbled upon his quarry and was headed for a final showdown. But it worried him that Quint had somehow found out everything about the case, his partner and himself. A stable worker was much more anonymous; no one noticed them – an advantage.

They were in Medina, another town on the Erie Canal. Beau had driven directly to the livery stable, and Alex had gone to the general store for supplies. He had the blacksmith re-shoe his horse and tend to a few minor repairs on the wagon. As the man worked, Beau kept up a running conversation, making meaningless small talk, like farmers usually do when in town.

The man looked up from his work to answer Beau's question. It seemed like part of his job was to socialize with every farmer and horseman who came through town. He was used to it, like a bartender who tolerates the drunks who sit at his bar, passing the time.

"Oh, yeah," he said through some horseshoe nails held in his teeth. "All kinds of people stop here on their travels. Mostly good people; locals in town for the day, looking to get their horses fed, groomed, re-shoed and get their wagons repaired. You from around here?"

"Batavia," Beau said. "Heading to Ridgeway to look at some land. We're sharecropping now."

"Ah, I did that for a while before I was able to buy this place. You don't save a lot of money 'cropping."

"That's for sure," Beau said absently. He was looking over the horses in the stalls. The blacksmith noticed.

"Got horses for sale or rent. You could double team that wagon. Easier on your horse. A single horse works fine for a light wagon, but yours is a little heavy. I could rent you one."

Beau laughed to himself. If anyone knew anything about horses, it was the Arapaho. The wagon he had was light and lightly loaded. Alex weighed very little, and he was not overweight. "Thanks, but we'll be alright," he said. Nice try, he thought.

The blacksmith smiled and went back to work. "Some people don't know how to treat horses," he said absently. "Take that old nag in the third stall. Guy came in here to put it up for a night. Big, heavy Irishman; and he didn't sit the horse well either. Poor beast was worn out. I convinced him to leave it here to recover and rented him a plow horse in the meantime. Like those two over there," he pointed toward two extremely large, bay-colored horses toward the back of the stable. "They're Clydesdales. Bred to carry armored knights into battle during the Middle Ages. 18 hands tall, 2,000 pounds. For sale or rent," he added.

Beau shook his head. "I'll need every penny I have to buy land, but I may be back once I'm established. I might need a good plow horse. Mind if I take a look?"

"Help yourself," the man said.

Beau walked over to the horse, patted it on the muzzle, ran his hands across its flanks and lifted a hoof. He got a good look at the horseshoe, its size, shape, and pattern. When he walked back to his horse, the blacksmith was done. Beau thanked the man, paid him, and promised to return when he could afford one of his Clydesdales.

Beau pulled the wagon up to the front of the general store, stopped, wrenched the brake on and got down to help Alex with the supplies. He went into the store and regarded Alex, toting up the prices of the goods she had bought. She was not happy.

"You're telling me that I owe you five dollars for two sacks of flour when your sign advertises 'flour, $1.75 a pound. That adds up to $3.50!"

"The sacks weigh more than a pound apiece, little lady," the man behind the counter said in a condescending tone. He was short, fat, and wore his hair slicked-back with some sort of pomade. A thin line of perspiration had sprung up on his forehead which he kept wiping away with a cotton handkerchief.

"Put them on the scale," Alex insisted.

"I already did," the man said dismissively. The totals are all there."

"I didn't see you put them on the scale," Alex said. To Beau's ear, she had adopted the tone of her aunt Ida Mae.

"I'm too busy for this," the man said, pushing the sacks forward a little. "You can pay me what you owe me, or you can take your business elsewhere."

Alex knew full well that this was the only general store in town. She picked up the two sacks as if to put them with her other purchases but then suddenly turned, walked behind the counter, and set the two sacks on the scale. She blocked the narrow aisle with her body, leaving the man with two choices, roughly push past her or stand there gawking. He gawked.

Alex moved the weights on the scale until the bar balanced. "One pound, fourteen ounces," she declared. "Without your thumb on the scale." She turned, took the two sacks to where her other items were, and pulled out her pocketbook. "By my calculation, I owe you three dollars and thirty-eight cents."

She counted out the money, set it firmly on the counter, and took the sacks over to the other items which she had already paid for. A small crowd of shoppers had gathered to witness the exchange.

"I suggest, Mr. Whipple, that you confine your cheating to the customers who won't check your figures."

She turned on her heel, hefted the box of goods, and walked toward the door. Beau could do nothing other than hold the door open for her.

"The nerve of that man!" Alex said as she plopped the box onto the bed of the wagon. "I bet he cheats everyone that way!"

Beau smiled and secured the load. He wanted to say, "now everyone has noticed you and will remember us," But he decided to stay silent.

They traveled the rest of the day, heading west. Mick seemed to have been heading toward Buffalo when the trail suddenly turned north, toward Lockport.

"Lockport is where the bottling works is," Alex said. "I don't understand!"

"Shipping new bottles to Albion by canal boat, which is safer for the bottles, and then shipping them back by land to the place of their origin." Beau said, shaking his head. "There must be something that I'm missing. This, and the random murders just doesn't add up."

"I think it's as simple as this," Alex said. "Whoever is making the cure-all wants to keep his location a secret, which means that Doctor Mulroney is tied in with Clara and Quint. What puzzles me is how a person like Clara got involved with a monster like Quint."

Beau followed Mick's trail all the way to the outskirts of the city, where they were finally swallowed up by the press of traffic. Their progress slowed and they were forced to stop frequently.

"He'll have gone to the livery stable first to put up his horse," Beau said. "I'll let you guess where he went next."

Alex laughed for a moment but then stopped, realizing something. "We can't go in the bar," she said. "We'd be recognized right away."

Beau nodded. "We'll have to go at this obliquely."

"Right, we'll have to avoid all the places we went last week."

They rode on in silence for a while. Finally, Alex spoke up, a pensive look on her face.

"Strange," she said. "We were here, closer than we thought. Somehow, we got off track."

"They had a mechanism in place that would throw off anyone who was getting close," Beau said. "We must be extremely careful from now on. Someone might be working for them that could describe us. We have to appear as nondescript as possible."

"I understand," Alex said. A shudder ran up her spine and stayed there. She felt as if they had stepped into a lion's den, a Bible story come real.

They drove into the city of Lockport for the second time in a week. The first time, they had taken a train and stayed at the best hotel in the city. This time they arrived in a dusty buckboard, posing as a farmer and his wife.

Beau dropped Alex off on Main Street and then drove to the livery stable, stopped the wagon, engaged the brake, and jumped down. The liveryman walked out from his shop, wiping his hands on his greasy apron.

Beau told him he'd like to park his wagon there for the day and turn his horse loose in the stable's corral.

The man told him how much, and Beau paid him.

"Drive your wagon around back and park it alongside the others. I'll be there to help directly." He turned and went back inside the stable.

Beau drove the wagon around back, where he saw dozens of wagons, carts, buggies, and other horse drawn conveyances. He parked the wagon in an empty slot and unhitched the horse. He led it to a large corral where other horses were grazing. He opened the gate, led the horse into the corral, turned it loose, and walked back out. As he was closing and fastening the gate, the liveryman came out from the rear of the stable.

"Looks like a full house today," Beau said to the man in a friendly manner.

"It's like this every Saturday," the man said. "People come from miles around for the farmer's market. It draws a lot of people."

"That's what we're here for," Beau said. "All the way from Batavia."

"Where are you staying?" the man asked.

"Can you recommend a hotel?" Beau said.

"Well, the Park is the best hotel in town, but it's expensive." He looked Beau up and down once, quickly, and then met Beau's eyes with a the Park is no place for you kind of look. Beau had seen it before. It didn't bother him.

"The Niagara is fairly cheap and has a tavern that serves a decent daily special."

"Thanks," Beau said, little distractedly. A very large plow horse at the far end of the corral had caught his eye. The liveryman noticed.

"Quite a horse," he said.

"Yes, it is," Beau said. "What sort of horse is it?"

"Clyde's Dale, something like that. A big Irishman rode in on it. Put it up and walked toward the bar. He hasn't returned. That horse has been eating me out of house and home."

"What happens if he doesn't come back?"

"I'll take possession. Get it verified by the sheriff and get paperwork from the judge. But God knows what I'll do with it."

Beau shrugged and laughed. "It would make a lot of glue," he said.

The liveryman laughed at the joke. But both men knew the big Clydesdale was far too valuable to be rendered for glue. And Beau knew that the man would make a pretty penny renting or selling it. He tipped his hat, turned, and walked toward the street, knowing that he had found out something important.

Beau met Alex on the street, where she'd been waiting. To his surprise she had shed her dutiful housewife outfit and was wearing a new set of clothes: black lace-up leather boots, a long, ruffled khaki skirt, a cream-colored blouse with a brown vest and a black plainsman's hat; her hair was loose and flowing beneath it. Her look reminded Beau of the women settlers who rode Conestoga wagons on the plains. They were tough, resourceful, and determined women, not your ordinary dutiful housewives. The look suited her, and Beau didn't comment.

They walked around a corner and out of earshot of any casual listeners.

"Whoever killed Mick disposed of the body," Beau said. "Probably weighted it down and dropped it in the canal."

"And that's important because?"

"Because Quint likes to leave his victims butchered, to leave a message. Leaving a scalped corpse would have been a sensation. The local paper would have been all over it. And the sheriff would have investigated. Mick wouldn't have died easily. He would have put up a fight. Such a violent death would have produced clues, witnesses even. Disposing of the body means that we're very close to them; and they don't want anyone sniffing around their backyard."

"But without Mick to tell us what he found, we will be searching and stumbling in the dark," Alex said.

"We just have to be careful not to stumble on something by accident," Beau said. "We need to stay ahead of events."

Alex nodded; the shudder still firmly embedded in her spine. The two of them strolled down the street through throngs of people. Alex tried to appear nonchalant as she window shopped, while Beau attended her dutifully, pretending to take interest in the various displays in the windows. They came to a pharmacy. Alex stopped and turned to Beau.

"I need to get a powder," she said. "All that jostling in the wagon has given me a headache."

"Ask for willow bark," Beau said. The pharmacist should have some."

"Another old Indian cure?"

"Something like that," Beau said.

She walked into the store.

A bell sounded as the door as she entered. There was no need, as the busy pharmacist was attending a line of people. Alex waited in line, noticing the various lotions, medicines, unguents, and cure-alls lining the shelves of the little store. The pharmacist was a short, fat man with a mousy mustache, weak chin, and slicked-back hair, parted in the middle. He wore a white shirt with arm gaiters and a floppy black bow tie.

"Yes?" he said to Alex as she approached the counter. He gave her a perfunctory smile, revealing stubby teeth with a wide gap in the middle.

"Willow bark, if you've got it," she said.

"Never heard of it," he said in a tired voice that said, I'm very busy, now, will there be anything else? He looked at a wall clock near the door, almost time to close.

Alex was not to be so easily dismissed.

"I think it's also called salicin," she said.

"Oh, you mean headache powder," he said. "How many packets?"

"Just one," Alex said.

The man turned and picked up a small paper bag from a shelf and laid it on the counter. "It comes in a package of five, is that all right?"

Alex thought about her pounding head and aching bottom. "Certainly," she said. She paid him, took the sack, turned, and walked toward the door. As she reached for the doorknob, someone pushed the door open from outside. Alex was forced to step back. The door hit the bell suspended from the ceiling, causing Alex to look up briefly. When she looked back down, she came face-to-face with Clara Comerford. Alex's eyes widened and her mouth worked soundlessly, trying to find words.

"Oh, excuse me," Clara said. "I didn't see you behind the door."

To Alex's surprise, Clara's face showed no sign of recollection at all. She brushed past Alex and walked directly to the counter. No one seemed to mind. As a matter of fact, several people smiled and said, "Good morning, Mrs. Billings."

Clara smiled at them deferentially. She accepted a package from the pharmacist.

"Thank you, Ira," she said. She turned and walked back toward the door. Alex, dumfounded, was still holding the door open.

"Thank you, Miss," Clara said as she breezed past. She walked out the door and got into a waiting carriage, the door held open by a footman. He closed and latched the door and deftly swung up onto the foot stand at the back of the carriage. The driver snapped the reins of the four-horse rig and drove down the street.

"Beautiful woman, isn't she?" an older woman standing next to Alex said, staring after the carriage. She had stepped to the door, which Alex was still holding open, like a doorman. The woman was dressed in the ubiquitous faded blue cotton dress, faced with white linen that seemed to be the uniform of the region for women. She wore high lace-up shoes and an off-white bonnet that was frayed around the edges. "She suits Doctor Billings so well. He owns most of the businesses in town," she added.

Alex nodded. "A lovely lady indeed."

Beau was standing in front of the hardware store, among a group of onlookers, watching workers unload sacks and bundles from a wagon. Alex signaled to him, and he approached at a leisurely pace. When he got close, she grabbed him by the arm.

"I have news," she whispered excitedly. She pulled him around the corner to a quiet alleyway.

He looked at her expectantly.

"She's here! Alex exclaimed. "I saw her in the pharmacy! Clara! We came face-to face!"

"Did she recognize you?"

"No! The strangest thing. She breezed past me without a glimmer of recognition."

"You never spent much time with her; and when you did, it was always in a formal setting. You were dressed differently, acted, and spoke in a certain way. She wouldn't expect to run into you in a different town, dressed as you are."

"Hmmm," Alex said. "I see your point. That would explain it, I guess. But here's the interesting point. She's married to the richest man in town, Doctor Billings. We need to warn him before he has an unfortunate accident! We also need to serve her the papers challenging the will. She needs to be brought to court before she disappears again."

"She needs to be arrested," Beau said. "To keep her from running. The question is, on what charge?"

"Impersonating a human being," Alex said.

Beau laughed. It was a mirthless laugh; he knew that things were about to get sticky. Alex was a lawyer, and lawyers did things by the book. The law was sacrosanct to them. But he knew that following the letter of the law was not always the best way to get results in his business. He took a serious tone with her.

"You must consider the situation as it exists in reality," he said. "Not how it should be, but how it is."

Alex looked at him with a puzzled look on her face.

"You will be bringing a case against a beloved member of this community. Her husband is a pillar of the city. We must assume that he loves his wife and won't believe that she's a con-artist. He has deep pockets and influence. What chance do you think you'll have in court when he hires the best lawyers around to fight your case?"

"But we'll be saving him from what befell my father, Clifton and who knows how many others."

"You're forgetting the wild card here," Beau said. "Quint. He is what befell your father and the others. If he's the mastermind behind her scams, he will have a plan in place to neutralize any threat to them. As he did with Mick."

"What do we do?" Alex said.

"We lay low and wait for Quint to show himself," Beau said. "By now he knows that I'm close. He can sense it, as I can sense him. Whoever blinks first loses."

"So, until then we camp?"

Beau shook his head. "Hotel," he said.

Alex smiled.

Beau didn't tell her what he planned to do, or what he had seen. He was certain that Mick had figured out the same thing, and it had gotten him killed. Extreme caution was called for, and he didn't want Alex caught in a crossfire. He would be gone for a while, maybe forever; the hotel was the safest place for her

40

The Niagara Hotel was a third-rate, seedy establishment well past its prime. There were crowds of workers, farmers and others loitering on the street, stairs and porch, smoking, chewing, and nipping at bottles. There was the smell of fresh manure from local fields and horse manure and dirt from the street. Alex and Beau walked up the stairs, past the throng of idlers on the porch, and into the lobby.

The lobby was a cacophony of voices, shouted orders, and greetings. The air was blue with tobacco smoke and smelled of stale beer, whiskey and sweat. Alex and Beau waited in line at the registration counter.

The clerk was a tall, burly man that Beau guessed doubled as a bouncer. Scars on his left cheek and forehead suggested some time spent as a bare-knuckled boxer. A grimace that was supposed to pass for a smile revealed two missing front teeth. He nodded to Beau, which was supposed to pass for a yes, can I help you?

"Single room, no share," Beau said. The man gave him a funny look.

"Cost you double," he said. "Most people share."

Beau said nothing and looked at the man as if to say so, how much?

"Five dollars," the man said. "In advance."

Beau fished in his pocket for a moment and pulled out a ten-dollar gold piece. He laid it with a soft clunk on the table. The man picked it up, looked at it with one squinted eye and bit it. He nodded and put it in his pocket rather than into the till box.

"Second floor, clean sheets," Beau said.

The man turned and whistled toward a woman who was obviously a maid. She walked over and the man said something in her ear. She nodded, turned, and walked away. The man took a key down from a large wooden pegboard and handed it to Beau.

"Room 217," he said as he turned the registration book around for Beau to sign and seemed surprised when he did.

"The room will be ready for you in about an hour," the man said.

Beau nodded and they went to the restaurant to have dinner in the meantime.

As they walked into the hotel restaurant, they were assailed with the sights, smells, and sounds of a typical western saloon. Bottles and glasses clanked, voices shouted, and tables and chairs screched as they were shifted. The air was blue with smoke and the smell of the smoke mixed with stale beer, sweat and cooking food. An out-of-tune piano was being pounded upon by a short man in a sweat-soaked white shirt with arm gaiters. He wore an old bowler tilted back and had a cigar stub clenched in his teeth. The tune he was playing was made tinkly by tacks pushed into the worn keypads. Alex could not tell which tune it was over the din of the crowd. There was a long bar up front and card games at tables in the back. Beau looked over at Alex and saw her struggle not to react to a scene she most likely had never encountered. They found a round, scarred wooden table next to a window and sat down. Alex took off her hat, shook out her hair and said: "Lovely."

Dinner was a grey slurry that was trying to pass as stew, a chunk of stale dark bread, a crumbly piece of cheese and a mug of warm, dark beer. There was no menu or any other choice. Alex dipped her spoon into the stew, raised it to her nose and sniffed. She set it back in the bowl and decided to get her sustenance from the beer. Beau did the same.

At the next table was a couple with two children, one, a small boy and the other, a beautiful girl in her late teens. She had golden blonde hair and cobalt-blue eyes that seemed to glisten with the excitement of youth. Several rough-looking men at the bar were leering at her, commenting rudely, and laughing. She looked away, embarrassed and uncomfortable. One of the men, a large man with too much hair and too much whiskey, staggered to his feet and stumbled towards the girl's table.

"You're too pretty to be sitting with this boring bunch," he said, gesturing toward her father, mother, and little brother. "Why don't you come and join us. I'll buy you a drink."

"We're Mormons, we don't drink," the father said firmly.

"I wasn't talking to you Homer," the man said. "I was talking to this little lady." He grabbed the girl by the elbow and tried to ease her to her feet. She pulled her arm away sharply, sat back down and looked at her mother.

"I'll thank you to keep your hands off my daughter," the mother said. She looked at the girl. "Pay him no mind, Elise," she said.

"Elise, is it?" the man said. "Well, I think it's high time Elise had a drink!" He grabbed the girl again, this time more roughly, and pulled at her. The father came to his feet and squared himself.

"I said we're Mormons, and we don't drink! Now let go of my daughter!"

The man pulled the girl to her feet with one hand and swatted at the father with the other, knocking his hat from his head. The men at the bar guffawed and shouted encouragement. Elise struggled to get free of the man, but he had a firm grip on her arm. Suddenly Beau stood and stepped over to the man.

"Let the girl go," he said easily, as if just making a suggestion. He smiled.

The man let go of the girl and shoved her toward her seat. "And who might you be, stranger?" he said, glaring at Beau. "You have the look of a half-breed to me."

Beau was tall, but the man stood head and shoulders over him. He outweighed Beau by at least a hundred pounds, if not more. He reached a hand to Beau's face and slid a knuckle over his cheek.

"Smooth as a baby's ass!" he said, looking over at the bar for encouragement from his friends. They laughed and guffawed, shouting for him to kick Beau's ass. The man laughed and turned, raising his hand to cuff Beau. It was a mistake. As he pulled back for the blow, he shouted.

"We killed plenty of your kind out west, but it looks like one of us must have taken a liking to your mother!"

He brought his fist around hard, but Beau deftly stepped aside, leaving the man nothing but air to strike. The action put him off balance and Beau shoved him lightly. The man pitched into a table full of half-empty pitchers and glasses. He tried to catch himself but ended up hugging the table and crashing to the floor with it, sprawling among the broken glass and spilled beer. His friends let out a whoop of delight at his expense. Beau turned to the table of Mormons.

"Are you alright?"

They nodded, shocked at what they had seen. That's when the big man made his second mistake. He struggled to his feet and pulled a Bowie knife from his belt. With a roar, he charged Beau.

Beau feinted left and then dodged right, ducking the big blade. He caught the man's arm, twisted, and dropped his weight sharply, snapping the man's arm at the elbow with a loud crack. The blade clattered to the floor and the man let out a roar of pain, dropping to his knees.

Like a flash, Beau pulled his own belt knife and swiped it toward the man's neck. A strong hand caught him.

"Easy, Lad," a deep voice said. It was the bouncer.

"I think you've had enough, haven't you Clyde?" he said, addressing the big man who suddenly realized he was a hair's breadth from death.

The man groaned and nodded, cradling his broken arm, and staggering to his feet. He slunk back toward the bar, his friends laughing at him. Beau sheathed his knife.

"I've never seen anyone face down Clyde and live to tell about it," the bouncer said. He looked over at the bar and saw Clyde sit down heavily, still cradling his arm. He let go of it and snatched a bottle of whiskey from the bar and drank deeply, the fight gone out of him. His friends turned away.

"It would be best if you left before his friends drink enough courage to try and avenge their friend," the bouncer said with a laugh. He looked over at the group and then back at Beau. "I don't think there are enough of them, but I don't need the mess."

Alex had watched the event with awe. She had never seen anyone move as fast as Beau and had never seen anyone so close to death than the man called Clyde. She was certain that, his blood up, Beau would have killed the man if the bouncer hadn't stopped him. She wondered if he had killed others. It seemed likely. There was the Cuthbert man, of course, but that was self-defence. But how many other men had he killed, and under what circumstances? Her thinking was forestalled by the arrival of a young man at her table. He nodded to her once and looked around furtively. Everyone's attention seemed to be focused on the unfortunate Clyde, nursing his broken arm. The young man dropped a folded slip of paper on the table in front of her and slipped away. Alex picked up the paper, unfolded it, and read it. It was written in a shaky hand. It read Beware! Things are not as they seem!

Puzzled, Alex watched the young man exit the room by a back door. She refolded the paper and put it into a pocket on her dress. Moments later, Beau returned to the table, apologized, and nodded toward the stairs. The Mormon couple stood, thanked Beau, and headed out of the tavern by the front door.

As they passed the registration table, Beau paused for a moment, whispered something to the bouncer, who had returned to his position, and laid a ten-dollar gold piece on the counter. The man nodded, picked the coin up, and slipped it into his pocket.

"What was that all about?" Alex said as they mounted the stairs.

Beau shrugged. "Just taking care of loose ends." He said no more.

The young man left the tavern, satisfied that he had left his message with the girl called Alex unseen. He had taken a big chance doing it, and he knew that if he was found out there'd be hell to pay. But he was glad he had. He wanted desperately to escape the hold on him and the woman he loved. The Pinkerton named Beau seemed to be the man who could help him. Judging by what the man had done to Clyde, he was confident he had made the right choice. Now he had to get back to the carriage, where he had been left, with the order: "Wait for me here, I'll be back in an hour." Delivering the message had taken less than ten minutes. Plenty of time left.

He walked down a quiet side street and turned into a darkened alleyway that led to the street where he had left the carriage. As he stepped past a recess in one of the buildings, a hand snaked out and grabbed him by the throat. He struggled for a moment, but the man's grip was too tight. He was being lifted off the ground. "Delivered your message, did you?" The man said in a hollow, monotonal whisper. The young man felt his bladder release. His heart pounded so hard that it echoed in his head. Then his bowels released.

"Relax," the man said. "I won't kill you, not while you're still of use to me." His grip tightened, soft and insistent, like a constrictor squeezes its prey. The young man felt his eyes beginning to pop out. He struggled to breathe, but he could only breathe out, not in.

"Tell me what the message said," the man said. There was no malice in his voice. No anger; just a strange, inquisitiveness devoid of any emotion. The young man nodded. He was let go and he dropped to the ground, wheezing, and grabbing his neck. He gasped and told the man.

"Beware! Things are not as they seem!" the man repeated with a smile. "It's almost poetic. I couldn't have said it better myself." He laughed.

"You wanted to warn them so that the Pinkerton would try and take me out, like he almost did our friend Clyde. What a fool! Instead, what you've done is going to flush him out, and I'll be waiting. Now, clean yourself up and get into the carriage, we have some time to kill."

IN the room, Beau checked the locks on the door, opened the window and looked out, closed it, and locked it.

"Something had to be done," he said, looking down at the floor apologetically. "I gave the man a choice. An out. He chose not to take it."

Alex walked over to him and gently took his hand. "You were defending that poor girl's honor. Who knows what would have happened if he had forced her over to the bar? Those men, and that Clyde person, were monsters!"

"They were bullies," Beau said. "And the only way to deal with bullies is to face them down, whatever the cost."

Alex smiled and smoothed the section of Beau's cheek where the man had roughly rubbed his knuckle. She remembered the name he had called him. She reached up and kissed him.

Later, they availed themselves of the feather bed and clean sheets. At one point, Alex straddled Beau from above and let her hair envelope his head and face.

"I think I'm in love with you, Beau Starr," she said softly. He started to respond but she put her finger against his lips. "Shush," she said. She smothered him with kisses.

Beau wanted to respond, but he knew if he did, he would break her heart. There were several reasons. Professionalism was one, of course, but others had gotten around that. And there was the very distinct social gap between the two of them, but his mother had trained him well in the social graces. In time, he could feel at home in a drawing room, smoking cigars and drinking brandy; but he wasn't sure that Alex wanted that from him anyway. Of course, there was the memory of the love of his life, snuffed out by Quint and his gang. But Alex seemed to be crowding her into his distant memories. However, the most compelling and important reason was that he would be leaving her tonight after she fell asleep, and there was a very good chance that he might not return.

Alex's note had alarmed him. Beware! Things are not as they seem! it read. Doctor Billings seemed like a pillar of the community and at risk of being scammed by Clara. He needed to be warned, or so it seemed. But Beau had seen something earlier that afternoon that changed everything. As Beau watched Clara's carriage proceed down the street, it stopped in front of the bottling works. A large, barrel-chested man dressed in a three-piece suit and wearing a bowler stepped out of the doorway, followed closely by a tall, well-dressed man. Beau turned to a man standing next to him and casually inquired, "Who is that tall man?"

"You from out of town?" the man said, looking at Beau.

"Batavia," Beau said.

"The man shook his head as if to say oh, that explains it. "That's Doctor Billings," he said. "He owns half the town." He stopped thoughtfully and smiled. "Owns most of the town, as a matter of fact. This city owes him a lot, he single-handedly revived it."

"Who's the big fella ahead of him?" Beau said.

"Scary looking, isn't he?" the man said. "That's the Doctor's brother, Quint. He acts as a bodyguard for the Doctor and his wife."

Beau didn't tell Alex. What he had to do, he had to do on his own; it was far too risky to involve her. He would reconnoiter the Billings estate that night and take whatever actions he deemed necessary to neutralize Billings, capture Clara, and kill Quint. By his reconning, it would take him an hour to get there on foot, another hour to do his recon, and a third hour to get back. He needed to do that before first light, in case he had to postpone his mission. Hopefully, Alex would be safe and sound asleep when he got back. He had paid the bouncer ten dollars to keep watch over her door.

Later, when Alex was asleep, Beau unlocked the window, opened it, stepped out onto the small landing, closed the window, climbed down the fire escape ladder to where it was drawn up, and dropped to the ground. He went into a light and silent jog down the darkened alleyways and out into the countryside. It felt good to run, as he had when he was a young boy.

41

Alex woke with a start. It was the middle of the night, and she knew that something had woke her, but she didn't know what. She reached for Beau, but he wasn't there. She sat up, her heart pounding. Where was Beau, she wondered? Why had he left without telling her? Then she heard it, the noise that had woke her. It was a soft knock on the door. She got up, wrapped herself in a robe and padded over to the door.

"Who is it?" she whispered.

"Josh," a voice said. It sounded young and afraid. "I'm the one who gave you the message. I need to talk with you. Can I come in?"

Alex undid the latch and slid the deadbolt back. She opened the door a crack.

"Talk to me through the door," she said. "What is it you want?"

The door suddenly crashed open, sending her reeling back onto the bed. Her robe flew open, and Josh was on top of her. He smelled like he had soiled himself. A hand grabbed him by the nape of the neck and lifted him. "Good job," the man said to Josh as he flung him away like a used rag.

Alex saw a man that embodied all the nighttime fears she'd had as a little girl. He was a big man, and broad, with the barrel chest of a boxer. A deep scar on his mouth left him with a permanent sneer. There were other scars too, but they weren't what sent a wave of terror up her spine. It was the man's eyes. They were deep-set, and bottle green, like the eyes of a malevolent serpent. He regarded her nakedness openly and she wrapped the robe around herself. She knew instinctively that the man was Quint.

"Get dressed," he said in a raspy whisper. "There's someone I want you to meet."

As they left the room, they had to step over the body of the bouncer, sprawled in the hallway.

BEAU jogged lightly down a dirt lane; his progress lit only by the stars. Trees, limbs, and bushes threw pale shadows on the countryside. He could smell the slightly metallic fog that was drifting up from wet recesses in the hilly ground. Up ahead, he could see the Billings estate looming darkly atop a hill that overlooked extensive pastures, orchards and fields of wheat and corn. It reminded him of the Comerford and Brown estates. Money dating back for generations had built them. An owl hooted and night animals scrabbled in the underbrush. He heard the scream of a dying rabbit, most likely in the jaws of a fox or coyote. A small herd of deer regarded him from a hilltop.

He ran on, silently.

Suddenly he heard the clatter of horse hooves in the far distance behind him. He slipped off into the woods and waited to see who was out at such a late hour.

A carriage approached, jouncing and jostling, its yellow lanterns dancing crazily' like the eyes of some nighttime predator. Someone was in a hurry. The driver, a young man, was whipping the horses relentlessly as the carriage sped past. The curtains were drawn, and Beau couldn't see the occupants. The carriage turned onto the lane that led to the Billings estate, sped up it, and disappeared behind the big building.

Beau took to the woods, wary of being seen on the road from the hilltop. It would take him longer, but he figured he still had plenty of time.

As he reached the hilltop, he could see several large wagons parked behind a large barn. They were enclosed wooden structures with steps on the back. The type used by Gypsies; or medicine shows.

Silently, he approached the first one. It had a large canvas sheet on its side. Beau lifted it slightly and peered up at the writing. It was dark out and the lettering was hard to discern but, his night vision was acute, and he was able to read it. "Doctor Mulroney's Exemplary Elixir," it read. He let the canvas fall silently back into place and pondered the situation. So, he thought, Doctor Billings was Doctor Mulroney, purveyor of a cure-all that used bottles from his own bottling works. But why the secrecy? Why deliver bottles to an apothecary in the middle of the state and then secretly bring them back here? A tortured scream forestalled his thinking. It came from the other side of the house. Beau slipped away from the wagon and warily circled the building. The screams became louder and then turned into a strange gurgling sound. Then everything went silent.

Beau went into a crouch and inched closer. He could see someone tied to a tree, slumped. He got closer still and could see that it was the driver of the carriage. He had been stripped naked. Horrible things had been done to him. The boy groaned, still alive but not for long. Beau pulled his knife and approached the pathetic creature, intending to slit his jugular and put him out of his misery. He felt rather than heard a presence behind him. Too late, he started to turn. A strong hand from behind gripped his left shoulder, and another hand came around and covered his face with a wet cloth that reeked of chemicals.

"Caught you!" a man's voice proclaimed. Then everything went black.

42

Beau woke with a headache and bleary eyes. He was tied to a chair, his hands bound behind his back. He was in some sort of lab. Glass bottles and beakers were everywhere, some burbling over burners that emitted blue flames. The air reeked of chemicals. He saw Alex, also bound to a chair. Her eyes were wide and pleading. There was a rag tied over her mouth. Behind her sat Quint, a triumphant smile on his face. He had one foot planted on the back of Alex's chair, which was poised at the edge of a large pit from which loud rattles, buzzes and hisses could be heard. Quint had a look on his face that said, make one false move and I tip her chair into the pit. But he said nothing.

At the other side of the room, Doctor Billings was regarding him with interest. He was tall, fit, and handsome. He wore an expensive smoking jacket and a white silk shirt with a gold ascot at the neck. He was striding around the room like a businessman in a drawing room, his left hand in the pocket of his jacket, a snifter of brandy in his right hand.

"Ah, the notorious Beau Starr," he said. "The man who has given us so much trouble of late. Quint sent you a warning! Why didn't you heed it?" He shook his head sadly. His voice was smooth and mellow, the result of years of hawking his patented cure-all, Beau thought. But his phrases were disjointed, hinting at madness. He continued to pace, glancing around at his audience of three. He gestured toward the viper pit.

"My little friends," he said. "Crotalus adamanteus. The Eastern Diamond Rattlesnake, the largest venomous snake in the country. There are several dozens of them in the pit, the cover of which I removed as a courtesy to your friend, Alexandra Comerford." He nodded toward Alex, whose frightened eyes were as big as saucers.

"Let me tell you a story," he said, sipping his brandy. "It's about a family that owned a bottling works. In the family for generations. Profitable. Its profits put a young man through college where he earned a Ph.D. in chemistry. Allowed him to build this lab. He devised a way to separate the two components of rattlesnake venom: neurotoxin and hemotoxin. He was going to develop medicines from it. He would have been famous, a savior of mankind!" he paused for dramatic effect. "Yes, you guessed it! That young man was me.

"When my father died, I inherited the bottling works and this estate. But I was naïve. A company representative came to me and persuaded to take my business public. More profits, he told me. I did as he suggested. But then the company, Northeastern Acquisitions, bought enough stock to have a majority on the board. I was voted out. Of my own company!" He laughed. "My own company!" he repeated.

"They closed the bottling works, laid off the workers and sold off the equipment at auction. I was suddenly penniless. I sold this estate and, with the little money I had, I started my cure-all business. I was married, but my wife and I were unable to have children of our own. We had taken in orphans. They traveled with us. My wife was brilliant, and she schooled them assiduously. But being forced to live like Gypsies took its toll on her. Her health declined and she died. Murdered I say! By the men who ran Northeastern Acquisitions. and the men who invested in that company. I wanted revenge, but I had no way to achieve it. I traveled the countryside, making enough money to feed my family but not much more. Then, my brother Quint arrived and found me on the road. He had a plan, a plan to win back what I had once owned and get revenge on the men who had ruined me!"

He sipped his brandy and became more and more animated. Quint watched, an amused smile on his face.

"Quint is a resourceful man, and he learned many skills while in the west. He burned down the investment company building with the officers in it. We collected on the insurance. Then he came up with an idea to collect from the investors that ruined me! First, the tragic death of an investor's wife, accomplished by dose of chloroform to render her unconscious and then an injection of neurotoxin, there would be widespread damage to the central nervous system and death. It was always done outside; two injections on the lower ankle exactly 14.3 centimeters apart. Just like a snakebite. And just enough hemotoxin to produce some necrosis. A single injection might be noticed and indicate foul play, but two, if noticed would be attributed to a snakebite. But most doctors would not notice it and declare the death to be the result of an embolism, a heart attack, or a stroke."

The doctor paused again, pleased with his description. He continued to pace to and fro, sipping his brandy.

"Six months later, a beautiful young woman appears in town, alone. She meets a rich old widower who is starved for affection. A romance begins and a marriage results. Then, the tragic death of the old man and an altered will. No need to get the man to alter his will; I'm a master forger and Quint is a master safecracker. He simply replaced the real wills with forged ones.

"The money went into the account of my company, Ontario Securities, and was then used to buy back my estate, my bottling works and all the rest of the businesses I own in this city. I revived this city, and the people love me for it. I can't let that be threatened, and you, Mr. Starr, have been threatening it, as did your friends Mr. Cable and Mr. O'Shaughnessy."

He shook his head and looked at Beau and then at Alex.

"Such a waste. A beautiful young girl with a promising future. I fault you, Mr. Starr. You were consumed with revenge. You had a chance to walk away, and none of what is going to happen would have been necessary."

He looked at Quint, who smiled an emotionless smile. It was a smile of anticipation.

Billings drank off the contents of his snifter. He became dead serious.

"We can't have the two of you murdered or come up missing, your aunt would hire more Pinkertons, and I don't want the attention. So, I'll tell you a tragic story. There once was a Pinkerton agent with a shady past. He was hired to find a young lady's stepmother. But he fell in love with the young lady - let's call her Alex." Billings suddenly laughed, a high pitched, nervous chortle. Then he continued.

"When Alex rebuffed him, he brutally raped and killed her, leaving her mangled body on the side of the road in a distant town. Quint will take care of the brutal raping." The doctor again laughed his strange laugh and looked over at Quint, who simply smiled.

"Then, consumed by guilt for what he had done, the agent committed suicide by blowing his brains out."

He laughed again, a giggle this time, and turned to refill his brandy snifter. Just then the door of the lab behind him opened and a young man, who looked much like the young man Quint had butchered, burst into the room. He was holding a double-barreled shotgun. He aimed it at Quint.

"You killed Josh!" He screamed. "Butchered him!"

Billings spun and faced the lad. He held up both hands in a gesture intended to stop him.

"Jason…" he began. But the young man had already tightened his finger on the triggers.

Billings caught both barrels in the chest and neck. He was propelled backwards into a conglomeration of beakers and test tubes. He lay gurgling on the floor as Jason stood over him in surprise and shock. He had intended to kill Quint, not the doctor.

He turned to face Quint, who had been watching the event. Quint grinned.

"You've done me a favor, boy. Now this estate and all the money and holdings of my idiot brother are mine."

In his rage, Jason had pulled both triggers on the shotgun. It was empty. He broke it open and frantically fished in his pocket for more shells. Quint smiled and stood. He reached in his coat and withdrew a pistol from a shoulder holster. He raised the pistol as the boy fumbled.

"Drop the shotgun," Quint said in a strange hollow monotone.

Jason, facing Quint, began to tremble. He dropped the shotgun and it hit the floor with a clatter. He tried to speak but all that came out was a garbled stutter. Quint smiled.

"You killed your father," he said. His voice was soft and insistent, like that of a parent correcting a wayward child. "You'll be hanged for it."

Jason began blubbering, adding to his trembling. "I…I didn't mean to. He stepped in front of me!"

"Here's the story I'll tell the sheriff," Quint said. He looked over at Alex briefly. "After I take care of these two, that is. I'll tell him that you quarreled with your father and, in a fit of anger, shot him. Then, consumed with guilt, you threw yourself into the pit."

Jason stared at the pit, filled with snakes. "No, no, no, no, no, no!" He said. His knees felt weak, and he felt as if he was going to faint. "You can't make me do that," he managed.

Quint waved his pistol at Jason. "In," he said.

Jason fell to his knees, begging. Quint grinned again.

Beau had worked the bonds on his wrists loose, but his feet were still tied. Quint had his back to him. Beau had imagined many ways to kill Quint when he found him, but he hadn't imagined this one. He tilted his chair forward and perched on his toes. Silently, on his moccasins, he bounced across the room frog-like and slammed into Quint. The man let out a groan of surprise and toppled into the viper pit. Beau, Jason, and Alex stared as the man writhed desperately. The snakes bit him on the hands, the wrists, on his arms through his shirtsleeves and on the neck and face. He turned blue, foaming at the mouth, his eyes bugging out of his head. Then he went silent, the snakes slithering over his body, hissing, and rattling.

Beau untied his feet, walked over to Alex, and untied her bonds and removed the cloth from her mouth. She sobbed and fell into his arms. Jason stood still, shocked at what he had seen. He stared down into the pit for a long time, saying nothing.

The door to the lab opened a crack. Someone peeked through it, then opened it all the way. Everyone turned to look. It was Clara.

43

W HEN CLARA STEPPED fully into the room, she looked first at Alex.

"The girl from the apothecary," she said. Her voice was dull, and her tone was a nasally monotone. Hollow. She looked at Beau for a moment, then at Jason, who was still in a state of shock.

"Jason," she said, almost a whisper. "Where's your brother?"

The lad looked at her for a moment and then looked down into the viper pit. Clara followed his gaze and saw Quint. Her eyes widened. She stepped over to the pit and spat, a hateful look on her face. Then she looked around the room and saw Billings, lying on his back, dead. She screamed.

"No, no, no!" She ran to him, knelt, and began caressing him, wailing.

The door opened again. Clara emerged. Another Clara, the spit and image of the first. She saw her sister crying over the supine form of Billings and screamed. She ran to him, knelt, and began caressing him.

Then another Clara emerged and repeated the scene. Then another, and another, until there were six. All identical, all wailing, sobbing and caressing Billings. Alex and Beau stood stock still, shocked and confused by the scene before them.

"There's one more," Jason said to them. He nodded toward the door. Another Clara emerged. But slowly, deliberately. She looked directly at Alex.

"Alex," she said, a look of familiarity in her eyes. Then she looked at the viper pit. She made the sign of the cross and looked back at Alex.

"He was the most evil creature I've ever known," she said, her lips tight against her teeth. She looked over at the women huddled around Billings.

"My sisters," she said. "They are two sets of triplets. I'm the youngest. I hadn't yet fallen under Father's spell. I think we should leave them to their mourning. She nodded to Jason and left the room. He followed, as did Alex and Beau.

Later, sitting in Billing's drawing room, Clara explained. Jason sat next to her, holding her hand, and watching her. He was clearly in love with her, and Clara's demeanor indicated that she was in love with him.

"Doctor and Mrs. Billings were the kindest, most loving people I've ever known. My parents…" She hesitated briefly, troubled by the memory. "My mother died in childbirth with me. My father couldn't stand the pain of her death or the burden of seven children. He committed suicide. We were placed in an orphanage. But Mrs. Billings, hearing of our plight, took us in, as she did another set of twins, Jason, and Josh. They raised us and educated us. They loved us. Things seemed wonderful. My father was a brilliant chemist and was working on experiments to extract therapeutic substances from snake venom. But he invested unwisely and was cheated. Pauperized.

"With the few resources he had left, he developed and bottled a cure-all. He bought three gypsy wagons and we went on the road, traveling from town to town. To boost his sales, he had us cut our hair to different lengths. Each day in a particular town, one of us would buy a bottle of his cure-all. The next day, the sister with the next longest hair would show it off to the crowd and buy another bottle. This went on for a week, the sister with the longest hair going last. Then we would move on to a new town and repeat the process.

"My father made enough money to keep us fed and clothed, but the life of a gypsy was too hard on our mother. Her health failed and she died. Her death turned him into a bitter man, but he had no choice but to continue traveling and selling his cure-all. It seemed that life like that would go on forever. But then my father's brother, Quint, showed up."

Clara wanted to continue, but emotion was welling up inside her. With and effort, she went on.

"My father was a good man. Once. But the circumstances of his financial ruin, lifestyle change, and the death of my mother were too much for him. You've heard of the straw that broke the camel's back? Quint was that straw. He immediately joined our little gypsy caravan and began putting thoughts in my father's ear. Thoughts of revenge, retribution, and reclamation. The two of them developed the scam and Quint made sure it was carried out. They made a list of the investors in Northeastern Acquisitions. Then Quint set a fire in the company's office during mid-day, so that everyone was there. He made sure the doors were locked. He didn't worry about innocent secretaries, cleaning people or visiting business clients. He wanted collateral damage. It was fun for him.

"After the fire, he targeted each investor. If the man wasn't a widower, he made him one. He made sure they all looked like accidents. Chloroform to render the women unconscious and then a healthy injection of concentrated snake venom. Most of the deaths looked like heart attacks or aneurisms. After allowing for six months of mourning, my father would take his medicine show into the target's town and stake out the bait. Us. Each day a different sister went to town, bought a bottle of elixir, booked a room at the best hotel in town and had an expensive and private dinner. The rest you know."

"You were bait for my father?" Alex said, her voice rising." You set him up to be murdered?"

"You don't understand," Jason said. It was the first time he had spoken. He said it firmly, staring straight at Alex.

"Quint made sure that all of us did our jobs. To fail or resist would lead to what became of my brother. He increased the amount of opiates in the cure-all and made us all drink a bottle every day. We became zombies. At first, Clara did as she was told. I met her with a bottle during her daily buggy rides. But, after a few weeks, something changed. Clara confided in me that she had fallen in love with your family, and your father. I was secretly in love with Clara and was devastated. But, out of love for her, I did what she asked. We stalled, we stopped drinking the cure-all, and we made a pact. We would try to keep your father safe for as long as we could. We would try to figure something out and, in the meantime, we would stall."

Alex looked directly at Clara, her lips tight against her teeth.

"You could have warned him!" she shouted. "He would have called the sheriff in and stopped Quint. He would still be alive!"

Clara put her face in her hands and sobbed. She couldn't speak. Beau did.

"Quint would have killed him anyway, and Clara and Josh. The sheriff too if he was brought in. The will would have been forged to make the holding company the recipient; the same company that was used for your uncle's legacy. They had no choice but to wait, stall and hope."

Clara pulled herself together. She looked up, bleary eyed and explained herself.

"It wasn't supposed to happen so soon. Quint must have suspected I was stalling. He told Jason it wouldn't happen for a few weeks. I planned to tell your father then, to give him a chance, even if it cost me my own life. We were on our Saturday buggy ride and John walked off in the brush to relieve himself. It was then that Quint jumped him. I already explained his method: chloroform and concentrated snake venom. Quint carried him out from the brush. Then he grinned at me and threw John up into the buggy. I drove as fast as I could to the doctor's office, hoping that he could save John. But it was too late."

Alex nodded. A plausible explanation. But was it just another scam? Would Clara try to escape once again? Clara seemed to read her thoughts.

"What I said the day of the reading of the will was true, and still is. I intended to sign the papers as soon as you had drawn them up."

"Why did you leave if what you say is true?" Alex said.

Clara shook her head. "I was kidnapped," she said. "Quint had figured out that I ... we ... were stalling." She glanced over at Jason. He looked down at the floor.

"He came in the night with his chloroform. He carried me out like a sack of potatoes." She hesitated again and cleared her throat. "I paid a heavy price for my crime, as did Jason. He was an animal, and he used us, all of us, as his private harem. His depravity knew no limits."

At that Clara burst into tears. Jason tried to comfort her, but it was obvious that the whole affair had left him traumatized. He just shook his head and stared at the floor.

"I murdered my father," he said. "It was an accident, but I'll hang for it."

"You didn't kill him," Beau said. Jason looked at him in surprise.

"Quint killed him. Shot him and then staggered backwards into the viper pit."

"But the sheriff will have questions about my brother and…"

"You won't have to answer them," Beau said. "I'll throw the shotgun into the pit, and we'll be gone." Beau grew pensive for a moment. "A fitting end, don't you think?" Beau said. "A snake in the grass killed by snakes."

"Nemo me impone lacesst," Clara said.

44

THE CARRIAGE BOUNCED and jostled down the dirt road, making good speed. Jason sat up top, the reins in his hands. The four horses were big and powerful and responsive. For the first time in a long time, he felt good. Inside, Alex, Beau and Clara sat. They were heading toward the Comerford Estate, now fully owned by Alex. She would be able to finish her law degree. Clara would again take up her post as tutor for the Comerford children. She had inherited one-seventh of Doctor Billings' legacy, including stocks, bonds and profits from the bottling works, restaurant, and other businesses. She intended to use some of that money to re-establish the families that Dr. Billings and Quint had pauperized.

Beau had agreed to accompany them, his last act as a hired Pinkerton on Alex's case. She wondered what he would do when they arrived, and the case was officially closed. She knew that he had feelings for her, but would they fade as the reality of being a country gentleman took hold? He was half Arapaho Indian and no doubt longed to return to the plains. She knew that, if she tried to hold him, it would only make matters worse.

Beau looked over at Alex and knew what she was thinking. He was conflicted. Part of him wanted to return to his homeland on the plains and another part wanted to stay with Alex. He laughed to himself. No part of him wanted to remain a Pinkerton. He grasped his spirit stone and sought its advice. He closed his eyes and saw the old shaman, One Ear, beckoning to him. But then the shaman faded, and his mother appeared. She was smiling. She had prepared him well for his new life

Epilogue

The sheriff and his deputies rode up the long driveway to the Billings estate. Neighbors had complained of a terrible smell coming from the old house. He knew what it was.

He and his men held handkerchiefs over their faces as they approached the door. He grabbed the big brass doorknocker and banged it three times. He waited a while for a response but got none. He banged it again, harder. Still no response. He nodded to his men, who had brought a large pry bar and two sledgehammers. They broke down the door in a matter of minutes.

Inside, they heard chanting from the front room. The parlor. They walked toward the sound, the sheriff leading. In the room, they found six women dressed in identical mourning black. Candles flickered as they chanted. They were arrayed around a body, dressed in a fine suit but badly decomposed. The stench was overwhelming. One of the deputies retched. The sheriff spoke, and the sisters turned as one to regard him. They were ghostly pale and gaunt, their black hair hanging in stringy strands. A cloud of flies buzzed around them. They stared at the men standing before them.

"Ladies," the sheriff repeated in a soft voice. "You must come with us."

"Nooo," one of them said in a hollow monotone. The others picked it up. It rose as a chant, higher and louder. The stench seeming to rise with it. The sheriff had anticipated such a confrontation and had brought several deputies with him.

"To the kitchen," he said, nodding to his men. They seemed reluctant to move. "Now!" he said firmly. "Lock them in there," he added.

The deputies seized the bony arms of the women, who were too weak to resist. They escorted them into the kitchen, locked the door, and stood waiting. The sheriff walked to the outside door and gestured to two men waiting in a one-horse wagon. They nodded, got down from the wagon, and unloaded a stretcher from the bed of the wagon. The sheriff spoke to them as they approached the door.

"In the parlor," he said, gesturing toward the front room.

"Just follow the smell, right sheriff?" one of the men said, laughing. He was a buck-toothed man one small step away from being a full-on idiot. He was short, stooped and had a lazy eye.

"Shut up Clem," his partner said. His voice was somewhat nasally from the pieces of rag stuffed in each nostril. He was at the rear end of the stretcher and wanted to get the job done as quickly as possible. He shoved at the stretcher, causing Clem to stumble a little. Clem let out a silly laugh and walked on.

The women, locked in the kitchen, began wailing. It was an eerie sound that put the deputies on edge. The sheriff waited in nervous anticipation. *The sooner this is over, the better,* he thought. *This was not the kind of duty he enjoyed.*

A few moments later the two grave diggers emerged from the parlor, the body of Doctor Billings on the stretcher. The sheriff glanced once at the gaunt, decomposed face and wished he hadn't.

"A sad ending for a great man," he said to the nervous deputies. The wailing had grown louder and more strident and they were looking at each other and at the sheriff with impatient eyes.

"It'll be over soon, lads. We just have to wait 'till they put him in the ground in the family cemetery. They've already dug the hole." He knew that the mayor would arrange an elaborate funeral event in town. After all, Billings was a hero to the citizens; he had single-handedly resurrected the city with his unselfish efforts. There would most likely be an ornate statue erected in the central park of the city. He deserved no less.

Two weeks later, the sheriff, deputies and gravediggers were back at the house. Buzzards circled high in the summer sky and the stench of rotting flesh suffused the land. The sisters had exhumed the body and placed it back in their parlor. This time, the sheriff muscled his way past the wailing, clutching wraiths that surrounded the body. Empty bottles of cure-all littered the floor, and it was clear that the sisters had been living on nothing but the syrupy liquid. They looked like prisoners of war who had been systematically starved by a vengeful enemy.

"You can't have him!" one of the sisters shrieked as the gravediggers put the sagging bag of rotted flesh and bone onto their stretcher. "You'll see! He won't let you! He can't be buried!"

That night the sky west of the city flickered with the flames of a burning house. Firefighters were unable to get near the Billings estate, which was fully engulfed in a roaring fire. Onlookers could hear the dying shrieks of the sisters, who refused to leave. By morning, the estate and all its outbuildings were a smoldering ruin. Two days later, the charred bodies of the six sisters were unceremoniously committed to a common grave in the family graveyard. For years afterward, people claimed that they could hear the shrieks of the sisters on certain stormy nights.

Doctor Billings was accorded a funeral with full honors, The body, covered in lime and sealed in a metal coffin, lay in state as the mayor, sheriff, aldermen and various city luminaries made long speeches about the good doctor. A large procession wound its way to the Cold Springs Cemetery, where it was interred beneath a large headstone, bearing his likeness, and inscribed with the words "A MAN FOR HIS CITY, A MAN FOR HIS TIME AND A MAN GONE TOO SOON."

Two weeks later, a flash flood washed away the hillside on which Doctor Billings was buried. His coffin was washed down the hill, where it popped open, exposing the decomposed body of Doctor Billings, standing as if ready to address a crowd of the dead.

THE END

Postscript: this novel was inspired by the story of The Seven Sutherland siters, a singing group from Lockport, New York, featured in Barnum and Baily's. They developed a tonic called "The Seven Sutherland Sisters Hair Grower," to which they attributed their luxurious long hair. They made a fortune and built a mansion in Warren's Corners.

About the Author

Marshall Seddon graduated from Fredonia State University in 1971. He served six years in the New York State National Guard, taught history at Brocton Central School for forty years and was a founding member of the Blackhorse Rugby Football Club. He enjoys fly fishing and playing jazz guitar. He and his wife Heidi live in Fredonia, New York. They have eight children, two golden retrievers and a cat named Twist.